Serenity Inn Series

Lilia's Haven

Kay D. Rizzo

BROADMAN
& HOLMAN
PUBLISHERS

Nashville, Tennessee

0-8054-1685-4

Published by Broadman & Holman Publishers, Nashville, Tennessee
Editorial Team: Vicki Crumpton, Janis Whipple, Kim Overcash
Page Design: Sam Gantt Graphic Design Group
Typesetting: PerfecType, Nashville, Tennessee

Dewey Decimal Classification: 813
Subject Heading: FICTION
Library of Congress Card Catalog Number: 99-23956

Library of Congress Cataloging-in-Publication Data
Rizzo, Kay D., 1943–
    Lilia's haven / Kay D. Rizzo.
            p.   cm. — (The Serenity Inn series ; bk. 4)
        ISBN 0-8054-1685-4 (pb)
        I. Title. II. Series: Rizzo, Kay D., 1943– Serenity Inn series;
    bk. 4.
    PS3568.I836L55   1999
    813'.54—dc21
                                                    99-23956
                                                        CIP

1 2 3 4 5 03 02 01 00 99

— *Dedication* —

To Diana Haynes: A sweetheart
of a niece—love ya!

Contents

CONTENTS

-Prologue-
Eulilia's
Rendezvous

HEAVY STORM CLOUDS THREATENED BUT NOT in the skies over the azure blue Ohio River. There, a full moon flooded the night with its dazzling light. Yet, as Wade Cooper, the rogue son of an Irish potato farmer, brooded in the shadows of the paddle wheeler's gambling lounge, he felt the weight of thunder clouds pressing in on him.

Wade had experienced such a weight as a child when he endured the beatings of a drunken father, so he had stowed away on a ship heading for America. In the hold of the ship with only dried bread and a flask of fresh water, he endured the cold and discomfort, vowing that once he arrived in the New World, he would never be cold or hungry again.

Yet the thunder clouds pressed in on him again, like they had every evening for the last few weeks. This woman had ruined it—his string of good luck at the gaming tables. The woman he'd made his wife! Eulilia Northrop of the Virginia Northrops! Had it been only a month since he whisked her from her father's home in Norfolk in the middle of the night to take their vows before the itinerant preacher on the train ride to Philadelphia? Romantic! That's what she called it. *Hmmph! Call it what you will, little girl, I call it good business sense.*

He'd been so proud of his coup at the time. But lately things weren't going as he planned. He'd been certain that the prestigious Northrops would grudgingly accept him into their family womb and fortune once he'd stolen their daughter's heart. That was his plan. Instead, when the young couple declared their love for one another, the parents had thrown him off their estate.

Wade's face burned with indignation when he remembered being tossed out the front door of their mansion with the help of the Northrop's son and the family's head butler. Imagine! Tossed out on his dignity, he was. He rubbed his backsides. Still fresh was the painful memory of landing on the red brick portico.

Wade leaned against the doorjamb of the paddle wheeler's gaming room. He eyed the assembly of America's wealthy class strolling by—ladies of leisure in their diamonds and furs, draping the arms of aging dandies who were puffing on their imported French cigarettes and sporting solid-gold watch fobs and diamond stickpins.

He'd seen the likes of them all before, dropping off their little darlings at Martha Van Horne's Finishing School for Young Ladies. He'd schemed and he'd planned. The belligerent Eulilia Northrop, daughter of "old money," at least two generations old, would be his ticket to a life of wealth and leisure.

Courting her while under the watchful eyes of the school staff had been challenging. Stolen kisses behind the stables, clandestine meetings by moonlight on the school's riding trails, promises of eternal love, and the girl was his for the taking. The immigrant stable hand could have dallied with her like he had with other girls at the academy, but from Eulilia Northrop of the Norfolk Northrops he wanted more than a tumble in the hay. Wade knew there'd be a scene at the Northrop's Virginia mansion—tears, shouting, threats—but he was certain that Eulilia's doting papa would give in to his little girl's pleas and Wade would gain part of the family's financial largess.

He'd heard tales about the sons and sons-in-law of Southern dandies spending their days and nights at the gaming tables and brothels while their little wives stayed home tending to their needlepoint and a succession of babies. That was his plan.

Instead, the evening he arrived at the Northrop Estate, Mr. Northrop erupted into a rage. Eulilia retaliated, her temper as violent as her father's. The two went at one another like cocks in the ring.

Threats like, "You will not bring that common stable boy into our family!" and "I will never allow a daughter of mine to marry so far beneath her!" pounded his ego again and again like the clank of the blacksmith's hammer striking hot molten iron.

Wade remembered standing in the shadows beneath the eaves of the Northrop mansion, certain she would come to him, yet fearful she might not. Despite the clouds that had settled into his head, he knew he'd have to implement plan number two. They'd elope. Once he returned their despoiled daughter, the Northrops would have to accept him as their son-in-law.

Wade waited until the house grew dark and a dim light appeared in Eulilia's second-story window. He'd used his time to plan his route. With practiced ease, Wade slipped through an open French door into the family library.

Quickly, he located the father's rare coin collection displayed in a glass case on a stand beside the fireplace. The fire had died down to glowing embers casting a giant shadow of him on the wall as he crouched over the glass display case.

Eulilia had boasted of her father's rare collection. Apparently her words had been correct. One coin had the head of a Roman Caesar engraved on it. Another one, misshapen with age, appeared to have a horse and cart imprint, and a third a sheaf of wheat. While Wade couldn't read the engraved words, he had no doubt the coins were very old and worth a goodly portion of the old man Northrop's wealth.

After scooping the coins into a leather pouch, he stuffed the pouch in his jacket pocket. Satisfied with his take, he retraced his steps through the French doors and around the side of the mansion to the rambling rose bush and trellis beneath Eulilia's bedroom window. Wade preened himself just thinking about the dimpled lass with the flaxen blond curls, flashing green eyes, and the high blush that filled her cheeks every time he stole a kiss. She was his "golden goose," he told his stable-hand friends—his ticket out of poverty.

They laughed and took bets on his success. "You're a stable hand, pure and simple," the manager of the stables reminded him. "And that's all you'll ever be. These girls come, flirt with you, then go home to the wealthy men from their own class."

Wade smiled as he stood beside the rose trellis. The delight of being able to go back to the school and collect his bets was almost as exciting as showing up Old Man Northrop. And the stable hand would show him up, one way or another. Yes, Wade nodded, he would. He'd prove to everyone—everyone who ever laughed, smirked, or denigrated him—that he was a somebody.

For a moment, as he felt the weight of the coins in his coat pocket, Wade considered forgetting the girl and disappearing into the night with the coins. But no, after the indignation of the evening, he had something to prove to the old man. Wade Cooper was more than a stable hand. He was a power with which to contend.

And Eulilia was a delightful morsel of beauty. He licked his lips in anticipation. The day may come when he'd make good such an escape, but not as long as there was anything left for the "pickin's." He laughed to himself as he gazed up at her window.

Beyond the tall hedge that surrounded the mansion, a horse whinnied. Wade froze for a moment until he was certain no one inside the house stirred. Eulilia's bedroom window slid open. He could see the gentle form of the young heiress, silhouetted against the ceiling by candlelight.

The young man could have climbed the graceful marble staircase to the second floor where Eulilia's room was, but he knew such an entrance would not be as romantic as an escape in the night through the bedroom window. And if Wade knew anything, he knew that the thrill of romance was the primary lure to entice little Miss Northrop from her father's clutches.

Wade whispered words of undying love to the girl leaning out of her window. "Hurry, my love, we must be gone before dawn." He made himself sound breathless with anticipation although he knew there were still seven hours before the sun came up over the waters of the Atlantic Ocean behind the estate.

When Eulilia heaved her trunk over the edge of the balcony and it thudded to the ground, Wade glanced about nervously. He was afraid the entire community would awaken and be after them before they'd left the Northrop property. With a flash, he signaled to a waiting groomsman to load the trunk aboard the rented coach, then assisted Eulilia in climbing down the rose trellis.

Her feet had barely hit the soft green lawn when a light came on in the upstairs hallway. "Ssh! Ssh!" he ordered, drawing her into his arms. He could feel her heart beating against his chest, a bird caught in a trap. When the light went out, he grabbed her hand and ran across the expansive lawn to the waiting coach. He lifted her into the carriage and leaped in after her. "Go! Go!" he shouted to the driver. The horses sprang forward as the mansion's front door swung opened and someone carrying a lantern stepped out onto the front porch.

Too late, old man! Wade chuckled to himself, nuzzling Eulilia's neck. The girl giggled and planted her lips on his. He kissed her with unrestrained passion.

She wiggled in his arms. "Wade! Not here!"

Chuckling, he ignored her protests. *Too late, little girl. To avoid a scandal, your old man is going to accept me into the family or pay me off.*

When she protested further, Wade backed off. Timing was important. *First things first,* he decided. Eulilia must become his wife before her father could catch up with them. Until they were out of the region, they would go by different names. *Kale, yes, that's a good name,* he thought. *Wade and Eulilia Kale. No, Eulilia is too out of the ordinary, too noticeable.*

As she snuggled into his arms, he leaned back against the seat and decided to convince her to change her first name. *Lilia, much less pretentious,* he thought. By the time they reached Richmond, Eulilia had accepted the name change as part of the intrigue of their elopement.

Good fortune shined on Wade when an itinerant preacher boarded the same stagecoach going from Richmond to Philadelphia. Sitting across from the minister, Lilia's cheeks flushed with excitement as she promised to love and obey. Wade smiled down at the young girl clinging to his arm as she repeated the words "till death us do part."

That was four weeks ago. How had he ended up on the deck of the paddle wheeler *Cameo* heading for the West? As Wade stood on the deck of the riverboat in the moonlight and watched the mighty Ohio River glide past the sides of the craft, he thought of the words "till death us do part," and grimaced. It had been a rough two weeks. For the first time he wasn't sure how long his charm could hold his bride.

The steady rhythm of the paddles slapping the water and the engines snorting and clunking filled the night air. *Till death us do part—if that woman continues acting like she did tonight,* Wade thought, *"till death" will be sooner rather than later, regardless of her daddy's stinking wealth!*

Ever since Lilia had learned of the theft of her father's coins, there'd been no consoling her. The coins, he'd been told, were collected by Lilia's father when, as a young man, he sailed the Mediterranean. The coins were hundreds of years old she said, "Older than Jesus Christ!"

Lilia told him how, as a child, she had studied the coins, reverently running their cool surfaces between her tiny fingers, her imagination carrying her into the land of sheiks and princes and pharaohs. She'd been so proud when one Sunday her father brought his collection to church and shared the stories of the coins with her and her friends.

When she'd told him that, he'd almost regretted the theft, almost, but only for a moment. Since then, the woman was out of control. Lilia alternately cried, screamed, threatened, nagged, cajoled, and pleaded with him to return her and the coins to Virginia. He could see sparks of anger in the once pliant young woman's eyes.

In the middle of an argument, unable to stand more of her diatribes, he spilled the reason he married her—her father's money, plain and simple. Horrified she buried her face in her hands.

With the same icy tone, he added, "And we're not going back to Norfolk so I can rot in jail for the rest of my life."

Her head snapped up. The pride that had always been evident in her face had disappeared. The woman was pleading with him. A feeling of power surged through him.

"Daddy wouldn't do that!" she begged. "Please, let me go home." Her eyes were red and swollen from sobbing. "I know he wouldn't." Without warning, the woman gulped and ran for the chamber pot in the corner of their stateroom.

Thinking she was playacting, he stormed after her. "Like you knew he would allow us to marry, right? You stupid little biddy."

She threw him a pitiful glance, then buried her face in the porcelain bowl.

Great! he thought. *Wouldn't you know, she'd get seasick and her father a former sea captain!* In disgust, he looked down at the pitiful creature retching at his feet and, for the first time, wondered how he'd ever found her appealing. "This is getting tiresome," he announced and left the cabin, slamming the door behind him.

Following dinner that evening, they'd had another argument. She called him a liar and a thief. Furious, he grabbed her upper arm and dragged her out of the dining hall to their cabin. There, he announced he would be spending the evening at the gaming tables—again. He'd been there every night since they boarded. Her pleading didn't deter him. As he strode from the cabin, he realized that his luck at the tables hadn't been much better than his luck in marriage. Many of the precious coins had ended up in the pockets of the colorful professional gamblers that frequented the game rooms. But in his heart, Wade knew he was getting better with each session at the tables. His skills were being honed against the masters of the games.

Luck hadn't completely abandoned him. He found a merchant aboard the boat who said he'd been to the Middle East and knew about rare coins. The man was more than willing to convert the coins into currency for the tables and for other "delights" available aboard ship. The proceeds from one of the lesser coins had gone to a luscious little number who had offered to "massage his dignity" after one particularly bad night at the tables.

He'd returned to his cabin as the first streaks of dawn spread across the sky. Lilia pretended to be asleep, but he knew by the catches in her breathing she wasn't. They'd never discussed his little digression. And if he had his way, they never would.

Tonight . . . He jangled his cash in his right hand. The coins he kept locked in a strong box in the stateroom. *I'll get lucky again, one way or the other.*

As he caught a glimpse of himself in one of the long and narrow, silver-backed mirrors outside the *Cameo's* game room, he adjusted his cravat. "Hmm!" he mumbled aloud. "Take that, Mrs. Northrop. And you said I couldn't tie an English knot! The reason I wasn't good enough for your daughter." He'd come a long way since whisking Lilia from her Virginia home. He groomed his mustache with his fingers.

Twenty-four years old, Wade Cooper knew he cut a handsome and roguish figure for the females aboard the vessel. More than a few of the showgirls had gone out of their way to make their availability known to him. And he with a simpering wife! Unbidden, those clouds pressed again inside his head. He pounded his fist against the door-jamb, rattling the mirror panel dangerously.

What a mewling cow I married! Wade couldn't believe the change in the fiery adventurous Lilia since Philadelphia. The trip from Norfolk had been glorious. His little wife hung on every word that came from his lips. At the railway station in Philadelphia, he insisted she contact her parents. Maybe they'd had a change of heart and would welcome her back with tears and kisses. She'd sent a telegram to her younger brother, Carter. Her brother's reply was brief. "Father has put a $1,000.00 bounty on Wade's head for stealing his coin collection. How could you marry a cad like that?"

Lilia stared at Wade in shock. Disgusted, he snorted aloud. What did she think they'd been living on since leaving Norwalk? His money? Her good looks? He shook his head in disbelief.

She demanded he return all the coins he had left. "We can send them back ahead of us."

He refused.

"Let me take them home and smooth the waters. Then after a week or two you can follow me."

She begged and cried and he studied her with growing disgust.

"How stupid do you think I am?"

After one violent argument, she tried to run away, but she didn't get out of the railway station before he found her. One good slap across the face and she cowered into submission. He didn't want to do that. It reminded him of his father. He felt as if he would throw up.

But when he saw how quickly the bruise near her right eye healed, Wade decided Lilia should feel fortunate. The bruises Wade's mother had suffered from his father had sometimes lingered for weeks.

Instead of continuing their trip north to Boston, Wade made an abrupt turn west, first by train, then paddleboat. *Old Man Northrop will never think to look for us out West,* he reasoned.

Resigned to going with him wherever he went, Lilia reminded Wade that her ex-roommate, Serenity Cunard, lived in Independence, Missouri. "I'm sure she'll give us a place to stay until we can decide where to go next."

Wade remembered the delectable, ebony-haired beauty who stood watch for the couple during their first few clandestine meetings behind the school stables. He remembered comforting Lilia when her roommate left school because of a death in the girl's family. That was the first night Lilia allowed their lovemaking to go beyond schoolgirl kisses.

Lilia had a stack of letters in her trunk from Serenity—a treasure, she called them. At first, he snorted at the idea of going to Independence, but then reconsidered. Independence was the gateway to the West. It made sense.

Serenity Cunard's home would be a good place to dump his cumbersome wife while he high-tailed it to California on the first wagon train west. He'd start over, safely beyond Northrop's grasp and Lilia's whining. He would turn his little cache of gold into a fortune, then live to a ripe old age like a king, savoring the pleasure of wine, women, and sport. He suppressed a smile at the surprised look on Lilia's face when he encouraged her to send a telegram to her friend.

The raucous jangle of the ragtime piano music drifted out of the barroom beyond the gaming tables. Wade could hear the bawdy laughter and catcalls of the patrons as the breathy, nasal soprano voice of "Sapphire Smythe, with a *y*, from the shores of sultry Saint Croix," wailed out the lyrics to some Stephen Foster ditty. He wasn't sure which one.

Music had never been his forte. Pasting a sultry grin on his face, he pushed open the swinging doors and swaggered into the gaming room. The thunder clouds pressing in on him lifted as they always did whenever he entered a gaming room. A mist of stale smoke lingered in the air, creating an image of warmth, acceptance, and good times.

At the sight of the oak tables, hot adrenaline coursed through his veins. A sense of adventure lightened his step. And confidence that his streak of bad luck was over filled his heart.

The old-timers, as he called them, were already deep into a night of gambling, their chips stacked on the scarred tables before them. These were the dyed-in-the-wool professionals and the interminably hopeless losers. Wade Cooper categorized himself with the company of the professionals. The part-timers would arrive later, after the floor show, where they would be picked clean, like turkeys after the shoot.

Yes, it would be a good evening. Wade rubbed his hands with satisfaction. Tomorrow they'd be boarding a paddleboat on the Mississippi. There were always shops and stalls along the wharf selling shiny baubles. He would buy his bride a trinket from his winnings, as an apology.

— 1 —

Runaway Bride

THE OPTIONS FOR THE MODERN WOMAN OF the 1850s were limited to staying single and becoming someone's auntie or marrying the first man to show an interest. If the young woman was a debutante from a wealthy family, she might be able to hold out for suitor number two or three.

At eighteen, Eulilia Mae Northrop, recent graduate of Martha Van Horne's Finishing School of Young Ladies, fell into that class of women. For her and the rest of her classmates, the choice was simple—marry. It was the man Eulilia Mae Northrop chose to marry that upset the wealthy Northrop household and set the gold-encrusted tongues of Norfolk, Virginia's high society a-wagging.

Wade Kyle Cooper, the roguish young stable hand at Martha Van Horne's Finishing School for Young Ladies, had swept her off her feet with romantic tête-à-têtes behind the school's riding stables in the moonlight.

During her senior year at the school, Eulilia had perfected her nocturnal escape from the dormitory. Looking at her brash behavior a month into their marriage, she had to admit that 90 percent of their romance had been the adventure and intrigue, not that she hadn't been enamoured by the handsome and silver-tongued immigrant from Kildare, Ireland. Not that she hadn't ached to run her fingers through his reddish-brown curls whenever he helped her into her seat during riding lessons. Not that his kisses didn't excite her with a driving passion she'd never before experienced. Wade had been all of that and more. Eulilia remembered her classmates' envy when she regaled them with tales of secret trysts in the night and the titillating awe she saw in their eyes when she hinted at the possibility of an elopement should her parents object.

A month after her graduation and subsequent marriage, she lay curled up on a berth in her stateroom on the Ohio paddle wheeler *Cameo*. Beyond the portal, the sun shone high in the morning sky. Wade was gone for the day, or perhaps he'd never come back to their cabin last night. She neither knew nor cared.

Pulling herself up off the narrow bed, Eulilia caught a glimpse of herself in a mirror on the wall opposite the berth. She groaned at her reflection. One glance and she couldn't blame Wade for preferring the company of the barmaids. Her once golden-blond curls hung in dull strands about her face. Her usually peaches-and-cream complexion appeared gray and lifeless. The blush was gone from her cheeks. Her eyes were red and puffy from crying. The bruise on her left cheek stood out in bold relief against ghastly tones of pale green and gray. *At least* . . . She examined the bruise more closely. . . . *it's beginning to heal. All the rice powder in the world will never cover that one.* She was thankful it was only a bruise and wouldn't leave a scar.

Eulilia! She still couldn't get used to being called "Lilia" as her husband insisted on doing. *Eulilia, you need to pull yourself together if you intend to fight for your husband's love.* The thought caused her to pause. Did she actually want to fight for Wade's love and the abuse that went with it? She wasn't sure.

Yet Eulilia had never been a quitter. She reminded herself that she'd survived four years at Martha Van Horne's Finishing School—adequate proof of backbone for anyone. "And you're not going to quit now!" The words rung hollow in the cramped stateroom. In her heart, she decided she would make her marriage work or die trying.

She poured a small amount of cool water from the porcelain water pitcher into the matching washbasin. Taking a face cloth from the rack beside the washstand, she scrubbed her face clean of yesterday's tears.

Today would be a new day. She would do nothing to antagonize her husband. She would entice him into her arms, and possibly back into her bed, with light laughter and adoring compliments.

She couldn't blame the women aboard ship for being attracted to the brash and beautiful man she'd married. Even after all that had happened, her heart palpitated at the sight of him. As to the insults he'd hurled at her the night before, calling her a stupid cow, a simpering biddy, and as ugly as a guttersnipe, she forgave him.

She understood the pressure Wade was under trying to win their fortune at the gaming table. That he was doing so with her father's prized coin collection gave her a moment's discomfort. It wasn't as if her father needed the cash from the coins to live on, she reasoned. She knew Mr. Chauncy Northrop was as rich as Croesus. Grabbing her boar's-hair brush with the carved ivory handle, part of a vanity set her father had brought back from the Orient for her, she brushed vigorously through her tangled golden locks, shaking her mind free of any and all guilty thoughts that were bent on haunting her.

When the first wave of nausea hit, Lilia was halfway to the dining lounge. Catching herself on the riverboat's brass railing, she closed her eyes for a moment. She'd been surprised the first night aboard ship to learn that she, the daughter of a ship's captain, could become seasick—seasick on a river boat! As a young child she'd gone sailing with her grandfather and never felt a touch of *mal de mer*, as the French called it. But after three weeks living aboard the boat? Surely she should have grown accustomed to the paddle wheeler's movements and rhythm in that amount of time, or so Lilia thought. Fortunately the worst was over by midafternoon and she could enjoy the rest of the day in relative peace.

To take her mind off her discomfort until the feeling passed, she planned her day: a cup of tea and a slice of toast for breakfast, followed by a tour of the deck, hopefully with Wade; an hour or two sitting on deck reading; another tour around the ship's circumference; a light lunch with Wade; a nap in her cabin; then pack their belongings, for this was the day they would converge with the mighty Mississippi. They would change vessels for the voyage to the Missouri River, then change paddleboats again for the trip west to Independence.

Independence, even the city's name sounded frightfully impetuous, hence, exciting to the runaway bride. She tried to envision the town from her friend Serenity's penned descriptions. Tears glistened in Lilia's eyes at the thought of seeing her former roommate once again. Her chin quivered. She bit her lower lip to ward off her tears.

So many things were different since the last time they'd seen one another. Lilia remembered waving good-bye as

Serenity's coach departed from the school after the death of Serenity's mother. That was over a year ago. What if Serenity had changed? What if Lilia's one true friend, subsequently married and pregnant with her first child, had grown into someone else?

They'd exchanged letters as often as possible, but the mails were nothing like sharing secrets in a dorm room after the oil lamps had been extinguished. Penned words couldn't adequately express the joys and the sorrows of two schoolgirls maturing into the loves and responsibilities of marriage and womanhood.

And then there was the religion thing. While Serenity had always had a bent toward a Divine Being due to her mother's devout Quaker background, she never let it get in the way of their fun. But after marrying the son of an itinerant preacher, Serenity's tone in her letters had changed. She wrote freely of trusting God with her problems and thanking Him for everything, or so it seemed to Lilia.

Serenity wasn't the only one who had changed, Lilia reminded herself. "Lilia," she whispered, "I am Lilia!" She would get accustomed to her new moniker if it killed her. She would make Wade happy in every way possible.

Lilia made her way to the dining lounge and sat down at a table. When the waiter came she ordered a cup of mint tea. "And a slice of toast, without butter," she added. Her stomach rumbled threateningly. She glanced down at her waist. The soft, yellow, cotton batiste with nosegays of blue bells embroidered throughout the bodice and skirt had hung loose on her waist when she slipped into it that morning. She'd tied the broad, yellow, taffeta sash more tightly than usual. Before she left school the dress had been a snug fit. She appeared to be shedding the baby fat of adolescence.

As she caught a reflection of herself in one of the massive, silver-backed mirrors in the lounge, Lilia admitted that she appreciated the results. When the waiter brought her order, she nibbled on the toast, then nursed her tea until it grew cold.

The lounge was quiet at this time of the morning. Most of the passengers had long since finished their morning meal and moved on to other shipboard activities, of which there were many. The paddle wheeler was an elegant and ornate floating palace with gaming rooms, bars, shops, and most everything else a small city might offer.

One other passenger sat at a table across the room from her—a well-dressed blond man in his thirties, clean-shaven, except for a small, well-manicured mustache. When he smiled at her, his eyes sparkled with wit and good humor—and the most darling dimples deepened in his cheeks.

She cast him a coy smile, then returned her attention to the virtually empty teacup and saucer on the white, linen-draped table in front of her. That a man found her desirable enough to smile at her thrilled Lilia. Recently she'd felt so ugly about herself. Feeling unattractive and awkward were new emotions for the lovely Northrop girl. During her teens when her peers expressed feelings of insecurity, Lilia couldn't understand. The last few days with Wade had opened her eyes to a host of new feelings.

Intrigued, she looked up from her teacup for a second glance. The stranger was crossing the room toward her. A smile of curiosity and interest illuminated his face.

"Good morning," he said, standing behind the chair opposite hers. "Are you dining alone? Why haven't I seen you before today?"

Lilia batted her thick, long eyelashes modestly, a maneuver she had used on men since the cradle. "Excuse me, sir? Do I know you?" Her reply, if spoken in a less inviting tone, would have been a rebuff to the engaging young man.

"The name is Jeramy Briggs, ma'am, of Savannah, Georgia." The man's smile widened. "And you are?"

"Eulilia Mae Northrop, uh, er, make that Mrs. Lilia Mae Cooper, er, Kale. . . ." Her face reddened as she stumbled through the names she was supposed to remember.

The stranger laughed again. "Is there a Mr. Cooper, er, Kale?"

Lilia chuckled, batting her eyelashes provocatively. "You, Jeramy Briggs from Savannah, Georgia, are a tease, are you not?"

"I've been called worse, madam." Mr. Briggs drew the chair from the table and sat down. He waved for the waiter, then arched one eyebrow toward Lilia. "You haven't answered my question. Is it Miss or Missus?"

She cocked her head to one side and opened her mouth to reply when Wade's shadow filled the doorway. "Uh, it's Missus, I assure you! Now, if you will excuse me." She started to rise from her seat, but not before Wade stepped up behind Briggs's chair.

"Well, well, my dear," Wade snarled. "And who is your new playmate?"

"Wade!" Color filled Lilia's face. Jeramy Briggs of Savannah leaped to his feet and turned to face the angry husband.

"Sir, how do you do? I am Jeramy Briggs of—"

Wade adopted the stance of a bantam rooster. "I don't care who you are or where you're from, you get away from my wife and stay away!"

"Why, sir, I assure you that I had no—"

Wade eyes narrowed. "I know your intentions. Don't insult my intelligence. My wife may be a naïve chit but I certainly am not."

At the impact of Wade's tone, Briggs took a slight step backwards. "Pardon me, sir—" Realizing that Wade's anger was growing, Briggs gave a submissive gesture with his hand. "Sir? Madam? If you'll excuse me?"

Lilia held her breath as the handsome stranger rushed from the dining hall. "Wade, the man was only making small talk."

Wade grabbed her left upper arm and hauled her from the table. "Not with my wife, he isn't!" He shoved her toward the dining hall door. "You tramp! I turn my back for a few minutes and you're out carousing with a stranger!"

As he pushed her by the arm and back toward their cabin, she protested. "No, Wade. You know you're the only man I've ever loved. I'm not—"

"Be quiet! Do you want the entire ship to know of your indiscretions?" He hissed in her ear. "What were you doing out of the cabin anyway?"

"I was hungry," she mewed. He unlocked the cabin door and pushed her through.

"I'll tell you when you're hungry and when you're not!" He slammed his fist into her stomach. She cried and doubled over in pain. With his other hand he shoved her onto the berth. "You will stay here in the cabin until I come for you. Do you understand?"

She lifted her defiant eyes toward him. "You can't tell me what to do!"

Slamming her back against the mattress, he straddled her terrified body and pinned her shoulders to the bed.

Lifting his fist as if to strike her in the face, he growled. "I can and I will. You are my wife. You vowed to obey me until death us do part, remember? And you will obey me if you know what's good for you!"

Tears streaming down her cheeks, Lilia turned her face to one side and sobbed.

"Say it! I want to hear you say that you will obey me."

In broken sobs, Lilia wept, "I will . . . I promise I'll obey you."

He gave her shoulders a violent shake. "And don't you forget!"

"I-I-I won't . . ." A whimper escaped her throat. She hated the sound. It was as if it were coming from someone else, not her, not the once proud and confident Eulilia Mae Northrop.

Appearing satisfied, Wade climbed off the bed and strode across to the door. "I'll be back when we dock to switch boats. I expect you to get everything packed and ready to leave." He opened the door and slammed it behind him. She heard the key turn in the lock.

A vile-tasting panic arose in her throat. She dashed to the door and tried the knob. It didn't turn. Shaking the knob, she screamed, "Wade, don't do this. Don't lock me in. I'll obey you, but please, don't lock me in."

When her cries went unheeded, she slid to the floor, leaned her head against the locked door, and sobbed. Since childhood, nothing terrified her more than being confined in close quarters.

When she was about five, her father took her to tour one of his ships and she managed to get locked in a small, dark compartment in the bowels of the ship. Her father and his crew spent hours looking for her. When they found her, she'd fallen asleep crying. Ever since, Lilia had recurring nightmares of the terrifying event.

After several minutes of crying, Lilia realized no one was coming to her aid, least of all Wade. She crawled across the wooden cabin floor and hauled herself into her bed.

What had happened to the flattering and loving man she'd married? What had gone wrong in their marriage in a little more than a month? Was this what marriage was all about? Love, honor, and obey? Did every woman suffer at the hands of her spouse like this? She knew better. She'd never seen her father hit her mother for any reason.

"I can't completely blame Wade," she reasoned aloud in the empty cabin. "I should never have flirted with Mr. Briggs. That would make any husband angry. And I know that Wade is anxious over our money situation." She'd come to recognize the signs when Wade lost at the tables or won. When he lost, he returned to her cabin in drunken rage and abused her either physically or verbally. When he won, he returned to the cabin drunk but happy, demanding his husbandly rights. Only on the night he spent with the showgirl did his pattern change.

Yes, she knew about that night. During an argument, he threw his indiscretion in her face, telling her that if she'd been more loving and more obedient, he wouldn't have needed to turn to a cheap tart for affection.

There was no doubt about it, to both Wade and Lilia, the gilt was off their marriage and Lilia had no idea how to fix it. She thought of contacting her parents for help. If only she could run home to her father's arms where Wade couldn't hurt her. But no, *I've burned those bridges,* she thought. If she ever risked going back and her parents threw her out again, the rejection would kill her.

Lilia knew that whatever was wrong was somehow her fault. She had to be doing something wrong. She knew it. Yet she'd tried to play every role possible, from fighting back to acquiescing to his every command and nothing worked. And she had a lot of time to think about her situation. She suspected that Wade stopped gambling and returned to the cabin only long enough for the janitor crew to clean and straighten the gaming rooms. No matter how hard she tried, Lilia realized she couldn't compete with "Lady Luck."

Maybe things will be better when we reach Independence. *Maybe Serenity will know what I can do to make my marriage better,* she reasoned. Her spirits bruised and her heart broken, Lilia retreated to the safe little world of sleep.

~2~

On to the
Mud Hut

LILIA'S SPIRITS LIFTED WHEN WADE'S MOODS improved. She actually enjoyed the journey up the Mississippi River aboard the riverboat *Freedom*. Wade spent more time with her during the days at least.

He stopped locking the cabin door. "You seem pale lately," he told her. "You need to spend more time in the sunshine. There's a ladies' tea every afternoon in the forward dining lounge. I think you should attend."

Lilia didn't know what had come over him, but she wouldn't pass up the opportunity to escape the cabin, even for a ladies' tea. The women at the tea were all over forty or pregnant, but that didn't matter. She listened to their horrid tales of childbirth and silently vowed she'd never allow herself to become pregnant. How to stop that from happening, she wasn't certain.

The pleasant midsummer days on the Mississippi passed quickly. The couple disembarked the *Freedom* north of St. Louis. Before boarding the Missouri riverboat *Clementine*, Lilia insisted they telegraph Serenity of their arrival. "It's the proper thing to do." She knew how much Wade wanted to learn the ways of the wealthy and the cultured. And Lilia didn't mind using that desire to get her way.

Lilia saw her first sod house a few miles later after they left the metropolitan area. Walking back from dinner, she pointed in surprise at a tiny house set back from the river's edge. "Look at that!" she exclaimed to Wade. "Why, that's a mud hut!"

Wade glanced at the hut, then at his wife. "Not everyone is born in a Northrop mansion, you know." She could sense his sudden ire.

"I know that, dear, but I've never seen anyone living like that. Have you? And with a thatched roof, in fact."

A glower filled Wade's face. "It's about time you saw the world as others see it!"

She shot a surprised glance at her husband. "I'm sorry. I didn't mean to—"

"You never mean to do anything! Come on! I got to get you back to the cabin before I miss my first game." He chuckled to himself. "These rubes won't know what hit 'em when I get done with them."

"Wade, are you sure you know what you're doing? You've lost a lot of money. We're going to need something to live on when we get to Independence."

When his grip tightened on her upper arm, she knew she was in trouble again. He urged her forward, barely accommodating the way her tiny French heels and numerous skirts hampered her steps. "There you go meddling again. What a harping biddy you've turned out to be."

"I'm sorry. I didn't mean to. I just thought—"

"Then stop thinking, woman. Leave that area to me! I am the man you married, am I not?"

When he glared down at her, she managed a weak smile in return. "Yes, yes, I-I-I-I'm sorry. . . ."

He gritted his teeth and shot an impatient glare sky-
ward. "Sorry? Sorry! That's all you say any more. What a
moron you've become."

He left her that night as he had every other night since
they'd begun their cruise west. Alone in the cabin, she lit the
oil lamp, shed her cotton dress and her crinolines for her pink-
and-white flowered, batiste nightdress. Then she climbed into
the berth with a stack of Serenity's letters to comfort her.

. . . is so thoughtful. I love it when he comes
up behind me while I'm working and nibbles on
my ear or wraps his arms around me and whispers
silly nonsense in my ear. And Caleb is so funny.
The other night while he was helping me dry the
dinner dishes, we got into a water fight. We ran
screaming throughout the cabin. If anyone had
been around, they would have thought we were
killing each other.

But my favorite time of the day is when we finish dinner and he takes out a large family Bible
that used to be his grandmother's. His voice is so
rich and so sincere as he reads aloud the promises
of God in His Word. When Caleb reads, "I will
never leave you, nor forsake you," tears come to
my eyes. Yes, I know those are God's words, but
hearing them from my beloved's lips adds incredible dimensions to them.

Spring will soon be here. We're working night
and day converting the mission into an inn. Mrs.
Rich and the ladies at the Baptist church in town
have been making quilts for the rooms in the inn.
Serenity Inn has almost become a community
project.

As I told you in the last letter, there is a great need for such a place. Sin is blatantly rampant in Independence. Families wishing to protect their young from the seedier side of life will appreciate having a place like Serenity Inn.

You asked in your last letter why I would choose to become an innkeeper. I'll try to explain. Since finding Jesus as my personal Savior and Friend, I want to share Him with everyone I meet. He commissioned me to "Go into all the world," but I can't do that. So instead, He's bringing the world to my front door. Isn't that exciting? I figure I'll preach a little, talk a little, and love a lot.

I know this is foreign to you. It was to me, too, back when I was a student at dear Martha Van Horne's Finishing School for Young Ladies. Sometimes I wonder where that silly little foppet has gone. . . .

Tears fell as Lilia folded the pages of her friend's letter and inserted them in the envelope. Frightened and lonely, Lilia whispered into the shadows of the darkened stateroom, "I hope that dear little foppet hasn't disappeared all together. I need her so badly."

The journey across Missouri couldn't hasten fast enough for Lilia. Wade's moods improved with his luck at cards. And with his improved moods, the roguish nature with which she'd fallen in love returned. Their morning and afternoon strolls on the deck of the *Clementine* became moments she treasured during her evenings alone in the cabin.

Once she asked if she could accompany him, bring him good luck. She'd seen the lovely ladies decked out in their silk and finery strolling with their husbands toward the gaming rooms. His reply was abrupt and definite. "No! It's no place for a wife of mine!" he said.

She wanted to ask why it was all right for a husband of hers to be there, but not a wife of his. What made the difference? Of course Lilia knew the difference. Society's rules were simple and unforgiving. A scarlet woman was a scarlet woman for life. Knowing how sensitive Wade was to censure, Lilia wasn't surprised that he wouldn't want his wife bringing such embarrassment down on his head. Nothing was more berated in the world of married men than to have a wife disobey or dishonor the husband's name.

The prairie sun shone big and hot overhead as the riverboat *Clementine* chugged into the docks at Independence, Missouri. Lilia leaned over the railing to catch a better glimpse of the magical city she'd been dreaming about for so long. The bell clanged. The roar and rattle of the riverboat's engines died. The dock master, sweat gleaming in the sun, shouted to the workers on the riverboat. Dark-skinned longshoremen lingering nearby prepared to hoist and shove and carry the goods shipped in from St. Louis and beyond.

A crowd gathered on the docks as the deck hands wrestled the gangplank into place. Lilia scanned the crowd, hoping to see a familiar face. Even as she did, she knew Serenity wouldn't be there since Lilia had not given her friend an estimated time of her arrival. Lilia sighed and turned in time to see Wade slip a silver coin into the bodice of a tarty little barmaid with floozy, henna-colored hair and a missing front tooth.

What does he see in such women? Lilia wondered. When the woman lifted her gaze to meet Lilia's, the woman sneered, then planted a firm kiss on Wade's lips. Lilia turned her face away, her sight blurred with tears. Steeling herself against Wade's indiscretions, she focused her mind on seeing Serenity. When Wade returned to her side and escorted her off the riverboat, Lilia comforted herself with the thought that in less than an hour, she'd be with Serenity, who would know what to do.

Wade left her on the dock beside their luggage while he went to locate a carriage to rent. He returned with a carriage pulled by a shaggy nag. He brought with him a good-looking man with dark hair and eyes and an easy smile. She couldn't place it but the man's face seemed vaguely familiar.

"Lilia, you'll never guess who I ran into. I went into a bar to ask directions to your friend's place and guess what? The first man I asked is your friend Serenity's brother-in-law, Aaron Cunard." He turned toward the stranger and said, "Mr. Cunard, this is my wife, Lilia."

The man cocked his head to one side and touched the tip of his wide-brimmed brown felt hat. "Howdy, ma'am. It's a pleasure to meet you."

Lilia nodded primly, shielding her face from him with the stiff brim of her petal-pink, embroidered, poke bonnet. A lingering glance between them would set off Wade and, more than anything, she didn't want that to happen, not on this most important day.

While the longshoremen loaded Lilia and Wade's luggage into the boot, Wade helped her into the carriage, then climbed in next to her, allowing Aaron Cunard to drive the rig. "Wasn't it kind of Mr. Cunard to volunteer to drive us and our luggage to the inn?"

"No problem," Aaron drawled. "I was thinking of heading out that way later tonight anyway. I'm definitely ready for some of my sister-in-law's great cooking."

Lilia crinkled her nose and forehead and smiled. "Serenity cooks?"

Aaron grinned at the woman next to him. "Oh, yes, ma'am. Good enough to make me reconsider staying single."

Wade gave a loud chortle. "You'd better think that one through again, my good man. No vittles are that good!"

His words pierced Lilia's heart. A blush rose to her cheeks. She dropped her head once more. Hiding behind the brim of her poke-bonnet was fast becoming a convenient escape.

As they rode past a small sod house with boarded up windows, Lilia couldn't contain herself. "Do people actually live in those places?"

Her driver laughed aloud. "Absolutely! In the summer heat a soddy stays quite cool. And in the winter, if the windows and doors are tight, the temperatures will never drop below 50° or so. With wood at a premium here on the prairie, that's important."

"Dirt floors!" Lilia shuddered. "I can't imagine actually living like that."

Aaron chuckled again. "Well, you won't have to imagine. Serenity and Caleb's inn is made of sod as well, though it's much bigger than the average sod dwelling. It's two rectangular soddies joined to the main building to form a *U*. But why am I telling you this? You'll see it for yourself in about five minutes."

"Don't mind my wife, Mr. Cunard," Wade explained in condescending tones. "She was born wearing silver slippers. She has no idea how the average person lives."

"Oh, that's all right." Aaron glanced sideways at Wade. "Soddies shocked this old boy when I first saw them too.

Now I can appreciate their economical value. As to the dirt floors, the ground is trampled down so hard that an energetic housekeeper can sweep her kitchen with a broom and not stir up any dust." He shook the reins. "Come on, Molly. It's time you kicked up some dust." The mare responded with a good-natured whinny and continued at her chosen pace.

"Beyond this bend . . ." Aaron pointed in the general direction. ". . . to your right, you'll see Serenity Inn. You actually see the backside of the building complex."

"Yes, I see it—" Lilia fell silent at the first glimpse of her friend's earth-toned dwelling. The blocks of mud weren't so bad. It was the stalks of grass sprouting out from the sides and the roof that esthetically offended her.

"The ell on this side is the sleeping complex. The main structure houses the great room and the ell on the far side houses the kitchen, dining area, and pantry," Aaron explained.

"Your brother's got a mighty fine barn," Wade drawled with unmistakable sarcasm in his voice.

"All the buildings were here when Caleb and Serenity bought the place," Aaron retorted. Lilia didn't miss the man's sardonic reply. "On the north side of the barn, Caleb installed a furnace and blower for his blacksmith shop."

Lilia brightened. "My favorite grandpa had a blacksmith shop on his estate. I used to sit and watch him work when I was a kid."

"Woman, who cares about your doddering old grandfather and his blacksmith shop?" Wade snarled.

"My wife can babble on for hours about nothing if you encourage her," he said to the driver.

Aaron pulled on the reigns and engaged the brake as the carriage rolled up to the open barn door. A large black dog bounded from behind the barn, barking at the carriage. "Calm down, Onyx. It's oniy me," Aaron scolded.

"Whoa, girl." Aaron stood up in the carriage. "Anybody home?" he called. "Onyx, be quiet!" When no one answered, Aaron looped the reins over the brake handle and climbed down from the carriage. "Caleb probably can't hear me over the roar of the bellows."

Wade climbed down from the carriage and stretched, ignoring his wife perched alone on the seat of the carriage. When she realized her husband had no intentions of helping her, Lilia scrambled down from the carriage as best she could. Embarrassed with her husband's lack of etiquette, she glanced toward Aaron and blushed uncomfortably.

Aaron turned away to loop the reins around the hitching post as the man Lilia remembered meeting in Boston more than a year ago rounded the corner of the barn. "Brother! Welcome. We haven't seen you in a coon's age."

"Been busy, taking runs over to Kansas." Aaron hugged his older brother, thumping him on the back in a typically manly fashion.

"You brought company." Caleb tipped his hat to Lilia. "I know you, don't I? You're Serenity's friend from Boston." He sounded genuinely happy to see her. Her eyes misted with relief.

She regained her composure. "And this is my husband, Wade Cooper. Wade, this is Caleb Cunard, Serenity's husband and Aaron's brother." She gestured toward their driver.

Caleb extended his hand. "Good to meet you. You must be exhausted. Did you dock this afternoon? It's a long trip, isn't it?"

Lilia tried to answer all his questions, but they came at her so fast.

"Come!" Caleb gestured. "Serenity is so excited about your visit. She's talked of little else since she received your telegram. Aaron, you will stay for supper, won't you?"

Aaron grinned sheepishly at his brother. "Are you kidding? I wouldn't miss it for the world."

"And I needed to ask?" Caleb laughed and took Lilia's arm. "We are so glad to have you visit us, Lilia. And your husband as well." He glanced over his shoulder at Wade, then led her around to the front of the house. Onyx and Wade followed, each uneasy and suspicious of the other.

"I'll unhitch the wagon," Aaron called. "Be with you in five minutes."

Lilia missed the interaction between the Cunard brothers the moment she spied Serenity weeding her flowerbed beside the inn's front door. "Serenity!" Lilia squealed. "Is that you?"

Serenity looked up from the flowers she was trimming and screeched. "Eulilia!" The woman leaped to her feet with amazing agility and flew down the walk to Lilia'a open arms. The hug dislodged Lilia's silk bonnet. It slid to her shoulders, but neither woman cared. Onyx barked and leaped at the excited twosome while Caleb looked on in bemusement.

"Look at you," Eulilia squealed again. Her navy blue, silk, traveling gown rustled against Serenity's homespun, brown, calico dress.

"Aaiigh! You're so . . ." Lilia's eyes widened with wonder. "When? When are you due?"

"The beginning of September," Serenity's eyes sparkled with delight.

"I can't believe it. Look at you, little mama." Lilia squealed again and gave her friend another hug. "I am so happy for you."

Behind the excited women, Wade eyed them disdainfully while Caleb attempted to quiet Onyx. "Good boy. That's a good boy." Caleb patted the dog's head, trying to smooth the tense, wiry hairs on the dog's back. Despite his master's comforting, the dog bared his teeth and uttered a low, throaty growl.

"Onyx!" Caleb scolded. "Stop that!"

"Aren't you going to introduce us, Lilia?"

The two women stepped apart upon hearing the irritation in Wade's voice.

"Lilia?" Serenity inquired.

"Yes, Wade likes the nickname." Lilia tried to hide the sudden wave of sadness that swept across her face. "Doesn't it sound absolutely modern? That's me, a cosmopolitan woman of the '50s."

Onyx growled and made a threatening move toward Wade before Serenity replied, "Onyx, sh-sh-sh." Serenity reddened at the dog's obvious dislike for her friend's husband. "Sorry, he's still getting used to new people coming and going from the place. So welcome to our home." She gestured toward the house. "Shame on me for keeping you standing outside. Come in. Come in. You must be tired and hungry."

"Oh, of course." Lilia eyed her husband. She knew that he was in one of his snits again. And she had no idea as to why or what she might have done to cause it. *Of all times! Can't he at least try to be nice?*

Earlier, when they drove through town past the bars and gambling dens, Wade had wanted to stay. "We can go out to your friend's house tomorrow," he said.

Lilia had no intention of waiting another day before seeing her friend. In the short time they'd been married, Lilia had learned to pick her battles carefully. Upsetting Wade, she'd learned, could be physically as well as emotionally painful. But this time she hadn't backed down. Wade had shouted, pouted, threatened, and cajoled, but Lilia held firm. Beneath her eager anticipation at seeing Serenity was an ache to see someone who loved and remembered her from an earlier time, a time before she was Lilia Cooper.

Ignoring her husband's sulk, Lilia introduced her husband. "Serenity, you remember Wade? You met him at school."

Serenity reddened at the memory of the two girls' midnight escapades to the stable. "Yes, I remember him well."

Lilia smiled. "I thought you would. And Wade, you remember my best friend in the whole world, Serenity Louise Pownell, er, Cunard." Lilia blushed at her forgetfulness of Serenity's married name. If only she could forget her own. . . .

Serenity extended her hand toward her friend's husband. "Mr. Cooper, once I left school I never expected to see you again. Welcome to Serenity Inn. And this is my husband, Caleb Cunard, whom you've already met."

Onyx pressed against his master's legs, his distrust of the stranger visibly apparent in every muscle in the dog's body. "We're glad you had a safe journey, Mr. Cooper," Caleb said. "Is this your first journey West?"

"Aye, I was born and raised in Ireland. I immigrated to America ten years ago."

"Well, you are in for a treat. This country is unbelievable, as diverse as mankind itself." Caleb gestured toward Aaron. "Here comes my little brother. By the way, Serenity, I forgot to mention that Aaron was here too."

"No problem. Aaron is always welcome at our table." Serenity kissed her brother-in-law on the cheek. Aaron, standing to one side of Wade Cooper, nudged the brim of his worn brown felt hat back on his head with one knuckle. "Isn't she a darling?"

Lilia didn't miss the thatch of dark brown curls that escaped the brim of his hat and tumbled onto his forehead, nor the delightful twinkle in his teasing blue eyes. She could see why Serenity had once been attracted to her husband's younger brother. As if he could read her thoughts, Aaron gave a bemused grin. Lilia dipped her head in embarrassment.

Holding open the front door, Caleb put his arm around his wife and brushed his lips across her cheek. "Serenity has been like a kitten chasing her own tail ever since your telegram arrived. You know, the telegraph company just finished stringing the lines this spring and we've received at least four telegrams already. Isn't modern science incredible?"

Serenity's eyes sparkled at her husband's tender ministrations. Lilia noticed Caleb's gentleness as well and her heart grew sad. The look that passed between the two women said more than Lilia had intended.

Serenity took her friend's hand and led her into the house. "Come. Meet my dear friend, Annie. She's here to help me until after the baby comes. You remember Annie, don't you? I told you about her at school."

"You mean your parents' servant?" Lilia asked. "The colored girl you grew up with?"

"Yes, that's the one. Annie works for my folks, but she's helping me, not as a servant . . ."

Lilia didn't miss the emphatic note in Serenity's voice.

". . . *but out of the goodness of her heart.*"

"How . . . how nice," Lilia simpered, turning part way

to see the look on Wade's irritated face. Wade shot her a warning glare.

"Well, this is it, Serenity Inn. We've been filled up almost every night since March. We have two families here now, the Tates and the Berks. Both families are leaving on a wagon train for Utah in a day or two."

Lilia arched one eyebrow in question. Serenity smiled. "Yes, they're Mormons, but you know what? God loves Mormons almost as much as He loves you and me." She giggled at her wry humor. "Actually a few years ago, the townspeople of Independence ran a colony of Mormons out. And I suppose, if some of the landed gentry in these parts knew we were harboring them, they would become upset, to be sure. But, when Caleb and I founded the inn, we vowed that we'd never turn another human away from our door, regardless of his religion or color."

Lilia couldn't contain her disbelief. "Anyone? You'd take in anyone?"

Serenity shrugged. "Yes, I suppose we would, as long as they behave themselves."

"But you're a Christian!" Lilia relished turning Serenity's religious babble back on her.

"Precisely. It is because we love Jesus Christ that we choose to love our fellowmen. Hey! How did we get into a philosophical discussion anyway? I wanted to show you my home. I've had such fun decorating it as best I could." Serenity gestured toward the seating area in front of the large stone fireplace. The late afternoon sun flowing in through the open door illuminated the comfortably worn brown sofa, the multicolored crocheted afghan stretched across the back, a large oak rocker next to the hearth, the over-stuffed, faded, chintz-covered armchair with a matching ottoman. A large family Bible, a stack of books, and a bouquet of daisies arranged in a porcelain milk pitcher brightened the dark oak table behind the sofa.

Serenity hurried to the kitchen beyond the dining area. "Come. I'll introduce you to Annie. She must be in the pantry. Annie?"

Lilia cast a worried glance toward Wade as she reluctantly followed her friend. How had he taken their exchange? One moment Wade could be extremely tolerant of other people, and the next, belligerently rigid. She turned and captured his gaze for an instant. *Please behave yourself tonight, Wade. Please, if you ever loved me.*

Serenity seemed not to notice Lilia's hesitancy. Grabbing a red-and-white, calico, Mother Hubbard apron from a hook next to the massive cast-iron stove in the kitchen, she tied the string behind her back. "It's been an exciting spring around here, what with Caleb's parents heading west and my dad and his new wife arriving from the East. And then to have you show up! I feel so blessed." Serenity shot a loving gaze at Lilia. "I've missed you terribly. We have so much to talk about! Annie? Where are you?"

The pantry door leading to the backyard slammed.

"Annie?"

Annie's smiling light-brown face peered around the doorjamb. In her hands she held a colander of string beans. "Did you call me?"

"Yes, where'd you go?"

"When I saw the carriage pull up, I figured we'd have guests for supper so I went out to the garden to pick a few extra bush beans."

"You were right. Please, come meet my friend, Eulilia, er, I mean Lilia. Lilia, Annie."

The former slave girl smiled tentatively at the woman about whom Serenity had told her so much. Try as she might, Lilia couldn't contain her disdain at being expected to treat an inferior as an equal.

−3−

An Evening to Remember

Sitting around the massive oak trestle table and chatting with Serenity about old times had been delightful for the homesick Lilia. She had the other guests doubled with laughter when she told about the night the two girls stole old Herman's britches. And for a time, Lilia almost forgot the heaviness weighing on her spirits. Even Wade got into the spirit by describing the headmistress's penchant for purloined snacks in the school kitchen.

"If big Bertha had ever suspected someone, even Mrs. Jones, was trespassing in her kitchen while she slept, the woman would have crowned her with her rolling pin," Wade admitted. "That woman could swing a mean broom handle as well."

Lilia's eyes sparkled with happiness at her husband's obviously good humor. "Serenity, remember the time we sneaked down to the kitchen for a couple of gingersnaps?"

"Do I?" Serenity laughed. "And if I remember right, we almost got caught too."

Lilia giggled. "But they were certainly great tasting gingersnaps!"

At the end of the meal, the other guests excused themselves, saying they had an early departure. Annie did the same, explaining that she had a busy day planned the next morning.

Serenity and Lilia continued sharing old times while they washed the evening dishes. After Lilia described her and Wade's elopement in romantic terms, she listened while Serenity told her about her and Caleb's wedding.

"It was so simple, yet so beautiful, and the Richs were so sweet to us. Wait until you meet the Reverend and Mrs. Rich. If anyone is close to God, they are."

Lilia grimaced at the mention of God. Already she'd noticed how often the subject of God popped into Serenity's and Caleb's conversations. When Lilia told about her and Wade's flight from her father's house in the middle of the night, the rented coach, the train ride, and the itinerant preacher, Lilia tried to make it sound glamorous. She vented her anger at her parents for trying to prevent her and Wade from marrying. "We had to elope. They gave us no choice. If Daddy hadn't been so insistent that we not marry, I don't think I would . . ." As she placed a large platter on a pantry shelf, her words drifted off into the night.

The men had retired to the seating area by the fireplace where Caleb and Aaron tried talking for a while about horses and blacksmithing, neither of which interested Wade.

From the place where Lilia stood washing the tabletop, she could tell it wasn't going well with them. And her heart sank. How she'd hoped Wade and Caleb would become fast friends, but she could see that they were made of different fabric. Wade was more like Aaron, Caleb's brother.

Caleb brought up the subject of California's gold strike. "It's changing our country. Why, I wouldn't be surprised if in the next ten years or so, the railroads will link us together with the West."

"Yeah, Brother," Aaron added, "the wagon trains will be a thing of the past. Independence won't need as many blacksmiths when that happens."

Caleb laughed. "Well, railroads can only go where the tracks take them. I figure as long as people need horses to get them from their homes to the depot, they'll need blacksmiths."

Aaron laughed. "I suppose as long as men crave the demon rum, my job will be in demand."

Caleb and Serenity exchanged a look of pain. Lilia knew without asking the reason why. She'd already discovered that her friend and new husband were tee-totalin' Bible thumpin' Christians. Didn't Serenity Inn exist for families who didn't want to expose their children to the seamier side of living? She glanced toward her husband, expecting him to laugh at Aaron's joke, but the sullen Wade stared down at his hands, never attempting to join in the conversation.

Serenity placed a teapot of water on the stove to boil, then joined Lilia at the table. "So, how was your journey? You came over some of the same route we took, at least along the Ohio River and the Mississippi and, of course, the Missouri."

"Oh, it was, uh, nice. . . ." Lilia nervously glanced toward the men as they talked. She did so every few minutes.

"Isn't it terrible about the price of sugar in China?" Serenity asked, a pert smile pasted to her face.

"Huh? Oh, yes. Wade and I were just talking—"

Serenity laughed. "Lilia! You don't know anything about the price of sugar in China. Neither do I." She touched her friend's hand gently. "Lilia, is something wrong?"

Lilia flashed a broad smile across her face. "Oh, no, everything is fine."

Lilia knew she hadn't fooled her friend for an instant. Serenity could always break through Lilia's reluctance to talk. Of course, Lilia had seldom been reluctant to talk to anyone, or so her teachers at the school would have said.

"Come to my room and see what I've been working on." Serenity arose from the table.

Lilia followed.

"Mrs. Rich has been helping me sew baby sacques. And you know all that embroidering I hated at school? Well, let me show you."

Lilia paused at the doorway to her friend's bedroom. Her eyes misted. It wasn't fancy—nothing like the elegance of the room she'd abandoned to marry Wade. But, if she'd tried, Lilia couldn't have imagined a more lovely room to share with a mate. Throughout the journey, Lilia had excused Wade's bad manners and nasty moods by saying he would change once they were settled. *It's all my father's fault,* she told herself. *If he had treated Wade the way he should have, Wade and I wouldn't have had to elope. Wade wouldn't have had to steal the coins and we could have married with my parents' blessings.*

Tears flooded Lilia's eyes as she held each of the tiny garments Serenity placed in her hands. She traced one finger over a yellow duckling embroidered on the collar of a light-green flannel sacque. "It's beautiful." Her words came out in a whisper.

"Look on the back, hardly a trace of stitching." Serenity laughed. "Remember how Miss Petunia Pearle made me rip out my stitches? She said the back of the piece looked like a rat's nest."

Lilia gazed at the garment but said nothing. She knew her friend wanted to pry out of her what was wrong, but she prayed Serenity wouldn't try, at least not yet.

The whistle of the teakettle in the next room ended the conversation. "Tea time," Serenity announced, returning the garments to the wooden chest at the end of the bed. "Nothing better to help one sleep than a cup of chamomile tea."

Lilia rose to her feet and ran a hand across her forehead. "I doubt I'll need anything to help me sleep tonight."

As the women passed through the great room to the kitchen, the men looked up, as if relieved for the interruption. "Gentlemen, we ladies are having a cup of chamomile tea before bedtime," Serenity announced. "Would you like one as well?"

Aaron laughed out loud. "The last time I had a cup of tea, Mama was trying to break a high fever I'd gotten from the croup. I wish you had something stronger to drink."

Serenity grinned at her brother-in-law. "Some day-old coffee in the pot over there. That should be strong enough to curl your hair, Aaron, if it weren't already curled."

"Thanks anyway, Sister dear, but I'd best head back into town," Aaron said. He hauled in his long legs across the thick braided carpet in front of the sofa where he sat and rose to his feet.

"But it's late," Serenity insisted. "You can stay here for the night."

"Aaron, Serenity's right. You really should wait until morning to head back to town," Caleb agreed.

Wade came alive at the mention of town. "You live in Independence?" Serenity and Caleb exchanged knowing glances. Obviously Wade hadn't been listening to anything that had been said previously.

"Yes?" Aaron drawled, uncertain as to where the conversation was going. "I bartend at Shorty's Saloon."

"Oh yeah. I remember seeing it on Main Street on our way out here." Wade cast a quick glance at Lilia, then rose to his feet. "Mind if I ride along with you? I gotta take the horses and rig back tomorrow morning anyway. Might as well as do it tonight since I ain't the type to go to bed with the chickens."

"Wade," Lilia whispered, sneaking a nervous glance toward Serenity and her husband. "It would hardly be polite for you to . . ."

The sudden swing of Wade's head startled everyone. "Woman! Get off my back! I got you to where you wanted to go, didn't I? Now, give me some breathing room!" Aware of the surprised looks on everyone's faces, he glanced toward Caleb. "Women! You gotta' keep 'em in line right from the start or they'll take over your life." He gestured toward Aaron. "While you saddle up your mount, I'll grab my coat and gloves. Give me a couple of minutes and I'll be out to harness up the horses."

A mortified Lilia gulped back sudden tears, uttered an "Excuse me," and fled the room, but not before seeing the surprised looks on everyone's faces but Wade's. His remained grim as he stormed out of the room after her.

From the guest room at the end of the hall, Lilia prayed no one could hear Wade's angry shouts through the closed door. On board the riverboat, she'd suffered the sympathetic glances of other passengers each morning after the newlyweds had one of their brawls. But to fight here at the home of her dear friend and on their first night as guests was inexcusable. He knew how important making a good first impression was to her and deliberately did everything he could to upset her.

As he shouted at her from the foot of the massive, four-poster bed, she cringed on the far side of the bed in horror. *Please, God, if there is a God, don't let him hit me. Don't let him hit me,* she prayed silently as he rounded the end of the bed, his body shaking with anger. The fire in his eyes warned her that he was in one of his impossible moods. There would be no reasoning with him tonight.

Shaking his finger in her face, he snarled, "Don't you ever correct me in front of other people again. I'm not a milksop like your father, Lilia dear."

"Don't talk about my father like that. He was the kindest, gentlest—"

"So why did you leave him for me? Humph! My manners were exciting enough for you and your little trampy friends at Van Horne's. Where were those proper manners then when you begged me to kiss you and to love you? Now, suddenly, I don't measure up?" He gestured about the room. "I may have been a poor ignorant immigrant, but I've never had to live in a dirt hovel!"

"It's not dirt, it's sod. Many of the—" She didn't see the back of his hand coming. The slap sent her sprawling across the bed. Lilia's hand shot up to cover her burning cheek. "Oh, please, Wade, don't, not here," she whispered.

"You did it again; you corrected me! You don't listen!" He leaned toward her, his face red with excitement. "Maybe I'll stay here after all and teach you how to be an obedient wife."

Her skirts hampered her movements as she attempted to skitter away from him on the bed. Placing one knee on the bed, he grabbed her hands and pinned her down. "No! No! Not like this, Wade. Not like this," she pleaded, rivulets of tears staining her delicately painted cheeks.

A wicked smile touched the corners of his mouth. "Poor baby, all those tears. Let me hear you beg."

"No, oh no," she sobbed, turning her head from side to side in protest. "Not tonight."

He trapped her wrists over her head in one of his hands and slapped her face a second time with the other. She cried out in pain. Her cry brought laughter from him as he fumbled with the buttons on the bodice of her dress.

Suddenly someone banged a fist on the door. Lilia and Wade froze at the sound. He straightened and released her wrists, then growled, "Yes?"

"Excuse me." It was Caleb. "Serenity asked me to give you a set of fresh towels. Is everything all right?"

"Everything's fine! Just leave the towels by the door." Wade glared down at his wife's stark white face. With a snarl he climbed off the bed and grabbed his coat. "Your brother still out there?"

"Uh, no, at least not in the house." Caleb cleared his throat. "He's probably still in the barn saddling his horse."

"Could you tell him I'll be right out?" Wade eyed Lilia, daring her to protest.

From beyond the door, Caleb replied, "Sure. Sure. I'll go give him the message."

In relief, Lilia watched as Wade picked up his leather gloves from a nearby dresser and slipped them on his hands. "If I hear that you whined to your friends about me, you'll wish you'd been born mute."

He strode to the door, opened it, and shot a last warning look toward Lilia and he was gone. The door slammed closed behind him. She stared at the ceiling for several seconds expecting him to return and finish the beating he'd started. Tears saturated the pillow beneath her head.

Nothing was as she had hoped. While she couldn't imagine herself being happy living in a sod house like her friend Serenity, she envied the love she detected flowing between the two of them. *How ironic,* she thought, *that the friend I pitied for so long, I now envy, despite the mud hovel.*

Lilia knew after the few short weeks as Wade's wife that the grandest mansion in Virginia couldn't ease the problems between them. Too late she could see what her father saw the first time he met the young man from Boston. Too late she regretted ignoring her parents' tears and pleading.

One night on the Missouri River paddle wheeler she'd seriously considered leaping overboard. Only her fear of being maimed instead of killed by the giant paddles prevented her from doing so. In St. Louis, she'd considered running away from Wade, but she had no money. Where would she go? Who would help a young woman traveling alone? Good women didn't travel anywhere alone. She realized that her position as a wife, as far as the law was concerned, was no better than that of a runaway slave.

One evening, when Wade was losing at the tables, she had struck up a conversation with a male passenger traveling alone. She'd intended to ask him to help her escape from Wade. But Wade discovered her and the gentleman standing by the railing in the moonlight. She never saw the young man again. And she still ached from the bruises on her back and ribs left by the beating she incurred.

"So here you are, Miss Lilia," she muttered to herself, "in a sod house on the edge of the wilderness, afraid and alone, unless you intend to humiliate yourself further by admitting the truth about your marriage to Serenity."

Reason tried to tell her that, after Wade's outburst, Serenity and Caleb already knew. How could they not suspect things were bad with Wade's shouting and cursing?

Yet, pride inhibited her from telling Serenity the truth and possibly getting help. *Help?* The word stuck in her throat. She remembered one of Wade's warnings.

"No one's gonna' help you run away from me. You're my wife. Your place is by my side as long as I want you there. And there's nothing you or your daddy's money can do about it." His face brightened at the mention of money. "Of course, he can have you back for a price. But then, who would want a soiled piece of woman like you anyway?"

Lilia painfully sat up on the edge of the bed. She cupped her face in her hands. Her blond curls tumbled down into her face. "Not only soiled, but pregnant too," she whispered, fearful that saying it aloud would confirm it for all time. "Wade mustn't know, at least, not yet." If she was eager to leave Wade before, being pregnant with his child made her plight all the more desperate.

Serenity seemed so at peace with her pregnancy. Tears sprang in Lilia's eyes when she remembered a conversation she and her friend had had while at school, something about Serenity growing into her name, becoming serene.

She's done that, Lilia thought. *Serenity glows with happiness. Will I ever find such happiness?*

Feeling unsteady, Lilia arose to her feet and walked to the small bedroom window. She peered out into the darkness, grateful Wade was gone and fearful of his return.

~4~

A New Day

THE SUN SHONE HIGH IN THE SKY BEFORE Lilia opened her eyes the next morning. She gazed about the room for signs of Wade's return. There were none. She sighed with relief. She smiled to herself. *Maybe I'll just lie here and enjoy the moment.*

Outside her window, she could hear children playing instead of the rumble of the engines turning the giant paddle wheel. *Where am I?* Then she remembered the late night arrival at Serenity Inn, seeing her friend again, and the altercation with Wade.

The aroma of pancakes spurred her to life. She threw off her covers, leaped from the bed, and grabbed the chamber pot from beneath the foot of the bed. It had been the same for days. Nausea. Vomiting. Dizziness. Would it ever stop? At first she blamed it on the greasy food aboard the riverboat. Before long she knew better. She'd eavesdropped often enough on her mother and the other ladies as they discussed this woman's or that woman's "delicate condition" to know what was happening to her body.

She made her way to the washstand and poured the fresh water into the basin. *Towels?* She glanced about the room for towels. *They're still outside the door,* she realized. She padded across the room and opened the door a crack. A stack of fresh, white Turkish towels sat beside the door. She snagged the stack into the room, but not before she inhaled a fresh whiff of eggs frying in the kitchen. This sent her scrambling for the chamber pot again.

She heard a tap on the door. "Lilia, are you all right?" It was Serenity.

Lilia lifted her head and took a deep breath before answering. "Yes, I'm fine."

"Are you sure?" Serenity asked again.

"Yes, I'm sure. I'll be out in a few minutes."

"What are you hungry for this morning? Annie made a batch of walnut-raisin bread this morning. It's delicious."

Lilia groaned. "Some hot tea would be nice. I'm not very hungry, I'm afraid. All the traveling must have upset my appetite. But thank you."

"Did you sleep well?"

Will she ever go away? Lilia sighed. "I slept fine, thank you. Everything's fine." Lilia flinched at the edge that had come into her voice but she needed time to be alone and to think. "I'll be out in a few minutes."

"All right."

Oh no! She knew by the tone in Serenity's voice that she'd insulted her friend. She didn't want to alienate her last lifeline. Mechanically she washed and dressed, alternately regretting her words and justifying them.

By the time Lilia strode into the great room, Serenity's overnight guests had left for town to continue their preparations for heading west. The midmorning sun splashed through the windows of the kitchen where Serenity stood before the table kneading bread dough.

"Good morning. A hundred and one, a hundred and two . . ." She brushed a stray curl from her forehead with the back of her flour-coated hand. "Nothing satisfies me more than making a batch of bread. When I'm frustrated I pound the daylights out of the stuff." She laughed. "So how did you sleep? You didn't sound too well this morning."

Lilia smiled awkwardly at her friend. "I slept fine but I must have eaten something tainted yesterday." She massaged her stomach as she spoke.

"I have just the thing for you. In the early days of my pregnancy, I couldn't keep anything down for weeks. Forget morning sickness. I had afternoon and evening sickness as well. Doc Baker recommended mint tea and dry toast first thing each morning." She glanced at her friend and smiled. "Maybe it will work for your upset stomach as well."

Lilia took a chair at one end of the table where Serenity was working.

"So what do you say?" Serenity dusted her hands off on her green calico apron. "I keep dried bread in a cloth bag over the stove, just in case my nausea should return. Of course, I don't expect it to now that I'm past that stage."

Lilia massaged her forehead. "I'll give it a try. Something has to work." Surely her friend suspected her condition with all this talk about pregnancy. She eyed Serenity's rounded stomach and groaned. How would she deal with getting fat and ugly? How would Wade handle her being less than the beauty he married? A frightening thought came to her mind for the first time. Wade? Would he reject her further? Leave her? Maybe being pregnant wouldn't be so terrible after all.

She watched Serenity bustle about the kitchen preparing her tea. Serenity hovered over Lilia while she forced down a cup of mint tea and a piece of dry toast. Certain Serenity already suspected Lilia's pregnancy, Lilia decided to share her secret with her friend. Lilia pretended to be happy about the baby growing within her, but her admission reinforced the reality of her hopeless situation. Lilia arose from the table and wandered over to a window.

"It's kind of scary, isn't it? Becoming a mother?" Serenity finished rolling out the bread dough and putting it in the bread pans to rise. "I almost didn't marry Caleb for fear of childbirth." She placed the pans on the cool end of the massive iron stove. Noticing a splash of flour on the chrome of the stove, she lovingly dusted it clean.

Lilia noted the simple act of love. Her friend was an enigma to her. How could she be so happy, living on the edge of civilization in a mud hut and baking bread for strangers?

Serenity glanced up from the stove and smiled. "You can't imagine how much I appreciate that the couple we bought this place from invested in a beautiful stove like this. Many of my friends have to do all their cooking and baking over an open fire." She gestured toward the fireplace. "Can you imagine?"

Lilia frowned. "What changed your mind?"

Serenity glanced at her in surprise. "Excuse me? I don't follow you."

"What changed your mind about marrying Caleb and having babies?"

Serenity chuckled as she spread the clean tea towels on top of the pans of dough. "Love. I couldn't imagine living the rest of my life without Caleb. When he left to care for his father who'd been injured in Kansas, I missed him terribly. That's how I knew, babies or no, I couldn't imagine my life without him."

"Are you still afraid, of childbirth, I mean?"

"Uh-huh. I guess I am."

Lilia returned her attention to the activity outside the window. The wind had whipped a sheet from Annie's hands and she was chasing it across the field beside the house. Behind her the large black dog barked and chased after the woman. Lilia laughed. "Look. Come quick, Serenity. You've got to see this."

Serenity peered over her shoulder to see what had produced Lilia's laughter.

"Oh, no!" Serenity gasped and flew out the front door to Annie's aid. Lilia strode over to the open doorway and watched the two women struggle to control the renegade bedsheet. Within a short time, they'd wrestled the sheet to the clothesline and pinned it in place.

Lilia gazed at the prairie grass blowing in the breeze. A chicken hawk circled lazily overhead, searching for a mid-morning snack. She could hear the clank of Caleb's hammer coming from the barn. An empty buckboard sat beside the open barn door. She suspected that the horse, which had drawn the buckboard, was inside the barn getting re-shod. Lilia had to admit the scene held a certain rustic appeal, like a painting produced by one of those Dutch artists whose name she could never remember.

By late afternoon the Berks had returned from town with a loaded wagon and a fresh team of oxen. Mrs. Berk joined Serenity and Annie, who were in the kitchen preparing dinner. Lilia had just made herself comfortable before the raised stone hearth when Serenity plopped a bowl of string beans in her lap. "Here, sing for your supper."

Lilia looked at her in surprise. She'd never prepared a vegetable in her life. The young heiress had no idea what to do with the long green things in the pot before her.

Serenity read her friend's mind and laughed. "Don't worry. It's easy, see?" She demonstrated how the job was done. "The ends go in the waste bucket by the door and the edible parts go in the pot simmering on the stove. You were a guest yesterday; today you're family. At Serenity Inn everyone helps."

Serenity bustled about her kitchen, acting confident that Lilia would be able to perform the assigned task. "I remember popping my first string bean. It was last summer when I got home from school. Dory, our housekeeper sat me down in the summerhouse with a huge pot of string beans. 'This is where you start, if you want to run your father's home,' she said. At that time I was determined that Josephine Van der Mere would not marry my father and take over the operation of my home. I decided that the only way I could prevent their marriage was to show my father that he didn't need the woman." Serenity laughed aloud. "I was a tad naïve about love and marriage at the time."

Annie giggled. Lilia shot a surprised glance toward the servant girl. Annie seldom made a sound in her presence. Lilia had almost forgotten Annie was in the room.

"I'll never forget coming around the corner and seeing Mr. Pownell holding Josephine in his arms while she squirmed and kicked," Annie said. "At first we thought something was wrong. Then they said they were going to get married that very day!" She giggled again.

"Did I tell you," Serenity turned to Lilia, "that they spent their honeymoon on a riverboat on its way to Independence to see me? They live in town."

Lilia nodded. The emotions she experienced while popping the green beans amazed her. She went from irritation to anger, to feeling at home and a part of the group. Since she was doing her share, the other women began including her in their conversation.

"Mrs. Berk," Serenity asked, "when do you and your husband expect to hit the trail?"

"In a day or two, I imagine," the shy young mother replied. "We want to make it over the mountains before the first snow falls."

"Getting ready for the trip is such a big job," Serenity added. "All that shopping!"

Mrs. Berk nodded. Slowly the woman began to share information about the purchases she and her husband had made that day for their journey westward. As she opened up to the other women, she shared her fears as well.

"Why would you want to leave your comfortable home back East?" Lilia asked.

"This is Jed's dream, to find gold in California and buy a little place along the Russian River. He read all about it at the town library." She brushed a strand of hair from her forehead and continued stirring the pot of stew boiling on the stove. "My Jed's the youngest of four boys. They all work on their dad's farm. If dad divided the property in his will, there wouldn't be enough to make a go of the place, so Robert, the oldest, will probably take over the place. So you see, if we stayed on the homestead, we'd never have our own place."

"Is having your own place that important?" Lilia asked. She'd never thought of a life beyond her parents' palatial mansion in Norfolk. It certainly was big enough, and her father was wealthy enough to support her and her brother's families without any trouble.

Mrs. Berk smiled and shrugged. "It is to Jed. And, therefore, it is to me as well. Besides, California sounds like a great place to raise our sons." Suddenly, like mothers of all eras, Mrs.

Berk paused to listen. "Speaking of sons, I haven't seen mine in more than an hour. Did any of you see which way they went?"

Annie pointed toward the front door. "Jed Junior said they were going to the barn to find their daddy."

A worried frown crossed Mrs. Berk's face. "I'd better go check to make certain that's where they ended up. Knowing my youngest, he's likely to be playing hide 'n seek with a coyote or prairie dog or something."

"If Onyx went with them, they'll be safe." Serenity strode to the window near the front door and pulled back the curtain.

Mrs. Berk hurried out the front door.

As the door closed behind her, the other women could hear her calling her boys. Serenity glanced toward Lilia and chuckled. "Looks like fun, huh?"

Lilia groaned aloud and glanced down at her hands in amazement. They were wrinkled and scuffy looking like those of a charwoman! She still couldn't imagine surviving the drudgery of motherhood, let alone performing tasks like she'd seen Serenity do all morning. Lilia decided that one of the first things she and Wade would need to do once they settled into their own place was hire a servant to do all the unpleasant jobs about the place. And popping string beans was definitely one of those tasks!

Having popped the last bean in the pot, Lilia carried the pot over to Annie. "Now where did Serenity say to put the leftovers?"

Annie pointed to the pantry. "There's a wooden bucket beneath the counter where we put all food scraps. Yesterday's scraps, today's chicken feed, Sunday's chicken dinner."

From across the room, Serenity laughed. "I haven't heard that one in a long time."

Annie picked up a wooden spoon and dipped it into the large kettle on the stove. "Your mother used to remind the kitchen staff of that all the time."

Lilia stretched and arched her back to dispel a slight crook that had settled in it. She couldn't imagine how Annie and Serenity could work for so long without stopping, especially Serenity. She understood—according to her Southern perceptions—that Annie, being of Negroid descent, was created for heavy labor, but Serenity was cast from a gentler mold.

Serenity looked up from her task. "Lilia, you look restless, why don't you take a walk up to the cemetery and back. That always refreshes me."

"I am worried about Wade. I expected him back from town by now." A scowl deepened on her forehead.

"From the crest of the hill you can see a long ways down the road toward town, you know," Annie volunteered.

Serenity strode to the pantry and returned with a galvanized pail. "Would you please drop this off with Caleb on your way? He'll be wanting it at milking time."

Lilia took the pail and headed toward the barn. The exhilaration of escape filled her with joy. She had the wildest urge to twirl in circles like a schoolgirl. It hadn't been so long since she was a carefree child, playing at life. In a few short months, she'd left behind her childish innocence. Reality wasn't a game.

Not now! I won't think such thoughts right now, she told herself. *It's a beautiful day. And I intend to enjoy it.*

The noise of the blacksmith shop greeted her before she reached the open barn door. Inside she found Mrs. Berk watching her husband and Caleb repairing a spring on the Berk's wagon. The two older Berk boys stood fascinated by the sight of the fiery furnace. The youngest boy was off to one side, playing with Onyx.

Lilia set down the empty pail inside the doorway. When Caleb looked up, Lilia said, "Serenity asked me to bring this to you."

"Thanks." He nodded slightly and returned to his task.

Lilia could tell lately that Wade's disappearance had been the main topic of Caleb and Serenity's private conversations. But Caleb had never spoken a word of it to Lilia. Even now, he waved politely and continued his work. The Berks did as well. Lilia watched for a few minutes too, then slipped out of the barn into the late afternoon sunshine. Her many layers of crinolines swooshed about her ankles as she climbed the slight grade to the crest of the knoll, the highest point on the Cunard's property.

She climbed upon a big rock and gazed out over the prairie, so empty and desolate. The colorful butterflies flitting from wildflower to wildflower couldn't remove the sense of emptiness she felt.

She watched the prairie grass gently sway with the breeze, reminding her of the waves coming in off the ocean at her parents' summer place. The emptiness of the prairie continued in the direction of town, except for the narrow trail of wagon tracks breaking the subtle golden seascape.

She searched the horizon for a sign of Wade. *Where could he be?* She wondered if he'd taken the time to sleep or eat since he hit the gaming tables late last night. The thought that he'd deserted her for good flitted across her mind. If he had, she would never find him in this vast unknown land.

"Why should I care?" she snarled at a passing butterfly. "Maybe it would be for the best if he did leave."

She looked toward the east and home. She shook her head sadly. Her home was no longer in Norfolk, not with all she'd done to her parents. She knew they'd never want her back, especially her father.

Her mind turned inward to the unborn child she barely acknowledged. She could only imagine the reaction Wade would have to her pregnancy when she told him. The bleakness of her thoughts deepened as she sat down on the rock and hugged her legs to her body.

A wave of homesickness like she'd never before known washed over her. At school in Massachusetts she'd never been homesick. In fact, she'd always laughed at the girls who were. For the first time, she experienced the emotional nausea of loneliness. Was it so long ago she believed she had all the answers to life's knotty questions?

A prairie buzzard circled in the sky high above her head. "Not yet!" she shouted and shook her fist. "I'm not giving up yet." She'd find herself again when things in her life settled down. She and Wade had plans, big plans. She vowed she wouldn't live the mundane life her friend had chosen.

Lilia slid off the rock and scanned the little cluster of graves marked with simple wooden crosses. Serenity had told her of the young missionary buried there. She didn't blame the man's wife for heading back to the comfort of her family after he died. She'd head home in a minute if she thought there was any hope of forgiveness.

Her gaze lingered on the graves of the lost babies. Idly her hand rested on her abdomen for several seconds. She bent down to pull a few weeds growing at the base of the cross above the newest grave. A tear slid down her cheek, unbidden. "Poor little one," she cooed. "You've been abandoned by your mama and daddy, left to the elements and to God."

Suddenly the hairs on the back of her neck stood up. She had the sensation that someone was watching her. She hadn't heard or seen anyone come up the pathway from the house. Her breath caught in her throat. She listened. Nothing. *Stop being so fanciful,* she scolded. *It's probably one of those pesky Berk kids.*

She straightened and before she could turn to see who had come upon her grief, she felt a hand touch her shoulder. Expecting it must be Serenity, she turned to speak. "I can't imagine what—"

"Aiieegh!" Lilia's screech echoed across the prairie, awaking critter and fowl for miles. The sight that met her eyes came straight out of her worst nightmare. She felt the blood rush from her head. Then adrenaline hit her system. She scooped her skirts into her hands, whirled about, and stumbled down the path toward the house, all the while screaming full voice.

Breaking into a run, she charged down the narrow pathway toward the barn. She'd gone but a few feet when Caleb and the others ran out of the barn and up the hill toward her. Annie and Serenity burst out of the house as well.

By the time Caleb reached Lilia and silenced her shrieks, her speech was incoherent. Unable to understand Lilia's babble, he gazed up the hill at the reason for her hysterics.

Standing on the crest of the knoll was a woman with long gray braids hanging down from her head onto her roughly woven tan tunic and gathered skirt. On her feet were beaded moccasins. A band of brightly colored beads encircled her forehead. Her weathered brown face resembled a well-worn trail map. Behind her left shoulder was a man whose face appeared to be older than time itself. A bird's feather sprang out of the band on his jaunty hat.

Except for his plaid flannel shirt and canvas pants, he could have stepped out of the pages of an article in one of the popular Wild West magazines flooding the Eastern cities entitled, "A Savage of the Plains." Two large turkeys dangled from each of the man's hands.

Caleb's face broke into a smile at the sight of the couple. "Gray Sparrow, Joseph Blackwing, welcome to our home. It has been a long while since you came to visit."

He passed the sobbing Lilia into Serenity's arms and strode up the hill toward their Shawnee visitors.

"It's all right, Lilia. It's all right," Serenity soothed. "Mr. and Mrs. Blackwing are friends of ours. We kind of inherited them with the place. Let me introduce you."

"No! No!" She shimmied out of Serenity's arms.

"They won't hurt you, I promise."

Lilia trembled with fear. "I thought they were going to scalp me."

A chuckle escaped Serenity's lips. "I had the same reaction the first time I met them. But, trust me, the Blackwings are two of the kindest, gentlest people you will ever meet."

Caleb and the Blackwings walked down to where Serenity and Lilia stood. Caleb now held the four turkeys in his hands. "Look what Joseph brought us, Serenity."

"Oh, Joseph, Gray Sparrow, how very thoughtful of you! What a nice addition turkey will make to our meals. Caleb has been so busy with his blacksmithing, he hasn't had time to go hunting."

"That's what he was telling us." The Shoshone man grinned a picket-toothed grin. "Gray Sparrow wanted to be sure you were getting enough meat in your diet, what with the baby coming." The Indian woman smiled up at her husband, then at Serenity. Lilia shuddered in horror.

—5—

Lessons in
Loving

LILIA EYED THE SHOSHONE COUPLE WITH distrust. Like a frightened child, she wished she could hide somewhere, anywhere. She'd read stories in the newspapers of people being scalped, babies being run through with knives, women being kidnapped and turned into slaves, and Indian braves on the warpath, their faces slathered with war paint.

Acting unaware of her friend's discomfort, Serenity glanced toward Lilia and the Berks. "Oh, forgive my manners. Let me introduce our houseguests. First, this is Mr. and Mrs. Berk and their three boys."

"The other night I told the Berk boys about our friends, the Blackwings," Caleb interjected. "I'm glad they can meet you before they leave for California tomorrow morning."

"Tomorrow?" Joseph Blackwing shook the hands of each of the boys. "You folks have a long journey ahead of you."

"Yes, we do." Mr. Berk shook Joseph's hand. "And dangerous too. Bad weather, drought, wild animals, and . . ." His face reddened.

"It's all right. You can say it—Indian attacks." The Shoshone man nodded his head solemnly. "Some of my native brothers are not so forgiving of past injustices, I fear."

Serenity placed her hand on Gray Sparrow's shoulder and turned toward Lilia. "And this, the one who announced your arrival, is a friend from my childhood, Lilia Cooper. Lilia is from Norfolk, Virginia."

Lilia gulped and forced a smile. "Nice to meet you, er, Gray Sparrow. I'm sorry about the . . ."

The Indian woman tipped her head slightly and smiled, revealing an uneven row of yellowing teeth.

"My wife understands your fright. We did come upon you unawares." Joseph Blackwing tipped his black felt hat toward Lilia.

Serenity passed her quivering friend to Annie, then gave Gray Sparrow a big hug. "Come, we were about to sit down to supper. We would be honored to have you join us. Mr. Blackwing, perhaps you can tell our guests about that snow storm when you got trapped in a cave with a black bear."

The boys' eyes widened and their faces broke into broad grins. Their parents reacted with the same enthusiasm. As for Lilia, her heart fluttered, not with anticipation or fright, but with disgust at the idea of dining at the same table with wild savages.

Finding herself in the arms of a young Negro woman with scarred hands was cause enough to have heart palpitations, but no one seemed aware of her discomfort. Lilia shuddered as she shimmied away from Annie's touch.

Lilia was shocked by how Caleb, Serenity, the Berks, and the savages all started toward the inn as if it were an everyday occurrence. Lilia couldn't believe the way Serenity chatted up a storm with Gray Sparrow listening and nodding, as if they'd been friends forever.

Lilia whispered to Annie. "How can she do that?"

"What?" Annie looked bewildered.

"Nothing. You wouldn't understand." Lilia clamped shut her jaw. She was frustrated that no one noticed her displeasure. She made it as obvious as she dared under the circumstances. After a few more steps, she nudged Annie again. "Serenity speaks to Gray Sparrow, but the woman never answers. Doesn't she understand English?"

Annie laughed. "Oh, yes, she understands English very well. Her husband, Joseph Blackwing, was raised in the East by a merchant and his French-speaking wife. The man speaks fluent English as well as French and a smattering of Spanish."

"But, if she understands . . ." Lilia rolled her eyes toward the Shoshone woman. ". . . why doesn't she . . . you know?"

Annie slowed their pace before answering Lilia's question. "When Gray Sparrow was a young girl, she was attacked by a gang of drunk white trappers. When she tried to scream for help, they cut out her tongue," the young colored girl explained. "Gray Sparrow expresses herself through the things she does for people. If anyone is sick or needs help, Gray Sparrow is immediately there. She's a real Christian, all right." Annie's luminous brown eyes were filled with admiration. "No one can figure out how the woman learns about people's needs, but she does. It's like she has a sixth sense—giving love where it's needed."

As they strode past a briar bush, Annie's skirt caught on a bramble. She stopped to yank it free. "Gray Sparrow's a medicine woman, you know, herbs and such. She used to be involved in devil worship and the incantation stuff many Indian tribes practice. But Joseph led her to Christ. Now she and her husband worship God like we do."

Lilia eyed the couple with condescension. *Of course, such people would find comfort in Christianity. Anything's better than their native religion.* She followed Annie into the inn. While Serenity made their guests comfortable, Annie drew Lilia to the pantry and handed her a stack of plates to put on the table.

"Serenity and Caleb go to their village the first Sunday of every month to worship with the Blackwings and others of their people who've accepted Christianity," Annie confided, her eyes sparkling with compassion. "Gray Sparrow gave me an herbal balm to rub on my scars. See?" She held up her hands in front of Lilia's face. "The skin is much smoother already."

Lilia shuddered at the ugly scars on the girl's hands and arms. Although Serenity had written to Lilia about the fire at Serenity's old home and about Annie's bravery in trying to put it out, the sight of Annie's disfigured hands gave Lilia cold shivers.

The evening passed quickly as Joseph Blackwing kept the Berks and the others spellbound with his adventurous stories.

Mentally distancing herself from the group, Lilia watched in silence. She was pleased with herself for making it through the trying ordeal without having a fit that called for vapors.

With the supper dishes cleaned and returned to the pantry, Serenity suggested that everyone get comfortable on the upholstered furniture in front of the fireplace. Lilia glided across the room to the kitchen area once more. From there she could hear all that transpired as well as occasionally check for Wade's return.

At one point when she thought she heard a wagon approaching, she slipped out the front door and skipped to the corner of the house where she could see the barn and the town road. Sure enough, a buckboard pulled by two horses drew to a stop in front of the house.

"Wade?" she called in the darkness.

"No, ma'am, it's Aaron." The man climbed down from the wagon and hitched the reins to the hitching post. He strode over to Lilia. "Cooper isn't here?"

She shook her head and wrapped her arms about herself to ward off the chill from a light breeze sweeping across the prairie.

"Sorry, ma'am, but when he left the saloon last night, I thought he was headin' home."

"Last night?" she asked. "He hasn't been back since he left with you."

Aaron pushed his hat back on his head and scratched his forehead. "I don't know what to tell you, ma'am. I haven't seen hide nor hair of him all day."

"Oh—" A wave of tears filled her eyes. Fearing she would make a fool of herself and cry in front of Serenity's brother-in-law, she turned away.

"I'm sure he's all right, ma'am. I didn't hear of any shootings or mishaps. Such news travels through Independence faster than a chicken hawk can grab its prey. If you'll excuse me, ma'am, I came to speak with my brother."

"He has guests, at least that's what he calls them. They're savages as far as I'm concerned." An edge entered her voice.

"Oh, it must be the Blackwings. If you'll excuse me . . ." He tipped his hat and strode into the house leaving her standing alone in the shadows.

Lilia's indignation rose. She was not accustomed to being abandoned or ignored by men. The tears trickling down her cheeks intensified when she remembered she was no longer the desirable young daughter of the wealthy Northrops of Norfolk. Of course the handsome, young brother-in-law of her best friend ignored her. She was another man's wife, a pregnant wife, in fact.

Instinct told her to run, run and hide, but where would she go? Back up the hill? She shuddered at the thought. To town? Reality reminded her of the folly of walking six miles into town at night. Mr. Blackwing's tales of wild animals and poisonous snakes he'd encountered on the prairie capped her decision to slip back into the house and to her room. She'd wait until morning, then ask for Caleb's help in locating her husband.

Lilia made excuses to her hosts and their guests and hurried to her room. Her muscles ached as she slid between the crisp cotton sheets on the down-filled mattress. She'd worked hard that day, trying to keep up with Serenity and Annie. It had been exhausting, an experience she hoped never to repeat, especially the encounter with the Indians. By morning, the Blackwings would be nothing but a foul memory she hoped never to relive. She'd convince Caleb to take her to town where she'd find Wade and move to more civilized housing. Friend or no, Serenity's standard of living didn't come close to what Lilia was accustomed!

Sometime during the night, she was awakened by rafter-shaking thunder. A mighty wind accompanied by ponderous storm clouds rolled out of the west. Lightning bolts streaked across the sky, snapping and crackling with destructive energy. Then came the rain, not droplets of moisture but a deluge.

After a time, Lilia fell asleep once again. She awakened before dawn to a particularly violent thunderclap. Clutching the top sheet to her chest, she padded to the bedroom window and peered out at a raging violence she had never before seen. She'd experienced thunder and lightning storms in Virginia, but the destructive rage of this storm far surpassed its nearest challenger. Another loud thunder boomer sent her scurrying for the safety of the bed. Her teeth chattered from fear. A part of her doubted she'd make it through the night.

"I hate this place!" she growled as she burrowed under the downy quilt. Everything about the prairie seemed to be bigger, wilder, and more frightening than anything she'd experienced before. "The sooner I get out of here and back home, the better."

Home? An inner voice challenged. *You can't go home. Remember? You've burned those bridges, little girl. You know your father's anger. He'll never take you back into the family circle. He will never forgive you!* She tightened the covers about her body and cried herself to sleep.

The morning brought her customary nausea and vomiting. By the time she bathed, dressed, and made herself presentable, the rains had stopped. But one look out of the window and she knew there'd be no trip to town that day. The world outside was awash with mud. Even the thirsty, sundried Missouri soil couldn't absorb the enormous amount of water that had fallen during the hours before dawn.

One glance in the mirror at her ashen face told Lilia she wouldn't be up to taking a buggy ride any time soon anyway. *I have to get something in my stomach,* she decided. *Otherwise it can only get worse.*

Fighting the urge to tumble back into bed and bury her head beneath a pillow, she made her way out of the bedroom and down the hallway toward the great room. Lilia's big surprise came when she stumbled into the great room and found in addition to Serenity and Annie, not only Mrs. Berk and her youngest son, but Gray Sparrow as well. She guessed that the Berks' two older sons were in the barn with the men. She cast a long disdainful glance at Gray Sparrow before she padded into the room. *This is the start of a lovely day,* Lilia thought.

Serenity leaned over the hearth, stoking the fire in the fireplace. "Lilia, you are just in time for a cup of hot tea. Did you sleep through the storm last night? Wasn't it something? The lightning was almost magical."

"Tea would be nice. Thank you," Lilia mumbled. *So when does this morning sickness go away?* she wondered. Gingerly, she seated herself on the edge of a chair and sighed.

Out of the corner of her eye Lilia saw the Shoshone woman, who was sitting on the other side of the hearth from Serenity, rise to her feet and pad to the kitchen.

Serenity placed the poker in its holder beside the fireplace. "These late summer storms can really whip up a brew of noise, can't they?"

Lilia nodded, but kept her eyes on Gray Sparrow.

At the stove, Gray Sparrow reached into a leather pouch she wore hanging from her waist and extracted a smaller packet.

"What is it, Gray Sparrow?" Serenity asked. Lilia watched as Gray Sparrow, through a series of signs and grunts, explained to Serenity, then Serenity translated to Lilia that Gray Sparrow had an herbal potion that would ease nausea during the early stages of pregnancy.

Lilia's mouth dropped open in horror. Her secret was out. How did she know? Even worse was the potion Gray Sparrow was making for her to drink. Lilia searched her brain for an escape, any escape. How did this savage woman know about her delicate condition? Lilia suffered in silence while Serenity and Mrs. Berk chatted about the Berks' postponed departure.

"I do hope we will be able to leave tomorrow," Mrs. Berk confided. "Otherwise we may have to wait until Monday before leaving."

Serenity, ever the optimist, assured the woman that the roads would be dry enough for the oxen to haul the wagons safely in a day or so. Lilia barely took her eyes off Gray Sparrow while the Indian woman prepared the tea. When satisfied the liquid had steeped enough, Gray Sparrow carried the teacup to Lilia.

The young aristocrat was in a quandary. Good breeding demanded she accept the drink. Yet her innate fear of the woman caused her to cower from the idea.

"Go ahead," Serenity urged. "Gray Sparrow saved Caleb's sister's leg and possibly her life with her herbal potions. I'm sure the tea won't hurt you and it may make you feel a whole lot better."

Lilia's hands trembled as she took the cup of hot liquid from the Shoshone woman and muttered a barely articulate "Thank you." The women watched as Lilia lifted the cup to her lips and took a tiny sip.

"Go ahead," Serenity urged. "Try to drink it all. I didn't have much morning sickness with this baby."

Lilia cast her a doleful glance at her friend. If she weren't feeling so terrible, no one could have convinced her to drink the bitter-tasting brew. Deciding death to be a more desirable fate than living in her present condition, she quickly gulped down the hot liquid, emptying the cup in one swig.

The Indian woman took the cup from Lilia's willing hands and placed it on the wet sink by the window.

All eyes were on Lilia. "Well?" Serenity asked. "How do you feel?"

Lilia paused; her mouth dropped open in surprise. As soon as she swallowed the hot tea, her stomach stopped rumbling and her dizziness subsided. She could feel the color return to her face. "I-I-I feel much better. Thank you."

"Wonderful!" Serenity clapped her hands in delight. "Then you'll have a couple of my soda biscuits with gravy?"

Lilia heard her stomach growl from hunger, a good sign. "That would be nice."

"Let me get it for her, Serenity, while you relax a while. You've been going all morning, what with roasting those turkeys." Mrs. Berk arose from the sofa where she'd been knitting a sweater for her husband. "Just seat yourself at the table, Mrs. Cooper, and I'll have a plate of biscuits and gravy ready for you in a jiffy."

Lilia turned toward Gray Sparrow and gave the woman a shy smile. "Thank you so much, but may I ask what was in that tea? It worked so fast."

Gray Sparrow turned to Serenity and made a series of signs and motions.

When she stopped, Serenity translated for Lilia. "If I understand her correctly, it's comprised of dandelion greens, ginger root, and wild comfrey. Is that right?"

The Shoshone woman nodded and grinned, then padded across the room to the pantry, returning with a small bowl into which she poured the contents of her leather pouch. She then handed the bowl of herbs to Serenity. "For tomorrow?" Serenity asked.

Gray Sparrow nodded, then counted off seven fingers.

"Thank you." Serenity held up the bowl for Lilia to see. "Gray Sparrow is leaving enough of her tea leaves to last you all week."

Lilia blushed from the unexpected kindness. "Thank you," she whispered. "Thank you very much." Already the aroma of roasting turkey was making her mouth water.

The morning passed quickly for the women as Annie, Mrs. Berk, and Gray Sparrow helped Serenity with the morning chores. Feeling out of place working alongside the other women, Lilia watched from the safety of the rocker beside the fireplace. At one point, Serenity dumped a kettle of bush beans in Lilia's lap. Awkwardly Lilia snapped the beans into small cylinders. When she'd completed the stack of beans, she viewed the results with a note of pride.

The aroma of freshly baked bread and roasting turkeys filled the inn by the time the men came inside for the noon meal of turkey, mashed potatoes, gravy, buttered corn, and string beans. Once the table was cleared and the noon dishes were washed, the Blackwings said good-bye to return to their village. As she watched the middle-aged Indian couple leave, Lilia couldn't get the memory of Gray Sparrow out of her mind. The young woman knew she had been anything but kind to the Shoshone woman, yet the Indian woman had willingly, eagerly reached out to ease Lilia's misery.

That evening after Annie and the Berks headed for bed and Caleb had gone to the master bedroom with a book he'd been reading, Lilia and Serenity seated themselves on each end of the sofa. Serenity bent her knees and tucked her legs beside her and covered them with an afghan. Lilia, on the other hand, sat properly as if in the parlor of royalty. Without glancing Serenity's way, Lilia apologized for the distant way she'd treated Serenity's guests. "You have to understand, a Northrop woman is not accustomed to socializing with people of other, er, color, except as servants, that is."

Serenity gazed at her friend for several seconds before speaking. Her steady look unsettled Lilia. Finally Serenity spoke. "I don't know what plans you and Wade might have, but if you want to survive out here in the West, you will need to stop thinking like a Northrop woman and begin acting like a pioneer woman." Her tone was one of kindness and compassion. "This is a dangerous land. The weather is fierce and the prairie is lonely. There's no room for pride or haughtiness. We need each other to survive."

Lilia's expression hardened. She lifted her nose a trifle. "I'm afraid I will never adjust to such primitive living." The woman took a deep breath, then weighing her words carefully, she continued. "Serenity, as you've probably already figured out, I've made a grave mistake marrying Wade. He doesn't love me, and, and I'm not sure that I love him. I don't want to adjust to prairie life; I want to go home." A tear trickled down her cheek.

"Oh, honey." Serenity reached for her friend's hand. "I'm sure you don't mean that. Wade loves you, I'm sure of it. And you love him." Her words sounded hollow and unconvincing. "You're overwrought from the pregnancy. My first months of pregnancy I cried a lot too. Caleb hardly knew what to do with his suddenly emotional bride. But those feelings will pass, I promise."

Lilia swiped at the hated tears streaming down her face. "No, I don't think so. I'm not cut out for pioneer living. I know that now. I just want to go home. But even if I could, I know my parents will never want to see me again."

Serenity scooted closer to her friend. "I'm sure that's not true. And as far as pioneer living goes, you'll adjust." She handed Lilia a linen handkerchief from the pocket of her apron. Serenity waved an affected hand in the air and mimicked the accent of their former French teacher. "You survived Martha Van Horne's Finishing School for Young Ladies, didn't you?" Lilia giggled through her sniffles. "After that, you can survive anything, my dear."

"But there I had—"

"There you had to wear those ugly uniforms and practice how to walk with books on your head. Who in the world, may I ask, walks with a stack of books balanced on their head?"

Lilia giggled again.

"As to your husband, you're angry because he hasn't returned from town. I'm sure he'll be back tomorrow."

Lilia shook her head as she blew her nose. "You don't know Wade. He attracts trouble like clover attracts honeybees. I'm afraid something terrible has happened to him."

"See? That shows you do love him." Serenity seemed pleased with her observation.

Lilia realized that her friend could not possibly understand the complicated relationship she had with Wade. She, herself, couldn't always understand what drove her husband's fury. Lilia swallowed hard and lifted her eyes to meet Serenity's. "I-I-I guess you're right."

"Of course I am. I'm always right, remember?" Serenity beamed.

A chuckle erupted from Lilia as she leaned back to rest her head on the sofa. "Sure you are, like the time you snatched old Herman's britches from the bushes?"

"Excuse me? My only mistake was listening to you in the first place!" Serenity curled her legs under her Indian style, then smoothed her skirts around her. "And a lot of help you were, rolling on the lawn and laughing."

"I didn't roll on the lawn. And besides, what could I do? I couldn't stop laughing."

Serenity cast her a wry grin. "We did have fun, didn't we?"

Lilia bit her lip and lowered her gaze. "Sometimes, I wish . . ."

"Wish what?"

"I wish I'd never left the school. If only I could go back in time. Everything's gone wrong since I graduated," Lilia admitted.

"I know what you mean. I felt like that for a while. My mother's death, my father's engagement to Josephine, the house burning down . . . It was a difficult time for me. If it hadn't been for Aunt Fay, er, I mean Mom Cunard, leading me to my mother's God, I don't know what I would have done."

"Yes, well, frankly, Serenity, I'd rather not talk about your God. If there is a God, He has a nasty sense of humor."

—6—
Vain Regrets

EARLY THE NEXT MORNING THE BERKS LEFT the inn to join one of the last westbound wagon trains of the season. Lilia tagged after Annie and Serenity as they stripped the Berks' beds and washed the linens. It was hard work, work Lilia had no intention of ever doing herself. Why Serenity didn't leave the job to Annie, Lilia couldn't understand.

As Serenity worked, she and Lilia talked. Lilia appreciated her friend's wisdom and her listening ear. Annie volunteered to hang the wash on the clothesline behind the inn, leaving the two women alone.

"Whew!" Serenity wiped the sweat from her brow and arched her back. "I'm tired! Carrying around this baby is rough on my lower back. Let's sit down." She waddled into the living room and lowered her awkward body onto the sofa.

Lilia, who had been watching Serenity's gait, followed her to the sofa and seated herself on the far end. She tried to imagine herself as round, unsightly, and sweaty as her old school friend. It was more than she could bear. The dam broke. Her troubles tumbled out of her mouth like the spring runoff. She couldn't stop herself.

"Wade . . . er . . ." Lilia sniffed into the handkerchief again. "Wade can be very sweet, at times. Other times, he turns mean. That's the only way to say it—mean. Once I found his fiery nature exciting. But now, his outbursts are not so attractive, I fear."

She nibbled on her lower lip before continuing. "He had a rough childhood and sometimes he . . ." Lilia looked up, her chin jutted forward defiantly. She studied her friend's face for any sign of censure. "If I had some place to go, to get away from him, I would. And don't tell me, 'Whither thou goest' and all that rhetoric."

Serenity gently touched her friend's arm. "I wasn't going to."

Lilia shot an angry glare at her friend. "Come on. What with all your talk about God, you weren't going to say something about a wife's place being with her husband?"

Serenity shrugged her shoulders. "I don't need to say what you already know."

Lilia continued as if Serenity hadn't spoken. "I tried to leave him during the trip West, but he caught me and said he'd kill me if I ever pulled that stunt again." She rubbed her upper arms and shuddered. "That was before I knew about the baby."

"I'm so sorry."

Lilia knew there was very little her friend could say. The law was with Wade. If she ran, she would be treated by lawman and bounty hunter like a fugitive slave.

Serenity brushed a stray, damp curl from Lilia's forehead. "Honey, I know you won't want to hear this, but you need your mama and daddy. I'm sure they could help you somehow."

The mention of her parents unleashed a flood of fresh tears. "Oh, Serenity, if only it were that simple." She threw herself in her friend's arms. Between hiccups, she told Serenity about the strong words she'd exchanged with her parents the night she eloped with Wade, about her father's warning that if she married Wade she would no longer be his daughter, and about the stolen coin collection.

"See?" she sobbed. "I have no family to go home to. My father will never forgive me for marrying Wade. But worse yet, he loved his coin collection. They were the pride of his life."

"Oh, honey, people say things they don't mean when they're hurting or angry. You are more important to your dad than any coins. I'm sure they'd welcome you back with open arms."

Lilia wagged her head. "No! I know my parents. Mama might, but Daddy? Never!"

Serenity held Lilia in her arms for several minutes, comforting her as a mother would a young child. The slam of the pantry door brought their conversation to a close.

Annie strode into the great room, carrying a colander of fresh carrots. "I thought these would taste good for supper."

"Good idea. My goodness, where has the morning gone? I'd better heat the stew for lunch." Serenity rose to her feet, rubbed the small of her back with her hands, and padded to the kitchen. Suddenly Serenity winced. Her hands shot to her back.

"Sit down," Annie ordered. "You aren't doing so well, are you?" She led Serenity to the rocker and helped her sit down. "You rest while Lilia and I take care of lunch."

The colored woman's audacity offended Lilia. For a former slave girl to volunteer her services without asking piqued Lilia's sensitivities. If Serenity hadn't been in such obvious discomfort, Lilia would tell that snippy little slave a thing or two. But the society debutante from Virginia bit her tongue, for she knew that her friend Serenity did need her help.

By the time they'd finished lunch and Caleb had insisted Serenity go lie down, Lilia was certain that Annie had purposely dumped the worst jobs on her. If she didn't know better, Lilia would have thought that the former slave girl was enjoying her opportunity for power. "Give these people an inch and they become power hungry," she muttered as she scrubbed the charred bottom of a large baking pan with a hand full of river sand.

Annie, less than three feet from her, turned and smiled. "I'm sorry. Did you say something?"

"No!" Lilia growled and scraped at a streak of burned-on food.

When the lunch chores were completed, Lilia announced that she was going to take a walk up the hill to the cemetery. She grabbed her bonnet and tied it under her chin. She set out with determination. The winds whipped her skirts about her ankles. The cool breeze felt good on her face as she started up the hill. Halfway up to the top, she remembered Joseph Blackwing's tales of poisonous snakes. Suddenly she decided to turn back.

As she passed the barn, she heard the roar of the bellows and the rhythmic pounding of metal striking metal. Curious, she followed the sound, around the side of the barn to the open barn door where Caleb was working with his back to her. The familiar sight brought a sad little smile to her face.

Scattered about the shop were iron scraps and tools in various stages of repair. The sight, sounds, and smells of the blacksmith shop teased the corners of her mind. Memories of her favorite grandfather on her mother's side flooded her mind. As a child, she'd loved visiting his shop and watching him hammer out horseshoes or wagon parts for the people of the rural area surrounding Norfolk. She immediately recognized several of the tools: a collection of hammers, clamps, an anvil, a vise.

Lilia stepped inside the barn's darkened interior and seated herself on the tongue of a wagon in need of repair. She watched the flames dance in the forge as Caleb operated the bellows. Sparks flew when Caleb hammered the red-hot tip of an iron bar into shape. When he thrust the piece of molten iron into the vat of water, she smiled, hearing the sizzle and seeing the billowing steam.

At one point, Caleb glanced over his shoulder. He waved one hand and continued working. This pleased Lilia. She didn't want anyone interfering with the flow of her surprisingly pleasant memories. She could almost taste the hard candy mints that her grandfather would slip to her as she watched him work. If her grandfather were alive, she knew she'd have a place to go where Wade couldn't follow and she would be loved. But her grandfather was gone, gone like everyone else in her life.

Despite the heat, she gazed unabashedly at the deeply tanned Caleb as he worked. His sweat-stained shirt stretched tightly across his muscular back. With every movement his biceps rippled beneath his shirtsleeves. The man had no flaws that she could see. Except, she reminded herself, for his inordinate love for reading the Bible every morning and every evening after meals.

Without a word, Lilia slipped out of the blacksmith shop and into the afternoon sunlight. She rounded the corner of the barn. Shielding her eyes with one hand, she gazed down the empty road toward town. After a few seconds, the woman heaved a sigh. Feeling older and lonelier than she'd ever felt before, Lilia plodded over the worn pathway, back to the inn and to the privacy of her guest room, where she cried herself to sleep.

That evening, she awakened long enough to eat and to inquire if Caleb would take her to town to find Wade the next morning. He assured her that he would do so. Satisfied, she tumbled off to bed once more where she slept the best she had since leaving Virginia.

Before dawn the next morning, Lilia opened the door to her bedroom and heard Caleb's rich baritone voice.

"Wherefore, if God so clothe the grass of the field, which today is and tomorrow is cast into the oven, shall He not much more clothe you, O ye of little faith . . . the Father knoweth that ye have need of all of these things. But seek ye first the kingdom of God, and His righteousness; and all these things shall be added unto you."

Lilia paused at the entrance to the great room to see Caleb, Serenity, and Annie join hands around the table and bow their heads for prayer. The flame from the oil lamp in the center of the table cast a glow over the scene as Caleb asked for God's protection and guidance over the Berks as they journeyed west. Feeling uncomfortable, Lilia padded back to her room to wait until the prayer was over. Fully dressed, she climbed back into bed and drifted off to sleep once more. Kettles banging on the stove awakened her.

Annie was the only one in the room when Lilia arrived. She was clearing the table of the breakfast dishes. "Good morning. How are you feeling? I have hot water on the stove for your special tea."

"Thank you," Lilia mumbled, glancing about the room. "Where is everyone?"

Annie laughed. "Caleb and Serenity are outside gathering eggs."

Lilia ambled over to the door and opened it. She shivered in the early morning air. "Looks like it's going to be a beautiful day." She was trying to make conversation for Serenity's sake. "How is Serenity feeling this morning? I know she wasn't doing too well last night."

"She had a rough night, so I understand."

"What's with the Bible reading?"

Annie gave Lilia a blank stare. "Bible reading? Oh, you mean worship. We do that every morning and evening."

"I've noticed." Lilia hoped Annie hadn't missed her note of sarcasm.

"Yes, I suppose you have." Annie lips tightened into a narrow line of disapproval. Abruptly, she turned and carried a stack of dirty plates over to the wet sink beneath the kitchen window.

Lilia seated herself at the cleared end of the table. "May I please have a cup of that Indian woman's tea now?"

"Surely," Annie called over her shoulder as she poured hot water into the two dishpans. "The tea leaves are in the pantry on the shelf to your right. You can't miss them."

Lilia started in surprise. *She expects me to . . . of all the nerve!* She slid her chair back from the table and stomped to the pantry. Lilia found the package of tea immediately, but she moved things about and mumbled aloud to protest her treatment.

After purposely waiting a few minutes, Lilia emerged from the pantry, with cup and tea leaves in hand. "I'm sorry,

Annie, to disturb you, but I haven't the vaguest idea of how to make a cup of tea."

Annie dried her hands on a tea towel and smiled at Lilia. "Here, it's very easy. I'm sure you'll catch on right away."

Lilia blinked in surprise at the spunk coming from the shy little maid. She smiled to herself as Annie instructed her on the fine art of tea making. Perhaps this girl had more substance than Lilia had first thought.

She nibbled on a soda cracker while the tea steeped. Then gingerly, she took a sip of the hot liquid. She shuddered at the bitter taste, but, after adding a smidgen of cream, she drained the cup.

Her nausea subsided by the time Caleb and Serenity returned to the cabin. Lilia immediately leaped to her feet to help Annie finish the morning dishes. Serenity barely glanced her way but hurried from the great room toward her and Caleb's bedroom.

Caleb tossed his wide-brimmed felt hat on the hook behind the door. "Lilia, are you still feeling up to a ride into town this morning?"

His question took her by surprise.

"Absolutely!"

Caleb nodded, then picked up the large family Bible from the table where he'd been sitting earlier and returned it to the bookshelf beside the fireplace.

"Serenity has several things she needs to pick up at Cox's General Store and she wants to visit her folks to see how their new house is coming." With barely a break in his speech, he asked, "Annie? You'll want to come along too. I know you're dying to see Josephine again."

Annie's face crinkled into a grin. "I would appreciate that, Caleb. It is nice of you to ask. Thank you for including me."

"Including you?" Caleb stared at her in surprise. "Of course, we'd include you, Annie. You're part of the family, remember?"

Annie nodded; her eyes misted with tears.

Caleb strode toward his bedroom. "Now, can you ladies be ready in fifteen minutes?"

Lilia bustled to her room. Taking a few minutes to secure her ivory combs on each side of her head, she found her favorite, white crocheted shawl, her embroidered poke bonnet, and a fresh pair of white lace gloves. She examined herself in the small mirror hanging above the dresser. Earlier, she'd chosen to wear her mint-green dimity dress with the hand-tatted lace around the wide neckline because it was Wade's favorite. She took a closer look at her face. It was pale, far too pale. She pinched her cheeks and nibbled on her lips. Better. She'd never been at a loss for color in her cheeks before this pregnancy. She decided that she'd check in town for a tin of rice powder or some rouge. A glance out the window at the bright sunshine convinced her to take along her white lace parasol.

Hurrying from her room, Lilia was surprised to discover that everyone was waiting and ready to go. And she thought she was eager to leave!

Lilia wasn't too pleased to discover that she was relegated to sit in the back of the buckboard with Annie. Caleb apologized for the inconvenience as he helped her into the wagon. "I insist that Serenity ride up front with me—the baby, and all."

Lilia simpered her understanding, but pouted throughout the ride. She sneaked a peek at her traveling companion. Annie didn't appear to be in a talkative mood either. And that suited Lilia just fine.

Halfway to town, the sky to the west filled with massive thunderheads. A storm was coming—a storm to match Lilia's fretful mood. Lilia worried about the condition Wade would be in when she found him. Would he be angry with her for looking for him? Would she find him dead? What if she couldn't find him at all?

When the buckboard lumbered up to the partly constructed house, Josephine appeared in the doorway. Her face beamed with delight. She welcomed them profusely. After a tour of the house site, Caleb and Serenity told Josephine that they had some shopping to do in town and promised to return later.

"In time for supper, I hope." Josephine's eyes sparkled with delight. "I'm learning to make a whale of a stew, minus the whale, of course."

"I'd like to stay here with you," Annie volunteered, "and help."

Josephine wrapped her arm around the girl's waist. "I'd love that. I can show you the drapery fabric I bought to put in your bedroom. It's lavender. You told me you like lavender."

Caleb took Serenity's arm to help her into the wagon. "We'll be back in plenty of time since Serenity will need to take a rest before making the trip home."

Josephine cocked her head to one side. "Serenity, why not stay with us while Caleb takes care of the business? You can rest now, and later, we'll all go shopping together? You're invited as well, Lilia," she added.

"Lilia has business of her own," Caleb interjected.

"Caleb's right, but that shouldn't stop you, Serenity, from spending time with your family." Lilia assured her. "With Caleb as my guide, I'll be fine."

Serenity turned to her friend. "You sure you wouldn't mind? I am rather tired."

Almost relieved not to have Serenity along should she be embarrassed when she found Wade, Lilia reassured her. "I really don't mind. Honest!"

Lilia's fears proved to be accurate. When Caleb located his brother Aaron at his rented room behind the mercantile, Aaron told them that Wade had been arrested the night before.

"I don't know what happened though," Aaron defended. "I was on the road until dawn this morning." He shot a quick glance at his brother. "I didn't hear about the arrest until I got back into town."

"Where were you?" A streak of irritation crossed Caleb's face.

Aaron's face hardened. "Excuse me?" An angry glance flashed between the brothers. Caleb shook his head in frustration.

"You're at it again, aren't you?"

Aaron's eyes narrowed. His lips tightened into a thin hard line. "I *am* an adult. I don't need to check in with you, Big Brother."

"I'm sorry." Worry creased Caleb's brow. "Be careful, Aaron. Just be careful." Caleb pressed his hand against his forehead and closed his eyes momentarily. "Look! Mrs. Cooper's worried sick about her missing husband. Could you please go to the jail with us to see if your information is correct?"

Aaron started to protest until he read the concern on Lilia's face. "Oh," Aaron answered grudgingly, "all right."

~7~

Bars and Broken Promises

DEPUTY SHERIFF HOMER DODDS WAS ON DUTY at the county jail when Lilia and the Cunard brothers arrived. They found him leaning back against the wall in a chair, his feet, clad in scruffy cowboy boots, on top of the desk. He was reading the local newspaper.

When Lilia entered the office, the bushy-browed lawman, sporting a day-old beard and an unkempt mustache, leaped to his feet. "Ma'am." He ran his fingers through his tousled hair and grinned. He was missing a front tooth. Lilia suspected he'd lost it in a fight carrying out the duties of his office.

Caleb removed his hat and offered his hand to the lawman. "Mr. Dodds, my name is Caleb Cunard. My wife and I run Serenity Inn outside of town."

Dodds nodded and shook Caleb's hand. "I know the place, Mr. Cunard."

"Great! My brother tells me that you are detaining one of my guests, a Mr. Wade Cooper." Aaron and the deputy exchanged brief glances, barely acknowledging each other's presence. Caleb continued, "This here's Mrs. Cooper, the man's wife." He gestured toward Lilia.

Dodds' eyes lit up. Married or not, he appreciated a pretty woman. He ran his gaze appreciatively over Lilia.

"So what happened? Where's my husband?" she asked, struggling to maintain her composure against the man's gaze.

The deputy sheriff scratched the side of his face, then ran his tongue along the lining of his cheek. "Well, ma'am, it seems your husband, along with several other men, got into a brawl the other night. Sheriff and I just brought 'em in here to sober 'em up so's we can sort out who done what."

"Does Mr. Cooper need to clean up?" Caleb asked. "Can Mrs. Cooper see him? Talk to him?"

"He has a fine to pay, for room and board here the last two days and for damages."

"A fine? What size fine are we talking about?" Caleb asked.

The deputy shrugged. "Garvey didn't say. He intends to take it up with the judge when he swings back through town." The deputy reached for a large ring of brass keys hanging on the wall behind the desk. "Fred Garvey, the owner of the bar, is pressing charges against your husband, ma'am. Beggin' your pardon, but Cooper was accused by the others of cheatin'. He tried to slip an ace of spades into his hand from up his sleeve, he did."

Caleb narrowed his gaze at the lawman and challenged, "You don't know that for sure, do you, Sheriff?"

The news about Wade didn't surprise Lilia. She'd suspected as much from his slippery encounters on the riverboat. Caleb, however, was a different matter. To Lilia's surprise, he seemed ready to defend his guest until proven wrong.

Caleb continued, "And you mean to tell me that you intend to keep Mr. Cooper locked up until the circuit-riding judge shows up? That could be weeks." Agitated, Caleb twisted and untwisted the brim of his felt hat. "And I'm not so sure that's legal."

He turned to Lilia. "Why don't you wait here while we go get our friend Felix," Caleb explained. "He'll know what to do."

"Good idea, big brother!" Aaron enthused. It was apparent that Aaron wished to anywhere but in the local pokey talking with the deputy sheriff. Lilia had noticed him nervously shifting from one foot to the other during the entire conversation and wondered what would make him so uncomfortable. But her musings were cut short as Aaron turned and bolted for the door. Caleb assured Lilia they'd be right back, then followed Aaron out the door. He sensed that she wasn't sure she wanted to be left for long in the care of Deputy Dodds.

Lilia sniffled into her handkerchief. "Sheriff, I'd like to go to my husband."

Dodds shot a cocky smile her way. "It's pretty smelly back there, ma'am. Lots of sweatin' and pukin' goin' on."

Lilia's stomach lurched at the thought. She leaned against the desktop to steady herself. The young lawman watched her intently. "It might be a little much for a fine lady like yourself."

Dodds' attitude hardened her resolve. "He's my husband. I must go to him."

"Suit yourself." The deputy shrugged and rounded the cluttered desk. He unlocked the first iron gate, then held it open for her to pass through.

"I can do this. I can do this," she whispered to herself as she stepped beyond and the gate swung closed behind her. An acrid odor accosted her as she followed the sheriff down the jail corridor. Her determination wavered as she choked back the bile rising in her throat. The deputy squinted down at her. "Are you all right, ma'am?"

She nodded, not trusting herself to speak.

There were eight cells, four on each side of the corridor. Each held prisoners. In the first six cells she passed, the prisoners were curled up on bunks, asleep. One older man with graying hair and bleary eyes sat on the floor and watched her pass. She eyed him nervously.

"Most of 'em are sleeping off a drunk," the deputy explained, "except for Chester here."

Hard, bitter eyes looked out at her from under thick dark eyebrows and reluctantly merged into a scruffy bearded face. "Chester's waitin' for Judge York to come to town. Old Chester done shot and killed young Robbie Forster for comin' to court Maude, his only daughter." The deputy shook his head and clicked his tongue. "It ain't as if Maude's that great a looker or nothin' either."

Lilia paused to take a second look at the accused murderer. She thought of her father and wondered if he would have killed Wade had he caught up with them. She couldn't imagine her mild-mannered father doing such a thing, even though he'd been so angry the night they eloped.

"Here he is." Dodds pointed toward the last cell on the left.

She looked in the direction the deputy had pointed and gasped. "Wade?"

The prisoner sat hunched over on the edge of the wooden cot, his head in his hands. He looked up at the sound of his name.

"Ooh!" Lilia's flew to her mouth at the sight of her usually dapper young husband. Wade's left eye was swollen shut, his lip cut and bruised. A series of bruises covered the right side of his face. When he opened his mouth to speak, she noticed that two of his teeth were missing.

"Wade Cooper, your wife is here to see you." Deputy Dodds unlocked the cell gate and gestured to Lilia. "Gotta' lock you in, ma'am, him being my prisoner and all."

Lilia stepped into the six-by-eight-foot, red brick cell. Light and fresh air—if one could call the steamy, August, Midwest air fresh—came in through the eighteen-inch, square, barred window high on the outside wall.

Wade remained seated on the bare cot, which was chained to the wall. When she approached, he waved her away. "Don't! Don't come any closer. You don't belong in here. Why did you come anyway? To humiliate me further?"

"You're my husband, Wade. For better, for worse, remember?" she defended.

The deputy shuffled from one foot to the other. "I'll be down the hall if you need me, Mrs. Cooper. Just call when you're ready to leave."

"Uh, thank you, sir." *Ready to leave?* She was ready to leave right then. Every instinct in her body screamed for her to run away. She bit her lower lip and squared her shoulders. Lilia took a tentative step closer to Wade.

An unexpected wave of nausea overtook her from the smell of the metal chamber pot in the corner of the cell. Swallowing hard, she proceeded until she could reach out and touch Wade's shoulder. He flinched at the contact. She recoiled. "I don't know what to say," she mumbled, acutely aware of the man watching the drama from the cell across the corridor.

"I wasn't cheating. Honest. I didn't do what they said. They were mad for losing to a Yankee, that's all." He buried his face in his hands. Greasy locks of hair fell forward over his fingers. It was a Wade Cooper she'd never before seen.

She ached to brush the brown curls back with her hand, but instead whispered, "Yes, honey. I know. I know."

She knew that Wade had been accused of cheating at cards on the riverboat, but his accuser couldn't prove it. The game master had barred both Wade and his accuser from the game room for two nights. Wade had been unbearable until he was once again allowed back at the poker table.

"Did you lose everything?" Lilia asked. She knew they'd not paid Serenity and Caleb for her stay at the inn.

"Naw." His cut lip lifted into a sneer. "I got a stash hidden, don't worry. Those country yokels, I'll show 'em!" He gave a nasty little laugh.

"How much?"

"Don't worry! I still got a coin or two." He eyed her suspiciously. "Why? Why do you want to know?"

"I can't stay indefinitely at the inn without paying, Wade. I'm a guest now, a friend, but we can't expect the Cunards to put us up indefinitely. And, from what the deputy sheriff said, it's going cost to get you out of here. Then there are the damages at the bar."

He lifted his gaze to meet hers. He studied her face through narrow slits until she squirmed with discomfort. A sneer formed on his lips. "Hmmph! Maybe I got the money; maybe I don't."

She looked at him questioningly. "What do you mean by that?"

He dropped his gaze to the floor. "I mean I ain't gonna' confide the extent of my finances to no dumb female, wife or no wife."

Her face flooded with color. "I have a right to know, Wade."

He didn't move but continued staring at the wooden floor beneath his feet.

Finally Lilia spoke again. "Caleb and his brother Aaron went to find an attorney friend of theirs who might be able to get you out of here." She turned her back on him and rubbed her arms nervously. "Maybe I should wire my father for help."

"No! Don't even think that!" Wade leaped to his feet. Fury shot from his eyes. She cowered in the corner of the cell, expecting a blow from his balled fists.

"He'll have a warrant out for my arrest and I'll never get out of the pokey." The bitterness in his face subsided to contrition as quickly as it had appeared. He strode over to her and took her into his arms. His bruised hands ran up and down her cotton cambric sleeves. His tenderness brought sobs to her lips, but his words continued to slash and cut through to her heart. "Besides, after what you did, do you really think he would forgive you?" he asked. "You know what a hard man he is when it comes to his money."

Tears blurred her eyes as she melted into his arms despite the grit and dried blood on his leather vest and soiled plaid shirt. "Oh, Wade, I was so worried when you didn't come back to me," she wailed.

He caressed her back and nuzzled her neck. "Oh, baby, you smell so good." Lifting her chin until their eyes met, he gently touched his bruised lip to hers. "You never need to worry about me, baby. Wade Cooper always ends up on his feet."

At the sound of approaching footsteps, Wade pushed her away. "Be brave now. Everything's going to be fine."

"Wade Cooper?" It was Sheriff Prior. A gruff looking lawman with a handlebar mustache and a fierce gaze unlocked the cell door. He acknowledged Lilia's presence with a curt nod. "Mr. Bonner is here to bail you out of jail until Judge York swings by at the end of the month. You need to give him your word that you won't jump bail and head for parts unknown." The man's lower lip worked the mustache hairs above his mouth. "I've agreed to this arrangement against my better judgment."

The iron gate creaked open. The sheriff stepped inside the cell. Stone-faced, he eyed the lithesome young woman who held his prisoner's hand. "Now I understand why my deputy broke my rule about letting women in to see their men. You are a pretty little thing."

Color flooded Lilia's face. She released her husband's hand. She could sense rage flaring inside Wade. If he didn't lose control here in the cell by lashing out at the armed lawman, she would, sooner or later, feel the sting of his ire. Wade hated having any man comment about her beauty.

The lawman continued, directing his comments toward her. "I'll tell ya' up front, ma'am, I don't like your taste in men, no how. You could do much better than this pond scum, especially out here in the West, where pretty women are as rare as a drunkard at a Baptist revival meeting." Sheriff Prior chuckled at his little joke. Directing his glance toward Wade, his smile hardened. Through clenched teeth, he said, "That husband of yours is a weezily varmint, and the sooner he's out of my territory, the better I'm going to like it."

Lilia bristled at the sheriff's words. Was he trying to incite Wade to violence? "I beg your pardon, sir. You can't talk to my husband that way."

The sheriff tipped his head to one side. While his smile broadened, his eyes remained cold. "Why, ma'am, I can talk to him any way I like. I'm the sheriff in these parts. Purty or not, you'd do well to remember that."

"Yes, sir." Lilia meekly dipped her head. She glanced toward Caleb and his lawyer friend but found no sympathy on their faces.

Satisfied with Lilia's humility, the sheriff called to Wade's newly acquired attorney. "Bonner, I wish you luck. I'd get my money from this one up front if I were you."

Felix smiled and extended his hand. "Thank you, Sheriff. Mr. Cooper, if you'll come with me, we'll get you a shower and some clean clothes. Then we'll discuss the conditions of your release."

Wade broke into a big smile. He resumed his earlier cocky air. "Appreciate this, Mr. Bonner. I won't let you down, I promise."

Lilia cringed at his words. She'd heard his promises before. A tiny part inside of her hoped he meant what he said this time.

Wade continued to assure the attorney that he'd learned his lesson, that he planned to straighten up, get a job, and maybe even buy a little place on the edge of town for his wife.

She winced again. Lilia knew her husband well. Wade, become a farmer? She knew he was saying what the attorney and the sheriff wanted to hear, nothing more. Hadn't she been the object of his promises so many nights on board the riverboat—promises that he'd change, that he'd never go back to the den of thieves called the game room, that he'd never lift his hand to harm her?

While Wade cleaned up at his attorney's place, Aaron offered to drive Lilia back to Serenity's father's place. "I think I should stay here with Wade," she protested. "He may need me."

Attorney Bonner assured her that he would care for any needs her husband might have. "Wade and I need to have a good talk, Mrs. Cooper. Just he and I."

Wade agreed.

Reluctantly Lilia climbed into the wagon and rode back to the Pownell's place. It was almost evening before Caleb and Wade arrived to take the ladies back to the inn. Josephine insisted they eat a light supper before departing. By the frown on Serenity's father's face, Lilia knew the man didn't approve of Wade. The usually loquacious elder statesman was quiet throughout the meal.

As the two couples and Annie prepared to leave, Mr. Pownell stopped them at the front door. "Cooper, I have a proposition for you. I'm building a new house and need workers. Most of the able-bodied men in town have left for the West. I pay a fair wage for an honest day's work. Can you drive a straight nail?"

Though she never heard Wade's answer, and doubted he'd agree to work for Mr. Pownell, Lilia's eyes glistened. She knew Serenity had put her father up to hiring Wade. Although the thought stung Lilia's pride, she was grateful. *Perhaps if he has a good job,* she told herself, *perhaps, he'll . . . he'll what?* She didn't exactly know what it was she expected from her errant husband.

What she'd fallen in love with was Wade's reckless air and his prideful strut. He'd represented freedom from society's restraints and from her parents' outdated values. She recalled her father's disappointment upon meeting her intended. She frowned. Would Wade, could Wade ever be her parents' view of a perfect husband? And would she love him if he were?

On the way out of town, Wade insisted that Caleb stop at the Blue Nickel, a seedy bar and bordello beyond the town limits where he'd been staying. When Wade hopped down and started for the front door, Caleb joined him.

"You don't have to follow me, Cunard," Wade growled. "I ain't going to run."

Caleb shrugged and fell into step beside him anyway. The ladies waited in the wagon until both men emerged from the building and hopped on board again. Under Wade's arm was a bundle of clothing.

Lilia eyed the bundle, then smiled at her husband. He hadn't been lying. He did still have some of her father's coins left. She leaned her head against his shoulder and closed her eyes. She told herself that everything would be all right, just as her husband had promised. *Tomorrow,* she vowed, *tomorrow I'll tell him about the baby.* Once Wade learned about the child she was carrying, he'd settle down and become the kind of husband she knew he could be.

Having fallen asleep upon his shoulder, Lilia was surprised when the gentle rhythm of the wagon wheels rolling over the dusty road stopped and she found herself back at the inn.

~8~

For Parts Unknown

THE SUN WAS ALMOST BENEATH THE HORIZON as the buckboard came to a stop outside the blacksmith shop and inn. Lilia was surprised to see two oxen hitched to a covered wagon waiting in the barnyard. Guests for the inn, she supposed, but hadn't Serenity said the Berks had joined the last westbound wagon train? Lilia hurried past the couple with five children, who introduced themselves to Caleb and Serenity as the Hogans from Connecticut. Wade grasped her by the elbow and headed to their room.

Lilia knew she was in for more trouble. She entered the room and removed her gloves. The door had barely closed when Wade slapped her across the face. Stunned, Lilia fell across the bed.

"I can't trust you one minute out of my sight, woman. Flirting with the sheriff of all people! How desperate are you, anyhow? You little tramp!"

She pressed her hand against her stinging cheek. "Wade, I didn't flirt with the sheriff. You know I love only you."

"Oh yeah, you expect me to believe that?"

Tears slid down her face. She felt as if her heart would break. It was true. She deserved Wade's distrust. While she hadn't flirted with the sheriff, she had flirted with other men aboard the riverboat, mainly to get her husband's attention. And yes, she'd found both Caleb and Aaron attractive. Wade was right. A whimper escaped her lips. She did deserve his distrust.

Wade dropped his bundle of clothing onto the bed. Shedding his boots and canvas trousers, he plopped himself on the edge of the bed and opened his bundle. A shirt, an extra pair of pants—he tossed them on the floor in favor of the brown suede pouch beneath. He released the drawstrings in the pouch and tipped it upside down on the bed quilt. Out tumbled five coins.

Lilia caught her breath at the sight of golden coins glittering in the last rays of sunlight. She reached out to touch them and felt the sharp sting of Wade's slap on her hand. "Don't you ever touch these, woman!"

"But they were my father's—"

"They're mine now, do you understand? And believe me, I earned every one of them, putting up with your belly-aching all the way from Virginia. I've taken good care of you, haven't I?"

Nursing her wounded hand, Lilia could only nod her agreement.

"Here!" He tossed the smaller of the coins toward her. "This should cover your stay here with your friends so far."

Surprised, she caught the rare coin and examined it more closely. She fought to swallow the smile teasing at the corner of her lips. Obviously Wade didn't know the value of the coin he'd given her. The small ill-shaped piece of metal was the most valuable of all her father's collection. She pressed the coin to her breast and closed her eyes. She could hear her father's voice.

"This one, Lilly-bell . . ." Daddy always called her Lilly-bell. ". . . was minted in ancient Egypt, the land of the Pharaohs." Then he'd recount the time he rode on the back of one of the shaggy beasts called camels. In her mind's eye, she could almost see the graceful royal palm trees and the playful monkeys that wealthy ladies kept as pets.

A tear slid unbidden down her cheek.

"Now what? What are you bawling about now?"

She shook her head and looked away.

Behind her, Wade dropped the coins into the pouch, then tossed it onto the rough oak dresser in the corner of the room. He removed his shirt and slid beneath the bed covers.

"Come here, woman." He grabbed her arm and dragged her to him.

"Wait, Wade, I need to undress and wash up first." She hated the whine in her voice. "It will only take me a minute."

He smiled and lay back against the downy soft pillow. "Umm, a real bed feels good."

Quickly Lilia skirted the foot of the bed to the washstand. After placing the precious coin in one of the gloves she'd discarded earlier, she removed her dress and laid it across a straight back chair nearby, then stepped out of her many layers of crinolines. She removed her hairpins and combs, allowing her heavy golden locks to cascade down her back.

The cool water in the basin felt good on her hot and dusty skin. After drying off, she slipped into her embroidered chambray nightdress. Memories of her mother stitching each of the tiny rosebuds that circled the neck of the gown bought tears to her eyes. She turned to find her husband watching her. He was smiling.

"Is it any wonder I'm so jealous when another man looks at you? Can you blame me? You are so beautiful." His voice was husky with desire.

She glided into his arms. How she adored him when he was in a gentle mood. So tender, so affectionate. This was what she dreamed marriage would be—moonlight and roses, she and Wade locked in a loving embrace.

Several minutes later, after their lovemaking, as she lay in her husband's arms, Lilia decided it was time to tell him about the baby. While she hadn't been thrilled earlier with the prospect of raising a child, she now knew everything would be all right.

"Wade, honey," she began.

"Hmm?"

She could feel his steady heartbeat pulsating against her ear. She snuggled closer to his side. "Honey, I've got some good news."

"Oh?"

"I'm pregnant." Her words hung in the night air. She felt her husband grow tense. "We're going to have a baby. Isn't that wonderful?" she urged.

"A baby?"

"Yes, a baby."

He shot upright in the bed. Her head fell against the pillow. Grabbing her by the shoulders, he glared into her face. "How could you let that happen?"

Startled by his reaction, she couldn't think of what to say. "What do you mean, let that happen?"

His rigid form loomed menacingly over her. "How do I know it's my kid?"

"Know? Wade, there's never been another—"

"I don't know that for sure. You were a slut when you came to me."

A cry escaped her throat, along with a rush of tears. "Wade, you know better."

He swung out of the bed. "I don't know any such thing."

"Oh, Wade, please don't do this. Please . . . this isn't the way it should be."

"What?" He paced across the room to the window and drew back the curtain. She watched in fear as he ran his fingers through his unruly hair. He whirled about to face her. "If you're expecting me to turn into a wimp of a man like your friend's husband, forget it. Doesn't drink, doesn't smoke, doesn't gamble—shush! That's a man?"

She huddled in the corner of the bed. "I-I-I don't expect anything except for you to love me."

"Love you when your body is ugly and gross with child? Some brat who'll ruin all my plans?"

"No, no, it won't be like that. I mean, yes, I'll put on weight during the pregnancy, but afterward, you won't notice the difference. I promise." Lilia slid out of bed and hurried to him. "Please believe me."

"Talk about a ball and chain!" He shook himself free of her arms. "Get released from the pokey to come home to a life sentence!"

Not knowing what else to say, Lilia padded back to her side of the bed and slid under the covers. She fell asleep watching the hard silhouette of her husband as the moonlight flooded through the window.

Reluctantly Lilia awoke to a new morning. Of late her dreams were much more satisfying than the cold, hard reality of each new day. She gave a gentle sigh and idly reached for Wade. Her husband was anything but a morning person.

But the mattress beside her was empty and cold. Her eyes snapped open.

The first rays of morning were filling the tiny room. One glance and Lilia knew something was wrong. Wade's clothing, strewn about the floor the night before—gone! The leather pouch of coins he'd placed on the dresser the night before—gone! Every evidence of his presence had vanished. Noticing something sparkling on the dresser, she went to it. Beneath another of her father's coins was a note.

The words on the note danced and swam before her.

"Dear Lilia, I'm leaving. I can't be tied down to a wife and a baby. I gotta be free. I'm not leaving you penniless, however. Here's another coin to help you get a fresh start— you and the kid."

She picked up the coin, studying its face. She recognized it as a Greek drachma. Wild hope sprang up in her heart, hope that she might somehow catch him before he got too far away. She slammed the coin down on the bureau, yanked her dressing robe over her head, and flew out the door.

When Lilia burst into the great room, Annie who was stoking the fire in the stove jumped and squealed in surprise.

"Have you seen my husband, Annie?" Barefoot, Lilia darted across the room to the front door. Flinging the door open, Lilia dashed outside, tripping over Onyx, curled up on the doorstep. The dog yelped in surprise. She rushed down the pathway to the barn.

"Wade? Wade?" she called as her bare feet hit the cold, moist earthen floor inside the barn. "Oh, dear God, please let him be here."

"Lilia? Is that you?" A voice called.

She stopped and turned toward the milking stalls.

Caleb stood in the doorway, milking bucket in hand.

She gasped for a breath. "Caleb, have you seen Wade this morning?"

Her friend's husband set the partially filled milk pail on the floor. "No, should I have?"

"Are either of your horses missing?" Lilia could feel hysteria rising within her chest. Fear caused her breath to come in short gasps.

"Well, I don't rightly know." He strode out of the side door into the sunlight and disappeared around the corner of the barn. She ran after him to the field behind the barn. She slowed to a walk, for she could see that Molly, the Cunard's chestnut brown mare, was missing. A forlorn Midge, Molly's pulling partner, pressed her long snout against Caleb's hand.

Caleb patted Midge's nose. Through gritted teeth, he growled. "It's all right, old girl. It's all right. We'll find Molly, I promise."

A sob burst free from Lilia's quivering body. "I'm so sorry. I didn't know he would . . ."

Without a word, Caleb strode toward the barn.

She followed, apologizing for her husband's indiscretion. "Are you going to tell the sheriff? Are you going to turn him in?"

Caleb grabbed the only saddle left in the tack room, a blanket, and the reins and strode out to where Midge patiently waited. "Go tell Serenity what's happened. Tell her I'll be back as soon as I can."

"Yes." Lilia wrung her hands as she trotted behind Caleb. She barely noticed the guest, Mr. Hogan, hitching his oxen to his wagon and two of his older children loading the family's goods.

"Please don't turn him in to the sheriff, Caleb. Please? I have a valuable coin. I can pay for your horse and your other saddle." She'd never seen the man so angry.

He waved her away and mounted the waiting horse. "I wish your husband had tried to mount Midge. She would have given him the ride of his life!"

Onyx barked and pranced around the horse's feet until Caleb ordered him back to the house. With aching steps, Lilia plodded her way to the house where she found Serenity measuring flour for the day's bread. Annie stood in front of the stove stirring the breakfast porridge.

Mrs. Hogan was wrestling her youngest son into a pair of trousers. His younger sister sat in the middle of the great room floor looking at an atlas.

Serenity smiled at her friend. "Well, what got you up so early?"

Lilia shook her head. She could barely speak. "Caleb told me to tell you that he was going into town and didn't know when he'd be back."

"What?" Serenity lifted her hands out of the flour and strode toward the window in the direction of the barn. "Whatever for?"

"Wade borrowed your horse Molly." Lilia swallowed hard. All three women stopped what they were doing and looked at her in surprise. Even the little boy stopped squirming. "I don't think Caleb will find him. I think Wade's gone for good."

Mortified, she turned and fled to her room. When Serenity knocked on the bedroom door seconds later, Lilia begged to be left alone. She was relieved when Serenity did as she asked.

Several hours passed, hours of crying and pleading with God, a God in whom she'd never believed, to send Wade home to her. Exhausted, she fell into a fitful sleep.

"No, Daddy, no!" She screamed after the angry man on the other side of the bars. "Don't leave me here! It's me, your Lilly-bell."

"You're not my Lilly-bell! You stole my coins. You're no longer my daughter." Her father's face was filled with rage. Her mother stood behind him holding a bundle of pink and white in her arms.

Lilia screamed as her parents took her newborn, vowing never to allow her to see the child again. She slumped down on the rigid cot. From somewhere next to her she heard a whimper. She looked for the source of the cry but realized she was alone. That cry, that whimper was her own. She squeezed her eyes shut to block out the horrid jail cell and her parents' last words.

Mercifully, when Lilia opened her eyes, she found herself in her friend's guest room instead of a jail cell. Wade was gone. And his child had not yet been born.

She stared at the rough whitewashed ceiling and the dark oak beams stretching from one wall to the next. The dream had been so real, especially her parents and their hate-filled words. *You're not my daughter!* Her father's words rang through her mind again and again. *You're not my Lilly-bell!* Her head throbbed and her eyes stung from her tears. The dream had convinced her that Wade was right. Her parents would never taker her back.

Fear clutched at her heart. She'd never been truly alone in her life. Even at the school she'd always had someone— first Serenity, then Wade. Now Wade was gone and surely Serenity and her husband would want her gone as well.

Stealing a horse was a horrible crime. More than one man had been hung for such an act.

The words she'd heard Caleb read from the Bible resurfaced in her unwilling mind. *"I will never leave you nor forsake you."* Furious that she should recall an empty promise like that at a time like this, she punched Wade's pillow with her fist.

"Don't try to move in on me now, God. Not after everything that's happened." Suddenly she sat up and pushed the bedclothes from her body. "What am I doing talking to a Being who doesn't exist? Next thing you know, I'll be spouting the pious prayers Annie speaks." She clicked her tongue. "Stop acting like a fatuous filly and get hold of yourself."

She leaped from the bed and hurried to the dresser. *I won't be beholding. I'll give Serenity the coin and then, well, then I'll—the baby . . .* Her bravado drained out of her as quickly as it had come. "Then what?" Her question hung in the air, unanswered.

~9~

Life Goes On

THE DAYS FOLLOWING WADE'S DISAPPEARANCE dragged by for the grieving young woman. Getting up in the morning became more and more difficult. She used her morning sickness as an excuse. Caleb came home without Wade, though the sheriff and his posse continued the search. She felt Caleb's disgust, even though she knew he tried to hide it. Losing that horse had produced a hardship and she felt responsible. Serenity did all she could to make her friend comfortable, but it was as if Lilia's spirit had died.

When she tried to give them one of her father's coins, they refused. Caleb told her to hold onto it, that she could pay them when she found a buyer for it.

Serenity advised Lilia to send her folks a telegram. Lilia staunchly refused.

On her good days, Lilia did her best to assist with the chores at the inn, but she knew her efforts often hindered more than helped. She clung to Serenity for support and resented Annie's presence. At times she resented Caleb and the tenderness he showed to Serenity as well. When the family gathered around the shiny oak trestle table for evening worship following supper, Lilia escaped to her room, or on warm evenings she would take a walk to the top of the knoll and sit on the giant granite rock until dusk.

While Serenity never commented on Lilia's quick exits from the dinner table, Lilia felt the need to explain. "The last thing I want to hear about is your God."

She resented the changes in her body. She knew she could never go back to the carefree schoolgirl she'd been before she met Wade. That part of her life was lost forever. She resented her unborn child as well. "It's your fault Wade left me! It's your fault," she wailed into her pillow at night.

When Lilia offered to work to help pay for her keep, Serenity agreed. She assigned Lilia the task of washing dishes after each meal and Serenity taught her how to make the daily supply of bread.

At first, even though she'd asked for the work, Lilia was offended by having to labor. But once she learned how to knead the dough, she found it a great way to pound out her frustrations. When alone in the house, Lilia talked to the dough as if it were Wade. She'd slam the dough on the flour-coated surface to vent her anger. By the time the bread was molded and rising on the stove, she felt a strange peace in her heart. The compliments she received at the dinner table gave her a pleasant satisfaction as well. Even Caleb acknowledged the good tasting results.

Washing dirty dishes was another story. As her hands wrinkled and roughened and her nails split, she resented Annie all the more. *You should be the one doing these dishes, not me. It's your place, not mine.* It wasn't that Annie didn't do her share. She did, and more. Annie worked hard to ease Serenity's burdens.

With the passing of each hot and sticky August day, Serenity's waistline expanded until she looked like she'd swallowed an entire pumpkin. Lilia gazed at Serenity's distorted body, realizing that within a short time, she would be in the same condition.

Lilia marveled at her friend's ebullient spirit, despite the obvious discomfort. During the third week of August, in the middle of fruit-canning season, Serenity's ankles swelled so much she couldn't put on her shoes.

Fearing a danger to the baby, Caleb took her to the doctor and he ordered her to sit with her legs elevated throughout the day.

Yet more than anything, Lilia resented seeing Caleb's tender ministrations to Serenity and hearing his gentle words of encouragement—something she would never experience from the father of her child.

A week and a half after Wade disappeared, Aaron Cunard, Sheriff Prior, and Wade's attorney, Felix Bonner, arrived at the inn with the news that the law had given up hope of locating her errant husband.

"We lost his trail north of St. Joseph," the sheriff explained, "in Indian country." He nervously rolled and unrolled the brim of his hat. "Got reports of Indian uprising in the area."

At the mention of Indians, everyone looked at Lilia. Gathering up what little pride she had left, Lilia thanked the sheriff for his efforts, then turned to Felix Bonner, "Here, Mr. Bonner. This is a Greek drachma, a part of my father's rare coin collection." She dropped it into the lawyer's surprised hand. "It should cover the money you risked covering Wade's, er, fines. If you would, please take this and sell it. Should you get more from its sale than you put out, keep it. It's yours. If it's not quite enough, let me know and I'll try to make it right with you."

"No, no. I couldn't do that. I will try to sell it for you, but I wouldn't keep anything beyond my expenses, Mrs. Cooper." He stared at the shiny coin for several more seconds. "Are you sure you want to get rid of this?"

"Absolutely! Fair is fair. I don't want charity."

The lines in the attorney's forehead deepened. "Do you know how much this coin could be worth?"

"Enough, I hope. As I said, it belonged to my father." Lilia wrung her hands nervously. Her lower lip quivered; her eyes filled with tears at the mention of her father. "Please take it."

Felix Bonner eyed the woman for several seconds, then studied the coin a second time. With obvious reluctance, the lawyer pocketed the coin. "I'll tell you what I'll do for you. I'm heading for St. Louis at the end of the week. I'll have the coin appraised. Then before I actually sell the coin, we'll talk." He dropped the coin into his vest pocket.

Lilia nodded and excused herself. One minute longer and she knew she would have humiliated herself by crying, something she seemed to do with incredible regularity. She dashed down the corridor to her room and threw herself on the bed. To Lilia, using the rare and valuable coin to cover Wade's bail money had come to symbolize her own betrayal of her father and the subsequent loss of all she once treasured. Coming to herself, she admitted that she hadn't lost her parents with the sale of the coin. She'd lost them a long time ago.

She sat up and dried her eyes. After some time, she heard the lawyer and Caleb's brother Aaron leave the inn. They'd all looked at her with such pity—the lawyer, the brother, Serenity, Caleb, and worst of all, Annie! A former slave!

"Pity! I'll have no pity!" Lilia pounded a fist into the pillow. She hated pity! She was a Northrop. Northrops lived above pity. Pity was something her mother had for the scruffy little street urchins that begged for pennies in front of the milliner's shop in downtown Norfolk. Lilia would have none of it, especially from a lesser creature like Annie.

Not long after Aaron and the lawyer left, Serenity tapped on her door and called her to supper. Lilia pretended to be asleep. Hungry or not, she vowed not to suffer anymore of their pity, at least for one night. Frustrated and homesick, she drifted off into a restless sleep. The old nightmares returned.

Hours later when she awoke, the room was dark, filled with the unrelenting shadows of night. One lone shaft of moonlight fell across the foot of the bed. Sitting up on the edge of the down-filled mattress, she ran her fingers through her tangled hair. Most of her hairpins had fallen out as she slept. Her stomach growled with hunger. The thought of a slice of brown bread with honey on it caused her stomach to rumble a second time.

Realizing she was still fully dressed, Lilia tiptoed to the door, opened it, and listened. The door to Serenity and Caleb's bedroom was open a crack, allowing a stream of light and the sound of their voices to escape down the hallway.

As she tiptoed past the open door, she heard Caleb say, "I still think we should contact her parents, her being pregnant and all."

"Honey, she's an adult," Serenity reminded. "If she doesn't want to cable her parents, we can't make her."

"Technically she isn't an adult, you know. And I feel that she is my responsibility under the circumstances."

Lilia paused outside the door to hear the rest of Caleb's reply.

"I'll tell you what. That good-for-nothing husband of hers had better never show his face in these parts again."

"I know that. And you know that, but does Lilia know that?" Serenity's voice held a consoling note. "She must decide her future for herself and for her baby. Ooh!"

Lilia listened to what sounded like a groan of pain coming from her friend, followed by Caleb's anxious voice.

"What? What is it, honey? Are you all right?"

Serenity gasped a sigh of relief. "Just more of that pesky indigestion, I'm afraid. I should never have eaten that chili-pepper sauce Mrs. Rich sent out for us the other day."

Caleb's voice rose. "Are you sure? Should I go get the doc?"

"Why? Caleb, I still have at least two weeks to go."

"Can I get you something?"

"Perhaps a cup of chamomile tea to help me sleep."

At the sound of bare feet hitting the floor, Lilia dashed for the great room. Cherry-red coals glowed in the fireplace as she hurried to the kitchen and lit an oil lamp. By the time Caleb entered the room, she had the fire lit in the kitchen stove and was heating a teakettle of water.

"Well, hello there," she called. "I hope I didn't waken you."

"Huh?" the man looked surprised. "No, no, that's all right. Serenity needs a cup of tea to settle her stomach."

"Chamomile?" Lilia tilted her head to one side. Blond curls cascaded down the bodice of her dress. She cast him a perky smile. "I hope you don't mind, but I got hungry and thought some tea and a slice of bread would hold me till morning."

"Of course not. This is your home while you're with us." Caleb strode purposefully toward her.

Her breath caught in her throat. *What a lion of a man,* she thought.

As if reading her mind, he averted his eyes. "Did you find everything you need?"

The man's muscles bulged beneath his rolled-up shirt sleeves. He walked past her into the pantry.

"Do you know if there are any of Annie's oatmeal cookies left?" she called. "I could really go for a couple of those along with my cup of tea." Lilia snatched up the oil lamp and followed him into the pantry. She brushed past in the room's confining space. "I know Annie puts them in a jar in here somewhere."

Lilia found herself face-to-face with Caleb. Caleb started in surprise. At that instant, the kettle on the stove began to sing. "I'll get that," he croaked and darted from the pantry. A second later, the kettle ceased its song.

Lilia pressed herself against the cupboard and buried her eyes in her arm. Why had she done such a thing? What had come over her? Her face blazed with color. Pregnant or not, the unexpected encounter had obviously startled him as well. She touched her flushed cheek with the back of her hand.

A tangle of thoughts tumbled through her mind, mostly of shame and confusion. Flirting with men had always been the most natural behavior for the snappy little blond. Since before she could sit up, she'd practiced her wiles on her father and on every other male entering her life. Her father called her his little "heartbreaker."

After dallying with Wade, her innocent flirtations had changed to a frustrated compulsion for attention and affection. Lilia's hand shook as she removed the jar of cookies from the shelf.

From the other room, Caleb called, "Why don't you set the table for the three of us while I go get Serenity?"

Woodenly she did as he instructed—three cups, three saucers, and the same number of teaspoons. A mystical blend of light and darkness cast a dreamlike glow on the room. But Lilia knew what had happened had been not been part of a dream. She knew that she would relive the encounter many nights alone in her bedroom.

Lilia let the tea steep while she filled a creamer with some of the cream Annie had separated for the making of butter and pot cheese the next day. Carefully Lilia carried the cream and the matching sugar bowl to the table.

When Caleb returned with Serenity on his arm, he averted his eyes from Lilia's face. She did the same.

He led Serenity to the table and helped her sit down. Lilia watched as the concerned man poured his wife's tea and measured out a teaspoon of sugar and a dollop of cream. "How about a cookie, honey? You could just nibble it while you sip your tea?"

Rubbing her lower back with her hands, Serenity shook her head. "No, thank you. The tea will suffice—I think. I should never have tried to do the wash yesterday. Annie tried to warn me. My back is killing me."

Instead of sitting down at the head of the table, Caleb sat on one of the benches beside Serenity. Lilia could see the concern in his eyes. "Are you sure I shouldn't go get the doc? I don't like the sound of this."

Serenity's hand trembled as she took a sip of tea, then a second. "Umm, that taste's good. My stomach feels better already. Ah, the magic of chamomile tea."

Caleb smiled nervously at his wife, like a puma prepared to spring into action at the slightest provocation.

Lilia hovered nearby. She knew very little about birthing, but she, too, worried that Serenity might be ready to deliver. She certainly looked it from Lilia's perspective. "Caleb could be right, Serenity. Maybe he should go get the doctor."

"No, not yet."

Suddenly Caleb stood up. "Serenity, I've had it. For the last two weeks you've had back pains and cramps almost every night. Annie tells me she can't get you to slow down during the day." He paced to the fireplace and stoked the flames. When he turned around his jaw was set. "Come morning, I'm taking you to your father's place where you'll stay until this child arrives. If anyone can make you take it easy, Josephine can."

"Caleb, no." Serenity looked at her husband in surprise. "I have to get the last of the snap beans canned, and the corn, why, it's just beginning to tassel. The way I figure it, I can get a lot done in the next two weeks."

"He's right, Serenity." Lilia eyed her friend's burgeoning waist. "I can stay here and take care of the inn while Annie goes with you to your parents' place."

"No!" Caleb's sudden exclamation startled both women. Then realizing the force of his reaction, he explained, "No, Lilia, Annie knows more about running the inn. It makes more sense for you to go with Serenity and for Annie to take care of things here."

"Wait one minute!" Serenity glared first at Caleb, then at Lilia. Bringing her fist down on the table with a bang, she said, "Who says I'm going anywhere? I think I would know if—" Her determined face melted to a puddle of agony. She doubled over in pain. Caleb rushed to her side.

"I think I need to lie down," Serenity whimpered.

Caleb helped her to her feet and led her from the room.

"I'll take care of everything out here," Lilia called, uncertain either heard her offer. After washing the dishes and returning everything to its proper place, she scattered the remaining embers in the fireplace. She took a few minutes to glance about the warm cozy room. Her gaze fell on Caleb's open Bible on the small ash wood table in front of the sofa. Curious, she walked to the stand and picked up the book. In the semi-darkness, she read the familiar words in Luke two regarding Jesus' birth, words she'd heard every year at Christmas time.

"And it came to pass in those days, that there went out a decree from Caesar Augustus, that all the world should be taxed. . . ." The vision of a small Norfolk chapel flooded her memory. The aroma of candles burning, of her mother's French perfume, and of garlands of evergreens filled her senses. She could hear the rustle of her favorite blue taffeta skirt as she dangled her legs from the wooden pew. She saw her father's somber mustached face gazing at the preacher as the man of the cloth read the familiar words.

"And Joseph also went up to Galilee out of the city of Nazareth, into Judaea, unto the city of David which is called Bethlehem; because he was of the house and lineage of David. To be taxed with Mary his espoused wife, being great with child."

Lilia carried the Bible to the table nearer the oil lamp. Seating herself on the nearest bench, she read the story of Jesus' birth for the first time. When she read about the stable that would become the Savior's birthplace, Lilia glanced about the great room. She looked at the whitewashed sod walls, the hard dirt floor, the rough-hewn furniture, and remembered her father's stables—clean and refined enough to eat off the oiled oak floors. She was struck by the contrast.

Idly she massaged her slightly protruding stomach and wondered under what conditions her child would be born. Certainly no one would celebrate its arrival—least of all her, forever chained to the responsibility of motherhood. Wade wouldn't, wherever he was. Her parents would never learn of the child's existence if she could help it. An unexpected tear splotched the onionskin paper. She continued reading. When she reached the end, she thought, *What a pretty little fable. How can the world wander after this man called Jesus?* Yet, doubtful as she might be of the story's veracity, the lie existed after more than a thousand years. And it did more than exist, people continued to believe it. She couldn't understand. Disgusted, she arose from the table and carried the oil lamp to her bedroom. From the tone of Caleb's voice earlier, Lilia suspected that Serenity and she would be heading into town come sunrise. She set the lamp on the bedside table and undressed for bed.

Before hopping into bed, she decided it might be wise to pack her trunk. As she did, her fingers brushed against the last remaining coin from her father's collection. It was the one her father had loved most.

For a moment she considered returning the coin to him. She could send it by packet. But reason intervened. The coin represented the last means of support she possessed. She couldn't afford to be too generous, even with her father.

Furious with her moment of weakness, she slammed the trunk shut and climbed into bed. She'd barely closed her eyes when the sun broke over the eastern horizon and a new day began.

~10~

Beautiful
Beginnings

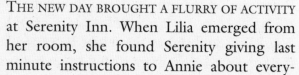

THE NEW DAY BROUGHT A FLURRY OF ACTIVITY at Serenity Inn. When Lilia emerged from her room, she found Serenity giving last minute instructions to Annie about everything from doing the weekly laundry to making Caleb's favorite applesauce. Annie, demonstrating the patience of a saint, listened and nodded, though she'd been doing menial chores much longer than had Serenity.

The last of the guests were gone. And it was unlikely there'd be more guests arriving at the inn so late in the season, but just in case, Serenity wanted to be certain Annie knew what to do.

When Caleb came in from milking the cows, he changed clothes, then sat down to the table for breakfast. Serenity continued her litany of instructions throughout breakfast, pausing only to bow her head while Caleb asked the blessing on the food.

Lilia couldn't believe her friend's concern over what to her were inconsequential details. Where had her easygoing, agreeable companion in pranks disappeared? Serenity had become a martinet! Lilia also marveled at Annie's good nature. If she'd been Annie, she'd have blown up at her friend. But then, Lilia reasoned, Annie's heritage was one of servitude. She was bred to follow directions.

"Caleb." Serenity started on her husband. "You will need to . . ." Patiently Caleb listened to the list of instructions his wife had for him as well.

To tune out Serenity's unending list, Lilia concentrated on devouring the stack of flapjacks on her plate. One thing she had to admit about Annie. The woman could certainly make delicious pancakes.

Lilia cut a piece of pancake with her fork and dipped it in a puddle of maple syrup, then put it in her mouth—delicious. She'd barely had time to savor the flavor when Caleb looked across the table at his wife and smiled.

"Serenity, darling, everything will be fine here, I promise. I know you hate leaving your home even for a day, but honestly, Annie knows what she's doing, and so do I."

"I . . . but . . ."

"All you need to worry about, sweetheart, is taking care of our little one. So relax, darling, enjoy Annie's scrumptious flapjacks." Caleb shot a smile toward Annie. "Great job, Annie. What did you add to these? Cinnamon?"

Annie grinned and nodded. "Something Serenity's mama taught me to do."

At the mention of Serenity's mother, Serenity bit her lower lip and sent an impish look at her husband. "You're right, Caleb. Maybe I'm afraid you'll do too well without me."

Caleb kicked back his chair and strode the length of the table. He knelt down on one knee and wrapped his arms around his wife's shoulders. "You foolish little love. You are my life. I can't live without you. And I promise you that Annie and I will visit you every day while you're in town, before and after our baby arrives." He placed a tender kiss on her cheek. "I need you more than breath itself, my love."

Tears trickled down Serenity's cheek. She buried her face in his shoulder. "I don't want to leave you. I'm so frightened."

"I know. I know," he cooed. "Honey, think about the good side. When I bring you home, you'll have our child in your arms. And I promise you that that baby will make it all worth it." He handed her his dinner napkin. "So dry those tears, sweetie. You, me, our child—we're all safe in God's hands, remember?"

She nodded.

He kissed her cheek once more, then returned to his chair at the other end of the table. Picking up the Cunard family Bible, he opened it to the Book of Proverbs.

"This is especially for you, sweetheart, Proverbs 31. 'Who can find a virtuous woman? For her price is far above rubies. The heart of her husband doth safely trust in her, so that he will have no need of spoil. She will do him good and not evil all the days of her life. . . .'"

Lilia listened to the words written by the wisest man who ever lived. While she'd heard them read before, she'd never really heard them. This time seeing them applied to her long-time friend gave their message new meaning. Her eyes misted at the thought of Wade, dear, foolish Wade, wherever he was. *We could have had a love like that,* she mused. *I would have done anything for you. Anything. I gave you all my love and you tossed it away.*

"'She is not afraid of the snow for her household; for all her household is clothed in scarlet. She maketh . . .'"

Images swirled around Lilia: the heady excitement of their clandestine meetings behind the stables at the academy, the thrill of stolen kisses, their promises to love forever.

Caleb's heavy baritone voice broke through her reverie. "'She openeth her mouth with wisdom, and in her tongue is the law of kindness. . . .'"

Kindness? Wisdom? Hardly descriptive of her own choices lately. Maybe if she'd been a better wife to Wade . . . maybe if she'd worked harder . . . shown him more love . . . argued less . . . supported him better . . . Idly she massaged the slight mound growing in her abdomen.

"'Her children rise up and call her blessed, her husband also and he praiseth her.'" Caleb paused to cast a loving gaze at his wife. "'Many daughters have done virtuously, but thou excellest them all. Favor is deceitful, and beauty is vain; but a woman that feareth the Lord, she will be praised. . . .'"

The book closed with a thud. Caleb knelt beside the table and folded his hands. Annie and Serenity followed his example. Automatically Lilia dropped to her knees as well. This was the part she hated. This moment was the one she most wanted to avoid.

It seemed so foolish, talking to a God you couldn't see. One might as well talk to the wind—isn't that what her own father once called prayer?

Lilia refused to close her eyes. She might kneel to avoid a confrontation, but close her eyes? Hardly. *Besides,* she reasoned, *no one would know unless they were peeking too.* She smiled to herself at the thought of catching Caleb or Serenity with their eyes partly open.

Caleb's prayer was short. At the amen, Lilia started to rise only to have Serenity begin to pray.

"Oh, dear Heavenly Father, I praise You for Your incredible love for us, Your children. I know how much You love us, including this tiny baby waiting to be born. Because You love me and know everything about me, You also know how frightened I am right now." Serenity's voice broke. She began to weep. Caleb rose to his feet and hurried to kneel by her side. "I can't, Caleb. I can't go through with this. I can't leave my home."

"Shh, shh. It's all right, darling, to be afraid. If I could, I'd go through it for you."

Lilia shot a quick glance toward the couple. Caleb was dotting his wife's face with tiny whisper-soft kisses as he spoke. "Darling, you know how much I love you, don't you? Well, God loves you that much and whole lot more. He promises to go with you through the valley of the shadow of death. . . ." The words hung heavy in the early morning air.

Fear coursed through Lilia. She knew the birth of a child held the threat of death for the mother, and possibly for the baby. She'd heard her mother's friends talk. She'd heard the horror stories of intense labor, of tearing, of hemorrhaging. This is what faced her friend in the next few days. And this is what she faced at the end of her term.

Serenity sniffed into the table napkin. "I'm afraid I may never come home again."

"Honey," Caleb encouraged, "it's natural for you to fear that after all you've lost during the last year. It's natural. And as much as I'd like to, I can't guarantee something tragic won't happen. But I can assure you that your mama went through it and lived, and my mother did the same, for-tunately for us."

Serenity giggled in spite of her fears.

Caleb continued. "You are strong, stronger than you think, and healthy too. You'll be surrounded by all the people you love most. Our love and God's love will give you courage, I promise."

Serenity nodded and sniffed. Caleb stood and helped his wife to her feet. She swayed a little. Her bulging stomach upset her center of balance. He slid his arm about her waist and helped her walk to the oak rocker. "You sit here while I hitch the horses and load the wagon. Lilia, are your things ready to go?"

"Yes." Lilia struggled to her feet, straightening the wrinkles incurred in the skirt of her French blue chambray dress.

"But, I have things to do. . . ." Serenity protested.

Annie rose from her knees and began gathering the breakfast dishes from the table. "I have everything under control. You just relax, you hear?"

Relief flooded Serenity's face. "Yes, ma'am." She eased against the back of the chair and closed her eyes. "This baby sure is eager to get born."

Annie's eyes widened in terror. "Not here, not now!"

"Soon," Serenity admitted, massaging her stomach with her hands. "Soon."

Lilia fled for her bedroom. She couldn't handle this. She thought her friend Serenity was confident and self-assured about childbirth. To find out how terrified Serenity was frightened Lilia more than she'd thought possible. *And she has a husband to be there for her.*

While Caleb transferred Serenity's and Lilia's luggage to the buckboard, he asked Lilia to spread out blankets for Serenity to lie on during the trip. "Just in case," he added.

"Just in case?" Lilia's eyes flew open at the suggestion that the baby might come when only she and Caleb were there to deliver it. She refused to accept such a thought. She

knew town was only four miles away. Four miles! Surely
Serenity could wait while they traveled four miles.

Caleb situated Serenity on the makeshift bed and
climbed down from the wagon.

Lilia gathered her skirts in her hands and let Caleb help
her climb aboard. "I'll stay here beside you," she told
Serenity. "Don't worry. We're here for you."

Serenity looked relieved. The pregnant woman rolled
onto her side and rested her head against the pillow Lilia
had prepared for her. "I hope I haven't waited too long,"
Serenity whimpered after an intense pain.

Lilia's voice shook. "Me too." To Lilia, the world had
shifted into an unreal, dream-like haze. Her mind couldn't
keep up with the reality swirling around her. She felt like she
was in a trance, like the Zombies of the Caribbean her father
had told stories about.

The sameness of the prairie fed her fantasy as the buckboard rumbled down the road. With Molly gone, Caleb had
had to buy a second horse he'd named Bertha. Suddenly
Serenity doubled over again in pain forcing Lilia back to
reality. The pain in Lilia's left hand, the one Serenity
clutched with the contraction, caused Lilia to come alive.
With her right hand, she patted her friend's back. As the
contraction eased, Lilia switched hands to relieve the pressure and restore the blood flow in her fingers.

Serenity's pains intensified. Whatever back pains she'd
been complaining about earlier had been forgotten in favor
of the newest onslaught. Lilia grimaced each time Serenity
doubled over, moaned, and gripped her friend's hand.
While Lilia didn't know much about childbirth, she knew
that Serenity's pains were coming too hard and too fast to
be ignored.

The wagon hit a rock with a thud. The jar sent Lilia sprawling on her backside. Her head hit the side of the wagon. She rubbed her head and thought all the invectives she'd like to hurl at Caleb. She included several for the horses and the buckboard manufacturer as well.

"Oh! Oh! It's coming!" Serenity shrieked. Her face was drenched with sweat. "The baby's coming."

"Not yet," Lilia begged. "You can't have the baby here in the road."

"Don't tell me I can't have this baby here. Don't you think I know it? It's not up to me." Serenity clutched her abdomen again, her face distorted with agony. "Stop! Stop the wagon! My water broke!" she screamed, clawing at her skirts. "Caleb, I need you now! Help me!"

"Stop the wagon!" Lilia shrieked over the rumble of the wheels. "Her water broke. The baby's coming!" Lilia had no idea what she was saying. She only knew Serenity put great importance on the broken water.

"Hold on," he called, cracking the whip above the horses' backs. "Just hold on!"

"I can't," Serenity wailed.

Lilia looked down at the puddle growing beneath her friend. "Oh no! What happens next?"

"The baby comes," Serenity snarled. "What do you think?"

Lilia scrambled over the luggage until she was directly behind Caleb. Pounding on his back with both her fists, she shouted. "Stop! You've got to stop!"

Caleb whirled his head about and looked at Lilia as if she were a phantom. His eyes were wide with terror. "Here? Now?"

"Here! Right now!" Lilia screamed. "What do I do? Help me!"

Caleb pulled on the reins and jammed on the vehicle's brake. The horses responded. As the wagon came to a stop, Caleb tossed the reins over the brake lever, leaped over the seat of the buckboard and the luggage, and landed at Serenity's side.

Serenity reached for her husband. Her words came in short, wispy gasps. "Help me, Caleb. The baby is coming. I can feel it." She pawed at her calico skirt and the cotton crinolines beneath.

"Honey," Caleb insisted. "Can't you wait until we get to the doc's house, or to your parents' place? It's just a little further."

"Caleb!" Her voice took on a strident tone. "It's too late!"

Lilia stood in the wagon waving her hands frantically in the air. "What do we do? What do we do?"

"Sit down, woman!" Caleb shouted. "You're only making things worse."

"And you're not?" Lilia snarled. "Telling her to wait? She's in pain. Can't you see that? Do something!"

"You do something useful, Lilia. Get my knife out of that toolbox beside you." Caleb began tearing the wet and soiled crinolines from Serenity's body and tossing them at Lilia.

"Knife? Why do you need a knife?"

"Just hand me the knife and pray!"

Lilia located the knife and handed it to him, then automatically began to pray as she folded Serenity's crinolines and laid them beside the trunks. "Oh, dear God, if You really do exist, please help this baby be born soon. Give Serenity relief from the pain—" *What am I doing? Praying to the wind? The first trace of trouble and I begin spouting nonsense to a Being who doesn't exist!*

"Lilia! Lilia!" Caleb's strident voice broke through her thoughts. "I need your help here!"

"Me?" The woman shrieked in terror. "I don't know anything about birthing babies!"

"Well, it's time you learn. Get up behind Serenity and cradle her head and shoulders in your lap."

Lilia scrambled to obey.

"Yeah, that's right," Caleb smiled through gritted teeth. Perspiration coated his brow. Fear filled his eyes. "It's not like I know so much. I've only seen my father help with the birthing of a colt. Fortunately the baby does most of the work, or so I understand. But I do know, Serenity, that you have to work with the contractions. When you feel like pushing, push. And in between pains, relax."

Agonized, hysterical laughter erupted from Serenity. "Relax? I'd like to see you relax in this position."

Caleb laughed in spite of himself. "Well, you must be doing fine. You still have your sense of humor."

"Oh really?" she moaned. "Is that what you call it?" And with that she cramped up again. "I've got to push! I've got to push."

Caleb disappeared behind Serenity's skirted knees. "I can see the head! I can see the baby's head!" He reappeared above the skirt. "Relax, honey. You're doing fine. Now relax until the next contraction comes."

Serenity slumped against Lilia's lap. "Easy for you to say." She licked her dry, parched lips. "I am so thirsty."

Lilia looked around her and spotted a leather water pouch fastened to the side of the wagon. Before she could free the pouch from its holder, Serenity was going into another contraction.

"Push, honey! Push!" Caleb cried, tears streaming down his face as he dipped behind the skirts once more. "Help her, Lilia. Forget the water and help her push."

"I am! I am!" Lilia shouted. "I'm here, Serenity. I'm here for you."

"Uh-huh," Serenity groaned as she fell back against Lilia once more.

Caleb appeared again. Lilia brushed an ebony curl from Serenity's strained, red face. "You're doing fine."

Another contraction doubled Serenity over before she could reply. Between gritted teeth she moaned, "Stop saying that! O-o-o-e-e-e-e!"

"It's coming, sweetheart! The baby's coming! Keep pushing!" Caleb shouted. "I have the baby's head in my hands. And now its shoulders—"

"A-i-i-i-e-gh!" Serenity screamed, giving one last grunt, then falling back against Lilia.

"Good girl. You did fine. The worst is over." Caleb encouraged. "It's a boy, honey, a healthy baby boy!" Caleb straightened. Tears streamed down his face as he held the slippery baby up for her to see.

A lusty squall filled the morning air, while indignation filled the infant's scrunched-up face. The child wanted no part of this strange new world.

Laughing and crying at the same time, Serenity gazed at her son. Caleb laid the screaming baby on its mother's chest. Serenity cooed softly to her son and the newborn quieted immediately.

"He knows your voice," Caleb said, his voice husky with emotion. Clearing his throat, he returned his attention to the needs of his wife. "Lilia, wrap the baby in one of Serenity's crinolines."

Lilia couldn't take her eyes off the tiny little miracle snuggled into the crux of Serenity's arm. She tenderly lifted the child from his mother's arms, wrapped him in a cotton eyelet crinoline, and returned him to his mother. The awe Lilia felt didn't match anything she'd ever experienced.

When Serenity attempted to sit up so she could better see the child's face, Caleb told her to stay put. "We're not done yet."

"Another baby?" Lilia shrieked in surprise.

Serenity laughed, then scrunched up her face and pushed. When Caleb assured her all was well, she explained, "No, it's the afterbirth, the sack the baby has been resting in for nine months. Mom Cunard explained it to me before she left."

Tears streamed down Lilia's face as Serenity examined each of the infant's tiny fingers. "You are so beautiful," she heard her friend say to the wee body. "Do you know how much I love you already?" Serenity lifted her gaze toward the clear summer sky. "Thank You, Father, thank You."

Caleb covered his wife and newborn son with a second crinoline and kissed them both. "We need to get you to the doctor and have him examine you and the baby to be sure everything's all right."

Reluctantly Caleb climbed over the luggage onto the bench of the buckboard. An unexplained tenderness filled Lilia as she cautiously reached out to caress one of the baby's arms. "He's so perfect. What are you going to name him?"

"We are naming him Caleb Samuel Eli Cunard, after his papa and both of his grandfathers. Sammy for short." Serenity didn't take her eyes away from her son's face as she spoke.

"Caleb Samuel Eli is a giant of a name for such a small body," Lilia said. She glanced down at Serenity's blood-soaked dress, then at her own blood-stained hands. She swallowed hard, fighting back a wave of nausea. *Miracle or no, birthing is a messy job,* she thought. *Funny, I didn't notice the blood until now.*

~11~

Grim Endings

THE NEWS OF BABY CUNARD'S BIRTH TRAVELED faster than the buckboard, or so it seemed to Lilia. First they stopped at the doctor's place. He insisted Serenity spend a week at her parents' place before returning to the inn. Next stop was the Pownell place. Josephine and Sam were delighted with their new grandson. The first-time grandparents showered baby Sammy with attention and love.

Lilia watched Serenity's father tote the tiny body about the parlor. She thought of her own father, who would never see his grandchild. But then, she doubted he would respond so kindly to her unwanted child.

Friends and neighbors began to arrive at the house. Lilia shied away from Reverend and Mrs. Rich. The last thing she wanted was to have the Baptist preacher set out to save her soul in front of half of the population of Independence.

With the baby born and her friend recuperating from the delivery, Lilia was grateful to be able to spend a few days in town. The city-bred lass was tired of taking a walk and seeing nothing but prairie and sky. She missed the bustle of cities like Boston and Norfolk. And she missed the shopping.

Once Caleb was certain Serenity was settled in with her folks, he made a trip back to the inn for Annie. With nothing to do for the first time in weeks and feeling out of place with Serenity's family and friends, Lilia decided to go shopping. Even a small community like Independence would have a dress shop or two, or a mercantile, she reasoned.

After choosing a lavender-and-white gingham dress with sprigs of white embroidered daisies on the bodice, she pulled her blond ringlets into a bun at the nape of her neck. She saw no sense in wasting time styling her hair only to cover it with a bonnet.

After informing Josephine of her intentions—Serenity and the baby were sleeping—Lilia donned her white eyelet bonnet, matching gloves, and white crocheted shawl. She slipped the cords of her gray leather purse, containing her last gold coin, over her wrist and strolled down the street toward the main part of town.

The light summer breeze whipped her skirts about her ankles as she walked. She passed the small Baptist church and wondered if the white two-story, wood-frame house next door was the parsonage where Serenity and Caleb said their vows.

The woman she'd been introduced to as Mrs. Rich sat on the porch swing paring apples. A young woman about Lilia's age sat on the front steps doing her mending. The younger woman waved as Lilia passed. Lilia returned the courtesy but didn't pause for conversation. The last thing Lilia wanted was to be trapped into a religious debate on such a beautiful day.

Lilia turned right on Main Street as Josephine had instructed and smashed against the third button of a black-and-gray cotton shirt. She staggered.

Strong arms caught her and kept her from falling from the impact. "Excuse me, ma'am," a decidedly masculine voice said.

Slowly she lifted her gaze past the open collar and the red neckerchief, past the scraggily beard, and equally scraggily mustache to the most beautiful blue eyes she'd ever seen. "Oh? I-I-I, it's you, Mr. Cunard."

Aaron Cunard's lips broke into a broad grin. "Mrs. Cooper? I didn't know you were still in town."

When Lilia explained about the baby's arrival, Aaron became excited. "I'm an uncle? I'm an uncle! Imagine that. Where is the little scamp? Back at the inn?"

"No, he's at the Pownell's," she explained.

"And Serenity is all right?"

Lilia nodded.

"And my brother? Does he know?"

Lilia laughed. "He should. He delivered Caleb Samuel Eli himself."

Aaron threw back his head and laughed. "That poor kid has quite a name to live up to—imagine a preacher, an assemblyman, and my brother, Mr. Perfect!"

Lilia noted the slight edge in the man's voice. "Excuse me, ma'am, but I gotta go see this kid." Aaron tipped his hat politely but didn't wait for her to respond. He dashed down the street from where she'd come. She watched him until he passed the church and turned onto the avenue where the Pownells were living until their new house was completed.

Hmm, Lilia thought, *that's one handsome man!* A wave of shame overtook her when she remembered she was married to Wade even if he had deserted her. *Till death us do part,* she reminded herself. "And besides, you love your husband, remember?"

When a passing cowboy cast a worried glance toward her, Lilia realized she'd spoken aloud. She smiled and adjusted her bonnet. The cowboy looked the other way and continued on down the busy street.

Mule-drawn wagons, riders on horseback, businessmen in pinstripe suits, and cowboys in canvas pants, homespun shirts, and wide-brimmed suede hats tramped along the congested street. Two Indian braves dressed in buckskin leaned against the wall of the town bank.

A group of middle-aged men stood arguing with one another in front of what she surmised was a bar and gambling house. Across the street she saw two women strolling and pushing baby carriages. A smile crept across her face. She enjoyed feeling the energy of city life.

She paused in front of the corner shop, a mercantile. Straightening her spine, she adjusted the shawl about her shoulders, lifted her chin defiantly, and marched into the store.

Saddlery and tin kettles hung from the ceiling of Pringle's Mercantile. Barrels of flower, sugar, and coffee lined the floor in front of the counter. On the other side of the aisle, housewares and farm wares were mingled together in careless disarray. The gray-haired clerk looked almost as dusty as the empty shelves behind his head.

The slightly disheveled mercantile clerk peered at her through wire-rimmed spectacles. "Waitin' on a shipment from the East," he explained. "But I still have lots of stuff to sell." And he was right. The general store carried everything the smart westbound traveler might need to guarantee his family's survival, none of which interested Lilia in the slightest.

The woman quickly left the shop and ambled down the street until she came to Dolittle's Apothecary. Immediately she noted the difference in cleanliness between the apothecary and the mercantile. A plump, apple-cheeked woman greeted her from behind the counter. "Good afternoon, Miss. Beautiful day, isn't it?"

Lilia ran her finger along the glass of the countertop as she studied the contents carefully. "Yes, it is."

"Are you from around here?" the woman asked. "Or just passing through?"

Lilia stopped short and shot an irritated glance at the woman. "Passing through, thank God!"

"A little late in the season to be heading west, don't you think? If you leave now, you won't make it over the mountains before the snow flies."

This stopped Lilia. Where was she heading? West? East? At the moment she didn't know. A jar of candy mints saved her from explaining. "How much do your mints—" She paused mid-sentence when she realized she had no money, except her father's coin. "Will you excuse me?" Blushing, she rushed from the shop, leaving the stunned clerk staring in surprise.

As she rushed past Jenny's Dress Shop, Lilia realized she had to get some money from somewhere. That's when she remembered the attorney, Mr. Felix Bonner. He'd promised to have the coin appraised and give her any extra cash he might get for it beyond Wade's fines.

Lilia gazed up the street, then down at the store signs. Since most Americans didn't read, shop owners used appropriate pictures on their signs to identify themselves: a shoe for the cobbler shop, a lady's dress for a dress shop, a pair of scissors for the barber. She didn't see a lawyer's shingle anywhere.

When a woman in a black-and-pink striped taffeta dress, carrying a matching parasol strolled by, Lilia stopped her.

Lilia had seen many such women aboard the steamboat. The woman was startled that a lady like Lilia would speak to her. She looked warily at the stranger.

Lilia didn't care. She was tired of being poor! "Excuse me, but do you know where the Bonner law office is?"

The woman pointed to the left. "Down Main Street, across from the sheriff's office," she muttered, looking around her as if afraid someone might see her talking with such a fine lady.

"Thank you." Lilia smiled and walked in the direction the woman had indicated. Her steps accelerated as she neared Mr. Bonner's office. The possibility of having cash in her possession again set her adrenaline flowing. She paused at the door of the office, suddenly fearful of what she would do if there were no money.

Her thoughts went back to Wade. Surely he would come home soon. But what if he didn't? Would she continue to sponge off Serenity and Caleb? Perhaps it was time she considered finding work. But what type of work could she do?

Since arriving at Serenity Inn, Lilia had learned many new household skills, none of which she wanted to pursue as a career. She could bake a fine loaf of bread or use sand from the yard to scour burned pots and pans. *My hands and nails prove that!* She laughed sarcastically to herself.

Martha Van Horne's Finishing School for Young Ladies hardly prepared her for gainful employment beyond conducting a proper tea party or choosing the correct fork to use with each course at a formal dinner party. The frontier town of Independence, Missouri, perched on the edge of America's vast wilderness, didn't have many tea parties or state dinners. "But if it ever does," she chuckled aloud, "I can always discuss European art in Italian or interior design in French with this bunch of codfish aristocrats!" The slur against the business people of Independence brought a contemptuous smile to her face.

Serenity had told Lilia about the Ladies' Book Club and the Garden Club in Independence, as well as the interest in the Suffragette movement. Lilia scoffed at the idea that these country yokels ever thought beyond the tasseling of their latest corn crop. She could only imagine the level of intellectual stimulation she'd find there.

As she climbed the steps to the attorney's office, a distinguished looking gentleman, wearing a top hat, string tie, and long coat, exited the offices. On seeing Lilia, he tipped his hat and held open the screened door for her. She nodded graciously and swept into the cool dark interior of the office.

The walls in the hallway and in the small waiting room were paneled in a glossy dark oak. A framed print of the Constitution of the United States and another of the Declaration of Independence hung on the wall facing the outside door. Shelves of leather-bound books filled a second wall. Beside the window in the third wall, giant Boston fern fronds cascaded down from the brass flowerpot that was perched on a pink marble pedestal. An oval floral print on each side of the window softened the angular lines of the room. And on the fourth wall, a gold filigree fireplace fan arched across the front of the cold and empty fireplace. A sumptuous Oriental carpet of reds and blues covered the dark, wide-planked hardwood floor in the center of the room.

Lilia was uncertain what to do next. She eyed the blue striped brocade sofa and two side chairs tastefully upholstered in rose, cream, and muted blue near the window.

Should she sit and wait to be acknowledged or knock on the carved oak panel door, which she assumed led to the attorney's inner office?

Her artistic eye was drawn to the intricately carved mahogany ladies' desk sitting in front of the bookshelves. A Federal style, two branch, pre-Revolutionary candlestick sat to one side on the desk alongside a teakwood pipe stand filled with an array of carved pipes. She paused to appreciate the pleasant aroma of expensive tobacco, an aroma associated with her father. The overall effect of the room gave her a sense of stability, security, and civility.

Tenderly she ran a gloved hand over the top of the finely carved mahogany desk. Living in a sod house with a dirt floor on the edge of the prairie for the last few weeks had unsettled her more than she'd imagined.

The sound of men conversing beyond the set of heavily carved oak doors caught her attention. A sudden wave of insecurity swept over her. *Lilia,* she coached herself, *you are a Northrop! And a Northrop is not intimidated by some backwoods lawyer!* She straightened her shoulders, strode to the closed doors, and knocked.

She heard a chair scrape and the sound of footsteps approaching the door. The door opened and Felix Bonner welcomed her and invited her into his office. The attorney's office reflected the same good taste evident in the waiting room. Stepping across the threshold, she immediately spotted the sheriff.

"Sheriff?" She nodded graciously as the man leaped to his feet and brushed a nervous hand through his unruly hair. His hat fell to the floor and he bent to reclaim it.

When he straightened, he avoided her gaze. "Ma'am, uh . . . it's nice to see you again."

"Here, Mrs. Cooper, please have a seat." The lawyer took her hand and led her to a comfortable looking burgundy upholstered chair. "We were just talking about you."

"Oh?" She arched one eyebrow as she caught a glimpse of the decidedly uncomfortable look on the sheriff's face.

"Actually, Sheriff Prior was just heading out to the inn to find you. I'm glad I managed to catch him before he left town." The handsome young lawyer cleared his throat and smoothed his carefully manicured beard and mustache. Lilia turned her face away. The gesture reminded her too much of her father. "Over at the Pownell house—I was there seeing Caleb and Serenity's new son—they said you were in town shopping."

"Yes, well, that's why I came to see you, Mr. Bonner." The fact that the sheriff had been coming out to the inn to see her escaped Lilia. She was intent on her mission. "Mr. Bonner, I came to discover what you found out about the coin I gave you. Until Wade gets back, I am short of cash and I was hoping—"

"That's why I was coming to see you, Mrs. Cooper," the sheriff interrupted. "Your husband."

Irritated that the sheriff would interrupt, she cast him a jaundiced glare. When he continued speaking, she credited his insensitivity to ignorance.

"Ma'am, I hate to have to tell you this, but two Shoshone braves arrived in town last night dragging a travois—"

"Excuse me, Sheriff, but . . ." Lilia clicked her tongue. "What is a travois and what does all this have to do with me?"

The sheriff cast a nervous glance at the attorney and cleared his throat again. "Well, ma'am, a travois is a blanket stretched between two poles hauled behind a horse or two. The Plains Indians use it to transport heavy loads."

Not understanding where the sheriff's explanation was leading, Lilia impatiently urged him to continue.

"Well . . ." Again he cleared his throat. "Your husband was on the travois."

"Wade? You found Wade?" She screeched, leaping to her feet. "Why didn't you say so? Where is he? Take me to him immediately!"

"It's not as simple as that, Mrs. Cooper." The sheriff twisted the collar of his blue cotton shirt. "You see, your husband had been badly injured, uh, er, burned, in fact, almost beyond recognition."

Lilia gasped. Her hand flew to her mouth. "How? Why? I don't understand."

"It seems the horse he escaped with stumbled in a hole and broke a leg. He had to shoot it."

Lilia staggered backward at the thought of her husband killing Molly.

"So," the sheriff continued, "Cooper, your husband, tried to steal a pony from the Shoshones. They caught him and, uh, uh, administered tribal justice." The sheriff's face reddened with discomfort. "And, uh, last night your husband died of his injuries."

"Died? Wade is dead?" Her breath caught in her throat. The room began to spin before her eyes. Tiny points of multicolored lights flashed around the edges of her vision. From somewhere, she heard a woman wail in pain, but she couldn't focus her mind on the source of the sound. She sank back into the chair.

She was hardly aware of anyone's presence when Sheriff Prior leaped to her aid. Felix Bonner dashed from the room and returned with a glass of water. "Here. Drink this!" The attorney shoved the crystal goblet to her lips. She felt an instant of pain as the glass trapped her lip between it and her lower teeth. She opened her mouth and let the refreshing water trickle down her throat.

"Take a deep breath, Mrs. Cooper." She could hear the attorney's words, but the racing of her heart refused to let her obey his command.

"Do you need to lie down?" the sheriff asked. "She needs to lie down, Felix. Do you have a couch or a bed nearby?"

"The sofa in the outer office!"

"No, no," she mumbled, feeling herself floating through the air or so it seemed. Then all went black.

When she awoke, Mrs. Pownell, Serenity's stepmother, and a softly rounded, middle-aged woman Lilia remembered seeing somewhere before were hovering over her. She heard Mrs. Pownell tell the other woman, "She's pregnant, you know."

The baby? Lilia stirred. "Is my baby all right?" she asked, slowly opening her eyes.

Instead of the dark oak paneling in the law office, the room was bright with whitewashed walls and white eyelet curtains. She was tucked beneath a light blue-and-white tulip bedspread in a four-poster, brass bed.

"She said something." The second woman leaned over her. A stray lock of hair tickled Lilia's nose, causing Lilia to wiggle her nose. "I couldn't make it out, could you?"

"I think it was something about her baby. Lilia, this is Josephine, Serenity's stepmother. You remember me, don't you?"

Lilia turned her head slowly toward the woman. "What happened? Where am I?"

Josephine brushed a wet washcloth across Lilia's forehead. "You passed out, honey. You're in Mrs. Rich's guest room. She's a friend of Serenity's. Felix and the sheriff brought you here."

Lilia turned her face toward her gracious hostess. "Thank you." A wisp of a smile crossed Lilia's face.

"Doctor Baker was here earlier and examined you. You went into shock. Both you and the baby should be fine." Mrs. Rich assured her. "He gave you something to help you relax."

Josephine smoothed the bedclothes over Lilia the same way Lilia's mother used to do. Lilia's eyes flooded with tears.

Lovingly Josephine brushed several stray curls from Lilia's sweaty face. "Serenity's been worried about you. The doctor won't let her get up so soon after birthing or she'd be here with you."

A wave of incredible tiredness swept over Lilia. She closed her eyes and drifted into unconsciousness, but not before she heard the woman talking about sending for the doctor again. She tried to assure the women she was all right, but her mouth felt as though it were full of cotton batting. She drifted into a numbing gray fog. With a whimper and a sigh, she succumbed.

-12-

A Time for Healing

"I LIFT THIS LOVELY CHILD TO THEE, LORD. Thou knowest how much her heart is hurting. Thou understands the pain she is going through. Place Thy beautiful healing hands of love on her. Show her that Thou lovest her and can restore joy, once more, to her heart."

Like layers of gauze lifted from a wound, Lilia's mind was released from bondage. She could hear an unfamiliar voice speaking, not to her, but to a third party. Her eyelids felt heavy against her dry and scaly eyes. Slowly she willed them to open.

A stranger with soft brown hair drawn back into a bun knelt beside her bed. The woman's head was bowed and her hands were folded. Lilia gazed about the unfamiliar room as the stranger continued to pray.

"Father, it was Thy precious Son who invited the little ones to come to Him to be blessed. So I ask Thee to bless the child growing within my dear sister. Keep it safe in Thy loving hands. Protect the babe from the grief and sadness of these last few days. Fill its yet unborn life with peace and joy."

"Who? Who are you?" Lilia licked her dried and chapped lips between words. "Where am I?"

The young woman lifted her head in surprise. "You're awake? Praise God! You're awake."

Lilia ran her hand across her throbbing temples. "Ooh! My head aches."

The young woman rose to her feet and rushed for the bedroom door. "Mama, come here! Mrs. Cooper is awake."

Lilia lifted herself up on an elbow and studied her surroundings—the brilliant sunlight streaming through the white eyelet curtains, the blue-and-white quilt covering her body, the brass headboard supporting her weight. Her mind began to clear. She was at the preacher's house. And the young woman wearing the brown calico dress with the narrow row of delicate, white tatting at the neckline must be the preacher's daughter.

Piece by piece it came back to her: hearing of Wade's death and fainting in the lawyer's office.

Wade. Wade, her husband, was dead. And she was in Independence, Missouri, more than a thousand miles from her family. She was pregnant and a widow at age eighteen. The enormity of her situation washed over her. She collapsed against the downy pillow, groaning in despair.

"Mrs. Cooper? Are you all right?" The preacher's daughter touched Lilia's cheek, then dashed for the doorway. "Mama, come quickly. I think something's wrong with Mrs. Cooper."

"What? What happened?" An older woman appeared in the doorway.

"She was alert and awake, then suddenly she was gone again," the girl explained. Mrs. Rich leaned over Lilia to listen to her breathing.

"I . . . I'm all right," Lilia mumbled, slowly opening her eyes. Snowy white hair formed a halo around the middle-aged woman's soft face. Her warm brown eyes were filled with concern.

She touched Lilia's forehead. "Mrs. Cooper, are you all right? Do you know where you are?"

Lilia nodded. "Yes, but I have a terrible headache."

The woman smiled and brushed a sweaty curl from her patient's forehead. "That's probably from the medicine Doc Baker gave you. Sometimes his cures are worse than the diseases." She gave a little chuckle and straightened. "You must be hungry. How does a bowl of Scotch broth sound to you? And a stack of soda crackers?"

Lilia struggled to make sense of the woman's words. Why she was talking about food at such a time, Lilia couldn't imagine. "What day is it? Where are they keeping . . ." Her voice caught. ". . . Wade's body?"

A shadow washed across the minister's wife's face. "Today is Friday. You've been in and out of consciousness for two days." She rose to her feet. "By the way, my name is Cora, Cora Rich. And this is my daughter, Esther. We named her after Queen Esther in the Bible, you know."

Esther peered around her mother's shoulder and smiled at Lilia. The younger woman's soft brown eyes mirrored her mother's. Light brown strands of hair that escaped from the net-covered wad at the nape of the woman's head did little to compliment an already plain face. Except for her generous smile and her doe-like eyes, nothing about the girl would stand out among women, despite her grandiose name.

Cora Rich smoothed the covers about Lilia's shoulders. "You rest. I'll be right back with your broth and crackers."

"But Wade? Where are they keeping my husband's body?"

The women exchanged worried glances. Cora Rich took a deep breath then smiled sadly. "Mrs. Cooper, we buried your husband yesterday, the weather being what it is and all."

"Buried? But that's impossible! I wasn't there to, to grieve for him." Lilia turned her head toward the wall. "Poor Wade. No one to mourn his passing."

Cora Rich sat down on the edge of the bed. She smoothed the wrinkles from the skirt of the dark-green cotton dress she was wearing. Slowly she lifted her eyes to meet Lilia's. "My husband conducted a lovely graveside service for your husband. The Pownells and the Cunards all attended, except for Serenity who is recovering from childbirth, as you know. Mr. Bonner and the sheriff were there too."

Lilia shook her head and closed her eyes. "Poor Wade, no one to mourn him, no one to care. . . ." Her words drifted off into a whimper. By the time she opened her eyes again the two women had slipped out of the room. Lilia stared at a portrait of a small child hanging on the wall at the foot of the bed. She wondered if it was Esther.

In a short time, Cora returned. Behind her, Esther carried a tray of food.

"Would you like to sit up in bed, or perhaps sit on the edge of the bed to eat, Mrs. Cooper?" Cora suggested.

"Call me Lilia." She struggled to sit up.

"Here, let me help you." Cora lifted Lilia to a sitting position and stuffed an extra pillow behind her back.

"Woo! I'm dizzy." Lilia placed her hands in each side of her head.

"That's the medicine again, I think," Cora volunteered. "Or it could be from not eating in a couple of days."

Esther placed the tray across Lilia's knees. "Mama's Scotch broth is the best in the county."

Cora clicked her tongue at her daughter. "Esther, broth is broth. I fear you are given to hyperbole."

"Yes, Mama." Esther ducked her head and blushed.

As Lilia sipped the hot, flavorful liquid, she suddenly remembered her friend. "Serenity? How are Serenity and her son doing?"

"Just fine." Cora beamed with happiness. "That little Sammy is the hungriest baby I've ever seen. He's going to sprout like prairie grass in the spring time." Cora plumped the pillows around Lilia as she spoke. "When you collapsed, Serenity asked the men to transport you to her parents' home. But I could see that Josephine had her hands full caring for the new mama and baby. So I volunteered to care for you here. I hope you don't mind."

Lilia studied the woman's face for several seconds. "Thank you. That was very generous of you, considering that I am a stranger."

Cora dismissed Lilia's thanks with a wave of her hand. "Stranger? Not anymore. We're all family in this house. Besides, you've been an angel."

Angel? No one had ever called her an angel. Devil more likely. Lilia giggled. "And I've been unconscious."

"Psaush!" Cora waved her self-deprecating remark away as she adjusted the tiebacks on the window curtains. Lilia watched her raise the shade several inches, then lower it again. "I always wanted a second daughter. Actually, when Charles and I married, we dreamed of having five little girls in a row, like stair steps. I planned to dress them in matching Sunday-go-to-meeting outfits." Her smile dimmed for an instant then returned brighter than before. "But God, in

His unerring wisdom, generously loaded all the best of traits and the most loving gifts possible into my one beautiful daughter, Esther. She is the joy of my life." Cora placed a gentle kiss on her daughter's blushing cheek. "Isn't she lovely? Could any mother ask for more?"

"Oh, Mama." Esther blushed again and slipped from the room. Cora watched her disappear down the hallway.

"She is such a good girl," Cora confided. "Someday she'll make some lucky man a lovely wife and mother."

Lilia sipped her broth and nibbled on the soda crackers. When she'd emptied the cup, she began, "Now that I'm feeling better, I need to think about—"

Cora gently pushed Lilia's shoulders back against the bed. "Regaining your strength!" She reached to the bedside table for Lilia's hairbrush. "Aaron Cunard brought your personal items from the Pownell's. He's been here twice every day checking up on you. He's mighty concerned."

The image of the rangy young man brought a smile to Lilia's face. Under other circumstances she might have found him intriguing. But now, she realized for the first time in her life that she needed to consider the needs of another human being before satisfying her own whims and desires.

Esther peeked around the edge of the doorjamb. "I started the water boiling on the stove."

Cora looked pleased with her daughter's forethought. "Let me take that tray to the kitchen while Esther brushes your hair for you. My girl possesses a gift of healing in her hands. When any of the ladies in the neighborhood are feeling under the weather, they always ask Esther for help." Cora took the tray and headed toward the doorway. "Don't stay too long, honey. Lilia needs her rest."

Esther smiled apprehensively at her patient. "I love brushing people's hair. If you don't mind, of course."

"I'd like that." Lilia turned her face toward the opposite wall so the woman could reach her hair.

Gently, silently, the woman brushed through the tangles in Lilia's blond tresses. The only sounds in the room were the hum of a fly trapped in a fold of the curtains and the soothing rasp of the ivory-handled hairbrush being drawn through her hair. Esther wove Lilia's blond tresses into one long braid down the woman's back. "You have the most beautiful hair. It's the color of corn silk." She tied off the braid with a thin yellow ribbon and placed the brush on the nightstand beside the bed. Slowly she rose to her feet. "Is there anything else I can do for you?" she asked.

"No, thank you. You've done more than enough." Lilia felt refreshed and exhilarated.

Esther cast Lilia a timid smile from the doorway. "I'll close the door so you can you rest for a while."

"That would be nice. Thank you."

Esther shyly tipped her head to one side. "If you need anything, ring that little bell." She pointed to a small brass bell sitting on the back of the nightstand. "I'm heating the water so you can take a hot bath. But in the meantime, rest."

Lilia smiled at the thought of how she might smell after three days being bedridden. "I'd like that."

With a tiny wave, the woman was gone and Lilia found herself alone once more, alone to think, alone to consider her losses. She began to enumerate her options.

Lilia would never understand how a human could be vibrantly alive one moment, then, an instant later be a corpse. She remembered attending her grandfather's funeral. One day his heart just stopped beating; the doctor attributed it to old age. Less than a day earlier, she'd visited him. They'd shared two of his favorite applesauce cookies. She'd confided in him how much she resented having to attend some girls' school in Massachusetts. He laughed and reminded her that she'd be home for summer break before she knew it. The conversation seemed to have occurred so long ago.

The night he was laid out in her mother's parlor, after the mourners had gone home, she climbed up on a footstool, leaned over, and kissed him on the cheek. Lilia shivered remembering the icy sensation when her lips touched his cold, dry skin.

The man who'd always greeted her with a jolly laugh and open arms lay in the shiny mahogany coffin, cold and stiff. The remembrance of the touch of her lips against cold skin unsettled her for months.

Her thoughts shifted to Wade. She imagined they'd placed him in a pine box, at best—the coffin of a pauper. Had Wade gone to some distant hereafter for all eternity or did he cease to exist? The body they buried in the town cemetery, like her grandfather, was nothing more than an empty shell.

With Wade gone, what should she do? Go back to her parents? Live with Serenity and Caleb until the baby was born? Then what? "Oh, dear God! I don't know what to do!" she wailed. Her words ricocheted off the ceiling.

No! If there is such a Being as God, He certainly couldn't care less about me and my baby. We're both legacies of deceit, theft, and fraud. Her thoughts rattled around in the emptiness of her heart.

Later that afternoon, Esther dragged a large oak wash tub into the bedroom, filled it with hot water, and sprinkled lemon-verbena bath powder on the surface. Gratefully Lilia eased herself into the tub. She closed her eyes. The sweet smelling aroma surrounded and engulfed her senses, and for a short time, displaced all the negative thoughts she'd had throughout the afternoon. She rested her head against the side of the tub and let the tingling hot water sooths away the aches and pains lodged in her bones and muscles from being bedridden for three days.

Beyond the drawn shade, streaks of red and orange filled the early evening sky. She'd barely closed her eyes again when Esther appeared with a stack of thirsty, snowy-white Turkish towels and Lilia realized her bath water had cooled to tepid.

"Mama says to tell you that dinner will be ready in fifteen minutes, if you feel up to coming to the table. If not, I'll be glad to bring you a tray of food."

Lilia smiled with gratitude at the patient woman. "Thank you, but I think I'll be able to make it to the table on my own," she said. "Didn't your mother say that Doctor Baker thought I should get out of bed as soon as I felt able?"

"Yes." Esther shyly dipped her head to one side. "But I don't mind."

"I'm sure you don't. You've been so good to me. I don't know what I'll do once I leave here."

"Leave?" Esther's eyes widened in surprise. "You needn't be talking of leaving. Mama and I are hoping you'll stay for a while, until you decide what you want to do now that your husband is . . ." She paused, looking uncomfortable.

"Dead. Wade is dead. You can say it." Lilia shrugged as if it didn't bother her. "After all, nothing we say or do will bring him back."

Esther placed the towels on the edge of the bed. "You're right. And I'm sorry."

Lilia drew herself out of the water and wrapped one of the towels about her body. "Why are you sorry? You didn't do anything wrong."

Esther averted her eyes. "I know, but . . ."

"Nonsense. Anything that happened to my husband, he brought on himself. And the same is true for me." Lilia dried herself off, then slipped into the camisole and bloomers Esther had laid out for her on the bed. "It's time I face the truth. I've made a mess of my life so far. And that was my choice. But unfortunately for my child, he or she is stuck with my bad choices." Lilia began to fasten the hooks in the back of the camisole.

"Let me help you." Esther took over where Lilia left off. After a few seconds, the camisole was buttoned.

"Women's clothing is a pain!" Lilia snorted as she pulled on a pair of cotton stockings and a pair of pink satin slippers. "I'd like to see men put up with all the fasteners and snaps, buttons and bows like we do."

Esther chuckled. "Yes, ma'am."

Seeing that the dresses from her trunk were now hanging in an open wardrobe in the corner of the room, she removed a pink-and-yellow flowered calico dress from a hanger and slipped the garment over her head. While Esther again helped with the fasteners in the back, Lilia squeezed in her waist. She couldn't help but notice that her waist size had changed in the last few days.

Brushing a few stray curls away from her face, Lilia turned to admire herself in the wall mirror.

"You look lovely, ma'am." Esther's face was filled with admiration.

"Why do you keep calling me ma'am? We must be close to the same age. You sound like you're addressing my mother! My name is Lilia." Lilia was amazed how comfortable she felt around the timid young woman. Lilia had always wanted a sister. Perhaps that was why she'd become so close to Serenity. But now, Serenity had Caleb and a new son. Lilia didn't want to become an additional problem for her friend.

Lilia felt strangely drawn toward this young woman who'd been born and brought up on the prairie. Esther had not attended a prestigious girls' school. She'd never been introduced to America's upper crust of society. Plus she'd been raised by religious parents! Lilia could excuse the first two drawbacks, but the religion part? Only time would tell.

~13~
The Face of Love

Dinner with the Richs proved to be less of a chore than Lilia feared. Having lived with Serenity and Caleb for a few weeks prepared her for the worship that followed the evening meal. That she was always mentioned in their prayers both impressed and dismayed her. Under the circumstances, she felt it would be poor taste to escape to her room the instant Reverend Rich picked up his Bible to read.

It's only for a few minutes each evening, she reminded herself as she folded her hands and bowed her head for prayer.

As they rose from their knees, Reverend Rich placed his Bible on a bookshelf near the dining room door and exchanged it for a copy of James Fenimore Cooper's book, *The Last of the Mohicans.* With a twinkle in his eye, he asked Lilia, "Would you care to join us in the parlor? Esther is going to entertain us with another chapter from *The Leatherstocking Tales.*"

Cora rushed to her guest's rescue. "Now, Charles, Mrs. Cooper might not feel much like socializing tonight. She needs her rest."

"I don't mind." Lilia smiled gratefully at her hostess.

"James Fenimore Cooper is one of my father's favorite authors as well. I think I might enjoy listening as Esther reads a chapter or two."

"Good!" A smile wreathed Reverend Rich's round cherubic face. "Come, come. Let's not dilly dally, then. We left off with the hero and his sidekick hiding in the forest outside the enemy soldiers' camp." He led Lilia into the parlor and seated her in a large, rose, chintz-covered, wing-backed chair near the darkened fireplace. The gently rounded man methodically lit the oil lanterns scattered about the room. Esther and her mother followed.

Reverend and Mrs. Rich seated themselves on a bur-gundy-covered loveseat while Esther chose to sit in the mahogany-armed upholstered rocker opposite Lilia and beside the best source of lighting in the room.

The preacher handed his daughter the book, leaned back, and folded his hands across his chest, ready to hear the latest chapter in the early American tale that had captivated Europe at the turn of the century.

When Esther reached the end of the chapter, her parents excused themselves and headed for their bedroom at the top of the stairs. She looked at Lilia shyly. "Before I go to my room, may I get you anything?"

Lilia stretched and smiled. "No, I don't need a thing. I'm going to sleep well tonight."

"I hope so." The girl placed the book on the stand next to her chair. "The last few nights you've tossed and turned all night long."

"How did you know?"

Esther dipped her head down to one side. "I've been sleeping in the rocker beside your bed to make certain you were all right."

"You have? How very kind of you." Lilia was astounded. She couldn't remember caring so tenderly for another human being during her lifetime.

"I wanted to. Besides, it gave me extra time to read my books," she explained.

The memory of someone reading aloud returned to Lilia, along with the memory of someone praying. "Why? Why do you care so much?"

A slow, sad smile replaced the earlier, carefree one. "Lilia, it is a pleasure to use the gift God has given me to care for you and your unborn. I'm not a woman of great beauty like yourself—"

Lilia started to protest.

But Esther waved her hand. "No, I'm a plain woman, born and raised on the prairie. I don't sing. I don't play the organ. I don't have the gift of speech. I haven't an artistic bone in my body." She averted her gaze from Lilia's. "And I don't ever expect to find a husband or have children of my own."

Lilia started to interrupt, but Esther continued without a break. "However, God honored me with one precious gift, the gift of healing. In some way my hands bring comfort to those who are ill. I can't explain it, but they do."

Lilia remembered the girl's gentle ministrations and she had to agree that Esther's touch was comforting, soothing, in fact.

"It is a joy to use that talent for Him. Do you understand?"

Lilia cast her a bemused smile. "Not really."

"Oh, sure you do. What talents, beside your beauty, has God given you?" The girl watched Lilia expectantly.

Lilia thought but could not think of a single skill or ability she possessed that could be considered a gift from God— not that she believed there was a God.

Esther rose to her feet and extinguished the flame in the nearest oil lantern. "I'm sure you have several. You haven't taken the time to think about them, that's all."

Lilia was reluctant to end the discussion. "Esther, you talk about God as if He's real. You speak as if this mythical creature society has invented actually cares about you. My friend Serenity does, too, but I don't understand."

Esther chuckled and sat down on the footstool at Lilia's feet. "First, the God I love is not a mythical creature society invented to comfort itself in times of trouble. I worship the Creator of all things—you, me, the mountains, the forest, the trees, the birds, the foxes, the rabbits, everything. For life alone, I praise Him. However, He's more than just my Creator. He's my Friend. I talk with Him several times a day. He's always with me. I can tell Him anything, and He listens and gives me direction on how to live my life."

"Direction?" Lilia snorted. "What direction is He giving you right now? To preach to me?"

Esther blushed. "I'm sorry. I didn't mean to preach. Please forgive me."

"No, I'm the one who should apologize. I asked you a question and you answered it. Seriously, Esther, about this direction thing, what is He directing you to do right now?"

The girl shrugged. "Just like you said. He wants me to sit here on this footstool and tell you about my Friend Jesus."

It was Lilia's turn to blush. The young woman in front of her was so busy carrying out God's plan in the minutia, she didn't seem to worry about the bigger concerns of what she would do with the rest of her life. When she'd spoken earlier about her future in regards to a husband and children, Esther hadn't sounded bitter or sad, or even resigned.

Since recognizing her own loss, Lilia had thought of little else but her future and that of the baby's.

Esther gazed into Lilia's eyes as if interpreting the real questions in her mind. "God leads me step by step. All I have to do is trust Him and thank Him for what I have instead of whining over what I don't have."

A country-bred philosopher, Lilia thought. "If you were in my shoes, Esther, would you talk so glibly about your future?"

A scowl knitted the young woman's brow. She appeared to be ruminating about the question. "I don't know for sure, but I hope I would. God promised, 'I will never leave you, nor forsake you.' That tells me everything I need to know."

Irritation rose in Lilia as she eyed the other woman. *God!* Lilia decided she'd heard enough about Him for one night. She excused herself and made her way to the guest room. *God! God! God! These people, as nice as they are, are a bunch of fanatics!*

Lilia hated to imagine that her friend Serenity had fallen into the same devious and deceitful mind-trap. As she slipped into her nightdress, Lilia decided that she needed to leave before their fables began to sound believable.

The next afternoon Cora and Esther invited Lilia to sit with them on the porch while they shucked corn for supper. While they chatted, a deacon from the church came by with a bushel basket of acorn squash and several cucumbers from his garden. Later, a lady from the church delivered several remnants of cloth for the Wednesday afternoon quilting circle.

"I've been making new school dresses for Abby," she explained. "Somehow, I always have remnants, no matter how carefully I figure the yardage."

Lilia watched and listened. That night, as she reviewed the events of the day, she had to admit that she liked the people she'd met. They were good people, well-intentioned, despite their spiritual delusions.

On Sunday morning, Esther invited her to attend church with them. Lilia demurred. That afternoon, when Cora suggested they visit Serenity and little Sammy, Lilia jumped at the opportunity to get out, especially to see her friend and the new baby.

Josephine Pownell enthusiastically welcomed the women into her home. After expressing condolences to Lilia for the loss of her husband, Josephine led the way to Serenity's first-floor bedroom. "This girl is next to impossible to keep down. The doctor wants her to stay off her feet for another week, but I don't know how he intends to make her do it. I tried to tell her that taking good care of her body now will pay off when she gets to middle-age."

"You're right," Cora confided, nodding her head as they walked past the parlor and into the library which had been converted into a temporary bedroom. "I've seen so many new mothers return to their chores too soon after delivery, and later pay for their folly with female problems long before their time. My mama always said you can't fool Mother Nature." Esther rolled her eyes toward Lilia and shared a conspiratorial grin.

They found Serenity sitting up in bed, her ebony curls piled high on her head. A pink satin ribbon held them in place. She looked like a queen receiving her subjects. A gentle breeze ruffled the lace curtains, bringing little comfort from the summer heat.

Caleb, who'd been sitting in a straight chair beside Serenity's bed since lunch, used their arrival as an opportunity to escape to the porch where it was much cooler. The three women greeted Serenity with kisses, then removed their bonnets. Lilia laid hers on the dresser beside the door. By not wearing her bonnet she felt ten degrees cooler.

The baby was asleep in a wicker bassinet between the bed and the lace-covered windows. A shock of black hair topped his tiny red face. Clad in only a diaper and lying on a light-green flannel receiving blanket, Sammy looked like he could pass as a Shawnee baby. Cora scooped him up, flannel blanket and all.

While Serenity told about the numbers of visitors they'd had and of the joys of middle-of-the-night feedings, Cora held the sleeping child for a few minutes, then passed him to Esther.

Suddenly, without warning, her friend's newborn was in Lilia's arms. She sent a worried glance toward Serenity, but her friend only smiled reassuringly.

The infant wiggled and gave a cock-eyed yawn. *It's alive,* Lilia thought as she fondled the baby's tiny fingers. *It's a real little person.* The thought that in six months she would be holding her own child sent a chill of fear through her. The baby stirred and opened his eyes.

"He has blue eyes," Serenity said proudly. "See his ears? They're shaped like my mother's. She used to call them pixie ears."

After what Lilia hoped was a respectable length of time, she returned the child to his bassinet and sighed with relief. The enormity of the responsibility of parenting that pressed in on Lilia's mind caused Sammy to feel heavier than his few pounds.

When Serenity asked her how she was feeling, Lilia assured her that the Richs were taking good care of her. Never one to be subtle, Serenity asked, "Have you thought of what you will do now that Wade is gone? Will you return to your home in Norfolk?"

"No!" Surprised by her strident tone, Lilia softened the remainder of her response. "That isn't an option for me, I'm afraid." She shot a quick glance toward Esther, then continued, "I suppose I'll return with you to the inn, if that's all right with you and Caleb, until . . ."

"Of course, it's all right," Serenity assured her. "You know you are welcome to stay as long as it takes for you to get on your feet."

"Actually," Cora interrupted, "Charles and I have been talking, and we'd like to invite you to stay with us, Lilia. Living in town, you might be able to find a job to help you get by. I spoke with Felix Bonner yesterday. He needs someone to clean his offices once or twice a week, light cleaning, of course."

A cleaning lady? Even light cleaning? The idea sounded laughable to Eulilia Mae Northrop of Norfolk, Virginia. But not so to the recently widowed Lilia Cooper. Serenity's stepmother suggested that Lilia try to find work with one of the wealthy families in town as a governess.

As Josephine, Serenity, and Cora discussed the possibilities available, Lilia became more and more discouraged. Any solution, however desirable or undesirable, would be temporary due to her pregnancy. Ladies didn't appear in public during the last months of a pregnancy. It just wasn't done, even in a backwater society like Independence, Missouri.

Lilia gazed through the lace curtains at a dog chasing a squirrel up the side of an oak tree. Could she truly have sunk to such a position? A tear slid down her cheek.

Surprised and disgusted with herself, she wiped it away. No matter what had happened or would happen, she refused to play the role of the weeping widow. She tightened her lips and shot a quick glance toward the other women.

Esther's gentle eyes told Lilia that she'd had read her thoughts. She could feel Esther's compassion. Lilia looked down at her feet.

Gratefully to Lilia, baby Sammy whimpered, drawing the women's attention from her and to the infant's immediate needs. Josephine lifted him from the bassinet. "Are you hungry, little one? Is it time for your din-din?"

Serenity untied the white satin ribbons on her bed jacket while Josephine changed the baby's wet diaper. Serenity's face beamed with the pride of a new young mother as she held out her arms to receive her child. "This little scamp is a great eater, every three hours, like clockwork."

"Ladies," Josephine strode toward the door. "Maybe we should give Serenity and Sammy a little privacy. How does a glass of cold mint tea sound?"

The woman chattered on as she led Cora, Esther, and Lilia from the room. "Samuel brought home a chunk of ice this morning. We might as well enjoy the last of it, don't you think?"

As the other two women followed their hostess into the parlor, Lilia wandered through the open front door onto the porch of the two-story white clapboard house.

Lost in thought about her friend's baby and the eventual arrival of her own, she didn't notice the man sitting in the wicker rocker at the far end of the porch.

"Hello there," Aaron called, leaping to his feet. His wide-brimmed felt hat fell to the floor in front of him. He stooped to pick it up. "Beautiful day, isn't it?"

Lilia whipped about in surprise.

Aaron's smile broadened, revealing an intriguing set of dimples. "Isn't my nephew something? Have you ever seen a more healthy lad?"

Lilia laughed nervously, though she didn't know why. "He is beautiful."

"Beautiful? You are calling my nephew beautiful, as if he were a girl?" Aaron's eyes sparkled with devilry. "Boys aren't beautiful; they're handsome."

"My apologies, kind sir." Lilia gave him a mock bow. "Please forgive my *faux pas*. He is indeed handsome."

"Foe-who?" Aaron knitted his brow.

Lilia laughed. "*Faux pas,* that's a French term for mistake."

"Ah, *faux pas*." He thought for a moment. "I like that. Faux pas." He rolled it around on his tongue several times. "I've got to remember that one. It sounds less accusing than the word *mistake*. So how many languages do you speak, besides English, that is?"

"My proper Bostonian English instructor would argue as to whether or not my Virginia twang qualifies as a dialect of the mother tongue." Her eyes sparkled when she laughed. "To answer your question, I speak two other languages—French and Italian. In my sophomore year of high school, I tried learning German but I couldn't get my tongue around some of the guttural sounding syllables. I switched to Latin." She giggled. "I seldom have cause to hold a conversation in the ancient tongue of Julius Caesar."

"I'm impressed." He gestured toward the second rocker. "Won't you join me?"

An unexpected awkwardness filled her with uncertainty. It had been a long while since a man other than Wade had complimented her. And Wade's compliments had disappeared soon after their wedding. She dipped her head like she'd seen Esther do, disgusted with herself even as she did so. "Thank you, but I don't think I will, sir."

Aaron shrugged. "Suit yourself." He made himself comfortable in the rocker he'd vacated while Lilia sat down on the top porch step. Hugging her knees to her chest, she rested her chin on them and studied the houses lining the quiet street, houses that could be transplanted to any number of communities throughout America.

Lilia was grateful for the shade from the porch's overhang. Out of the corner of her eye she watched Aaron Cunard sit quietly in the wicker rocking chair. She tried to ignore the presence of the persistent cowboy. And from her point of view, he was a cowboy. His clothing was as homespun as those of the ruffians she'd met on the Missouri River paddleboat heading west.

"It sure is a warm day today, ma'am." Aaron used his hat as a fan to cool his face. "But not unseasonably so, don't you think?"

Behind her, the screen door slammed shut. She turned and saw Esther carrying a tray with three icy cold glasses of mint tea. "Mrs. Pownell asked me to bring these out to you." She bent to allow Lilia to take the first glass. "She and Mama are talking babies still."

Esther straightened and walked shyly toward Aaron. "I brought a glass for you too, Mr. Cunard."

As Lilia watched Esther approach Aaron, it dawned on her that the minister's daughter had a crush on the younger Cunard brother. Lilia shook her head and glanced away. From what she'd seen of Aaron, Reverend and Mrs. Rich would frown upon such a union—not that Aaron would find the girl particularly attractive anyway.

Lilia guessed, because she knew he worked in a bar, that he found flashier women more to his liking. She'd seen more than her share of such women on the riverboats. Yet she never would have been able to fault him for the way he conversed with the plain young woman. Lilia couldn't decide if Aaron was making fun of the girl or being genuinely nice.

While he treated both her and Esther with courtesy and deference, Lilia detected a darker side to the man's personality. Wade had opened her eyes to men and to the art of deceit. This Cunard fellow displayed all the signs of duplicity as far as Lilia was concerned. She vowed to avoid such men at all costs.

-14-

Messengers from God

MESSENGERS FROM GOD COME IN ALL SHAPES and sizes, so Esther had told her during one of their more profound conversations. Lilia continued to scoff at the idea that an omnipotent God like Esther described could or would be interested in what happened in the life of one insignificant woman in America's remote outback. And all the Scripture texts that Esther quoted couldn't convince Lilia otherwise.

On Wednesday night of the first week in September, Lilia had cause to reevaluate her position on the matter. Reverend and Mrs. Rich returned from the midweek prayer meeting at the church with three middle-aged gentlemen callers. They'd come to see Esther. From their clothing and demeanor, Lilia figured them to be farmers.

Elder Moore, the most outspoken of the three, had a big voice, a brown beard, and a mustache full enough to house a family of cardinals, but he had not one strand of hair on the top of his head.

Mr. Farver, a small, stringy man with a scruffy week-old beard, barely spoke. When forced to contribute his opinions, his eyes filled with fear and his words came out in a stutter.

Lilia had doubts about the third visitor, Mr. Ted Tyler, who claimed to be from Liberty, Texas, but whose accent sounded like a North Carolinian to the Virginia-born lass. His eyes wandered over her too many times for her comfort.

As quickly as was polite, Lilia excused herself and escaped to her room, though her curiosity consumed her. She sat on the edge of her bed and tried to read from one of the leather-bound books she'd borrowed from Reverend Rich's library—stories by Washington Irving. She'd always admired the author's vivid character descriptions and his gift of humor. But this evening, the story of Rip Van Winkle couldn't hold her interest.

She knew it was none of her business what the three men wanted with Esther, but Lilia had never been one to keep her nose out of other people's lives, so her mother always said. Yet she tried to read.

"Rip Van Winkle was one of those happy mortals, of foolish, well-oiled dispositions, who take the world easy, eat white bread or brown, whichever can be got with least thought or trouble, and would rather starve on a penny than work for a pound."

Oh, forget it! She slammed the book closed. *The last thing I want to read about tonight is "starving for a penny."*

Money seemed to be her main concern of late, or perhaps, the lack of money. Mr. Bonner gave her a hefty sum as payment for her father's rare coin. She suspected he'd been more than generous with her, as he never did try to sell it in St. Louis. The sheriff had given her a gold coin, a Spanish doubloon from the last century, that he'd found on Wade's near dead body. She'd sell the doubloon if necessary, but the last coin, the one from ancient Palestine, the one that her father loved most, she hoped she'd never need to trade for food or lodging.

Admitting defeat, Lilia tossed the book on the bed and pressed her ear to the closed door. She could hear voices but couldn't make out the words. With a sigh, she ambled back to the bed and threw herself face down on the blue-and-white quilt. Deciding to try again, she picked up the book and opened it to the page where she'd left off. "Rip Van Winkle . . . of foolish . . . replying to all lectures . . . a henpecked husband." She idly skipped through the paragraphs.

She started at a sudden knock on the door. Hoping it was Esther coming to tell her about her evening visitors, Lilia sprang for the door. It was Cora, not Esther. Lilia managed to contain her disappointment. "Yes?"

"Lilia, our guests would like to talk with you, if you're willing?"

"Me?" Lilia's jaw dropped in surprise. "Why me?"

"They came to see my daughter, but she—why don't you come out here and let them explain." Cora led Lilia into the parlor. The men leaped to their feet as the women entered the room. "Here she is, gentlemen, my house guest, Lilia Cooper from Norfolk, Virginia."

The men nodded respectfully. Lilia sent a questioning glance toward Esther. The young woman looked miserable as she huddled in the corner of the sofa. Lilia couldn't imagine what these men had to say that had made the usually cheerful girl so unhappy.

"Mrs. Cooper, we understand you are recently widowed," the man introducing himself as Elder Moore said.

"Yes?" Lilia eyed him questioningly.

"And you can read, write, and figure?" he continued.

Lilia glanced at Reverend Rich and his wife, then at Esther. "Yes."

"Miss Rich tells us that you also speak French and Italian?"

Lilia opened her mouth to reply, but the man identified as Mr. Farver interrupted. "We don't care about those foreign t-t-tongues. W-w-we want our kids to speak good English!"

"Excuse me, sirs, but what is this all about?" She glanced at Esther whose face resembled that of a doe cornered by a pride of mountain lions.

"Mrs. Cooper, we represent the Sugar Creek school district and we are in a bind." Elder Moore glanced at the other two men, then back to Lilia. "The schoolteacher we hired, sight unseen, took sick on her way here from Maine. A doctor told her that she won't be able to continue west until November."

"School was scheduled to open last Monday. We have fifteen children, grades one through eight, but no teacher," Mr. Tyler added. "One of Pastor Rich's congregation suggested we hire Esther as a temporary teacher until the other one arrives, but . . ."

Lilia finally understood Esther's misery. Knowing Esther as she did, Lilia couldn't imagine the timid young woman controlling a classroom of rambunctious children for an hour, let alone three months or more.

Elder Moore leaned forward and leveled his gaze at Lilia. "When Esther refused, Mrs. Rich suggested that you might need a position for a few months after the death of your husband and all."

Lilia returned the man's steady gaze with a look of confidence and composure. Her air of calm hid the violent pounding going on inside her heart. A teacher? Her? Would Serenity ever laugh at this one! Of all people. Lilia had been the scourge of every teacher she'd ever had, from Norfolk to Boston. That she was interested in the position surprised her. "I'm a stranger here, sir. Forgive me, but where is Sugar Creek?"

Elder Moore leaned back in his chair knowing he'd read her response accurately. "The town is north and west of Independence a short distance. It's only a few miles from Serenity Inn in fact. Pastor Rich told us that you are friends with the couple operating the place."

"Yes, Mrs. Cunard was my roommate at the New England Finishing School I attended."

Mr. Farver quoted a sum of money she'd make every week, a pittance compared to what Lilia had been accustomed to carrying around in her pocket as a Northrop. He listed the rules they'd expect her to live by while employed by them, one of which was regular church attendance. When he finished, he asked, "Well? Are you prepared to accept our offer?"

"How soon would I start?" she asked.

Elder Moore glanced at the other two men, then back at Lilia. "We were hoping you could go with us tonight. There's a furnished two-room soddy next to the school."

Today? A soddy! Lilia couldn't believe her luck. She'd be living in a mud hut, after all she'd said to Wade about Serenity's place.

"We would expect you to take your evening meal, on a rotating basis, with each of the children's families."

Lilia grimaced at the idea of eating with strangers of differing social classes. "Is that a requirement?"

The three men exchanged glances. Elder Moore shook his head. "No, just a suggestion to save money and to help you become acquainted with the people of the community."

Lilia frowned. "If you waive the rotating meals, I'll fill in for you at the school."

"Very good, Mrs. Cooper." Elder Moore rubbed his hands together in satisfaction. "Very good. And you'll come with us tonight?"

"I would prefer to arrive tomorrow afternoon as I will need to shop for incidentals before I leave town. On Friday, I'll conduct a half day of classes. It will help me get acquainted with my students." She noted the look of displeasure on the preacher's face. She could tell the man was unaccustomed to being challenged, especially by a woman. "Is that all right with you, Elder Moore?"

The man's neck reddened. He shifted his gaze to the floor. "Y-y-yes ma'am."

"Good. Then it's settled." She rose to her feet. "I will arrive tomorrow afternoon in Sugar Creek." She extended her hand toward the preacher. Realizing they were being dismissed, the men awkwardly rose to their feet.

"I am looking forward to it, as are my wife and my children." Taking her small graceful hand in his, he smiled.

She shook hands with Mr. Farver, then reached for Mr. Tyler's hand. The man took her hand in his and lifted it to his lips, kissing her fingertips. "Until tomorrow. *Bon soir, madam.*" His devilish grin unnerved her momentarily.

"*Parlez vous en Francais?*" she asked, arching her eyebrow sarcastically.

The man cleared his throat and reddened. "Not really, ma'am. I just picked up that greeting from a Frenchie I wrangled cattle with as a boy." He cocked his head to one side and added, "Maybe you could teach me though. I'd be an apt student."

"I'm sure you would be, sir." Lilia straightened her spine and lifted her chin defiantly. She looked down her straight aquiline nose. "But as I'm sure you know, Mr. Tyler, I will be too busy teaching the children of Sugar Creek to instruct their parents."

While she stared Mr. Tyler down, Pastor Rich cleared his throat. "Well, gentlemen. It looks like your search is complete." Resting a hand on Tyler's shoulder, he guided the forward young man toward the front door.

Lilia stood with her feet nailed to the parlor floor while the men said their good-byes at the front door. The reality of what she'd done began to sink in. How could she be so foolish? Wrapping her arms about herself, she shivered against the cold reality of her hasty decision.

Delighted to be off the hook, Esther rushed to Lilia and gave her a hug. "Oh, Lilia, as soon as Elder Moore explained the reason of his visit, I knew you were the woman he was looking for. You will be such a good teacher to those little children."

"But if it doesn't work out," Cora warned, "you are welcome to return to us."

"Thank you." Lilia felt apprehension flooding her face.

"It's going to be all right, Mama. I know it will." Esther gave Lilia another squeeze. "Didn't I tell you that God watches out for His children? Didn't He promise to provide for your needs?"

Ever practical, Cora eyed Lilia's waistline. "You will have to keep your pregnancy as quiet as possible. Hopefully, since this is your first child, you won't show too soon." She tugged at the back of Lilia's skirt. "I know a few tailoring tricks that will help."

Pastor Rich had returned and stood in the doorway to the parlor. "Cora, I do hope you aren't encouraging Lilia to lie about her condition?"

"No, darling." She strode to his side and snuggled under his left arm. "But she doesn't need to advertise her pregnancy before it is necessary to do so either. You know how finicky people can be about a woman appearing in public in the last stages of pregnancy."

He planted a kiss on his wife's forehead. "Yes, dear, and you're no less finicky than the next woman." He gave Lilia an encouraging smile. "Listen to my wife. She knows about such things."

Cora beamed at her husband's compliment. Kissing his cheek, she bustled across the room to Lilia. "My ecru crocheted vest would be a perfect lightweight cover. A nip or a tuck here and there in your dresses, a few Mother Hubbard aprons made from my fabric remnants and no one will guess. By the time they figure it out, the new teacher will have arrived and be ready to begin teaching."

Regardless of the lateness of the hour, Lilia found herself caught up in Cora's whirlwind. It was after midnight before Lilia fell into bed, exhausted, yet strangely warmed by Cora's generosity and her overabundant enthusiasm.

When Lilia awoke the next morning, she discovered Cora had not only spent the rest of the night tailoring Lilia's entire wardrobe, but she'd also gone through her kitchen cupboards for utensils Lilia could use. Lilia's eyes filled with tears upon seeing the things Cora had stacked for her on the kitchen table. A wave of homesickness passed over her. The young woman could imagine her own mother doing the same thing for someone else's daughter.

Lilia and Esther giggled like schoolgirls as they shopped for the few necessities Lilia needed to purchase. At the mercantile, when Lilia paid for her purchases, Mr. Pringle gave them each a licorice stick for free. "You remind me of my two daughters when they were little. They're both grown and living in St. Louis now."

As the two women left Mr. Pringle's store, Lilia thought about how long it had been since she felt young. After they completed their shopping and dropped the parcels off at Esther's home, the women walked to the Pownell home to tell Serenity the good news.

Serenity was delighted for Lilia. She also had a great time teasing Lilia about becoming a schoolteacher. "Actually, you'll make a great teacher," Serenity remarked. "You'll be one step ahead of the children when it comes to pranks."

As Lilia prepared to leave, Serenity asked if they could have a special prayer for Lilia. What could Lilia say? Earlier Reverend and Mrs. Rich had done the same thing. If nothing else, she decided, she'd appreciate being away from all this religion stuff, even if that meant attending church once a week to keep the school board happy.

At the end of the prayer, Serenity gave her friend a hug. Then, holding her at arm's length, Serenity asked, "You'll be living quite close by, you know. Sugar Creek is only a hop, skip, and a jump from the inn. So you'll come over for Sunday dinner each week, won't you?"

"Not every Sunday," Esther interrupted. "Mama and I were hoping you'd come to our house once in a while too."

Surprised, they turned to Esther. She'd barely said a word since they arrived at the Pownell house.

"You are both such dear friends." Lilia linked her arms in both women's and started toward the door. "I'm sure there will be enough Sundays to go around."

Serenity leaned against the doorframe as the two other women stepped onto the porch. "I wish I could come with you to help you settle in."

"I know, and you're precious to offer, but you have your son to care for and . . ." Lilia gestured toward the other woman. "I have Esther here."

"And my mother," Esther reminded. "She wouldn't miss the opportunity to help Lilia settle into her new place."

Serenity smiled graciously at the unusually loquacious young woman. Turning to Lilia once again, Serenity added, "I can't believe you're doing this. What an adventure!"

Lilia paused to consider Serenity's remark. "You're right. It is quite the adventure, isn't it?" She gave Serenity a kiss on the cheek, then hurried down the front steps after Esther.

Back at the Rich's house they found Cora overseeing the loading of Lilia's goods on a buckboard Reverend Rich borrowed from one of his parishioners.

"I'm sorry I can't come with you to your new home, Lilia dear," Cora said, "but Mrs. Garvey, one of the oldest members of our congregation, needs my help this afternoon. But I'm sure you and Esther can do just fine without me."

Lilia thanked her hostess for all she'd done, then allowed Reverend Rich to help her and Esther aboard the wagon. If the truth be known, Lilia was relieved not to have Cora along. The woman had a gentle, but firm way of taking charge of every situation. And while it was true that Cora's organizational skills were superb, the older woman intimidated Lilia more than she wanted to admit.

"You'd better tie your bonnet on tightly," Cora called as the wagon lurched forward. "The streets are mighty bumpy this time of year."

Lilia smiled and waved. Being around Cora was like returning to one's childhood. She could see why Esther seemed afraid of her own shadow.

~15~

Home Sweet Home

REVEREND RICH RELEASED THE BRAKE ON the buckboard and shook the reins above the backs of the mismatched team of horses. The wagon lurched forward, hitting the wheel ruts made by a succession of covered wagons that had rolled through the town earlier in the season. Esther's and Lilia's hands flew to their bonnets, catching them before the wind caught the lightweight, cotton poke bonnets and sent them flying in the breeze.

The wagon rumbled through town creating a billowing cloud of dust behind it. Townspeople waved to the preacher and his daughter as they passed by. The Richs returned the greetings. Lilia sat primly on the loosely sprung buckboard seat beside Esther with one hand holding her bonnet in place and the other grasping the iron armrest at her side.

The main street of town was quiet. It was midday. Housewives had finished their shopping hours earlier, as had farmers who'd come in from the surrounding area. Three Mexican cowboys dressed in trousers, boots, and serapes, leaned against the wall by the telegraph office. Two business-men dressed in outdated black suits appropriate for a funeral sat outside the barbershop. They appeared to be having an intense discussion. A skinny brown dog, probably abandoned by a family heading west, slept with his head resting on his front paws on the boardwalk in front of the hardware store.

Later, when the sun went down, the area would come alive with cowboys from the cattle ranches in town for the big weekend, with women of the night advertising their trade, and with yokels, local and otherwise, out to make a fast buck in the gaming halls. A shadow in the form of Wade's self-assured face came to mind. Lilia straightened her spine and lifted her chin, determined not to let the memory of her dead husband ruin her resolve.

The wagon rolled past the mercantile, past the sheriff's office, and on to the western outskirts of town. Before them, deeply worn ruts cut through the tall prairie grass. A jackrabbit hopped across the road in front of the horses and disappeared into the thick grass. A crow called to his mate from a branch of a hollow tree trunk. A bee buzzed near Lilia's left ear. She swatted it with her gloved hand.

In no time at all the town was lost behind a cloud of dust. When they came to a branch in the road, Reverend Rich urged the horses to turn right on a lesser-traveled road headed northwest.

"Sugar Creek is a tiny community just north of Independence," Reverend Rich explained above the rumble of the wooden-spoke wheels. "I don't think the town has much more than twenty-five or thirty families. They have a community church pastored by Elder Moore from the Chesapeake area. You met him the other night at our house. He's the chairman of the school board as well as the pastor."

Lilia nodded, struggling to keep her balance as the wagon rumbled over rocks, dirt clods, and into gully-sized potholes.

"The town is only a stone's throw from the Kansas Territory. There's been some trouble between the abolitionists and the pro-slavers around here, but that won't affect you. You're here to teach the children." As Reverend Rich continued talking about Sugar Creek and its inhabitants, Lilia's mind wandered.

What did she know about teaching children to read or to figure? As the wheels of the wagon ground against the dusty roadway, her fears intensified. Act first, think later—this time Lilia knew she'd really done it. What if the children refused to listen to her? What if they hated her?

"There!" Reverend Rich pointed to a cluster of soddies ahead of them in the distance. "There's Sugar Creek. And, if I'm not mistaken, the school is that clapboard building with the bell tower. The school acts as the church on Sundays."

"O-o-oh!" The grimy little community looked as if it had risen like spring dirt clods erupt from the ground following a hard freeze. Butterflies fluttered in Lilia's stomach. She swallowed hard, trying not to think of vomiting. There was no turning back. Her adventure had begun.

The wagon rolled past a cluster of soddies sprinkled about the area. She imagined curious eyes staring out at her from behind glass-paned windows and open shutters.

A woman not much older than she stood in the doorway of one of the soddies. She was holding a baby on her hip and had a golden-haired toddler clinging to her skirts. The woman smiled and waved. Reverend Rich waved back. "That's Mrs. Page. You'll have her three older children in your classroom."

The horses stopped beside a one-room sod house. Beyond the soddy stood the unpainted schoolhouse with a squatty bell tower perched on the front of the roof. A patch of prairie grass, a narrow pathway, and a third building, an outhouse, separated the teacher's quarters from the school.

She was surprised when she saw the Cunard's buckboard and team of horses tied to the hitching post outside the soddy. In front of the soddy, she noted a wooden-covered well with a hand pump. Beside the well was a campfire with an iron kettle suspended over it. The soddy's two windows and the heavy wooden front door were flung open to the sunshine. Lilia leaped from the buckboard before Reverend Rich could bring the vehicle to a complete stop. She fell to her knees, but immediately bounded to the front door and peered into the soddy's dark interior where she found Annie scrubbing the inside windowpanes.

"Annie, what are you doing here?" Lilia screeched to a halt, barely catching her balance. "How did you get here before us?"

Annie laughed. "You'd barely left the Pownells' when Serenity and Josephine went into action. Serenity would have been here herself if she could. So I volunteered to come in her place."

As her eyes adjusted to the dim interior lighting, Lilia identified Caleb and Aaron beside the large, gray, stone fireplace at the rear of the soddy, constructing shelves. Her gaze fell on the stack of cow chips that filled a wooden crate on the far end of the hearth. She grimaced at the thought of collecting them for herself.

Her gaze rested on a well-worn horsehair sofa and the bright, yellow-and-orange crocheted afghan that had been spread across the back. A yellow-and-red sunburst knitted pillow rested on the seat of a scarred wooden rocker adjacent to the sofa.

She continued her initial inspection of her new home. A red, blue, yellow, and green crazy quilt covered a single bed, which was barely more than a cot in size. The vibrant colors tried valiantly to brighten the drab little room.

Two chairs and a table with chipped paint filled the middle of the room. And in the middle of the table, a bouquet of daisies and wild carrot blossoms arranged in a tin pot were resting on a white linen doily.

"This is a surprise!" Lilia exclaimed. "I don't know what to say."

The two men straightened and grinned. Caleb brushed sawdust off his pant legs. "Don't say anything. Just grab a rag and begin scrubbing something—though I doubt Annie has left you anything to scrub. She's kept us running for water all afternoon. I see where she's scrubbed the varnish off the front door."

"That's not true." Annie huffed indignantly at Caleb's teasing.

"If you didn't, it's not for lack of trying!" Aaron chided.

Uncomfortable with being the center of attention, Annie changed the subject. She gestured toward the bare dirt floor in front of the sofa. "The braided rug we found when we got here is out back drying. Aaron strung a new clothesline for you. I hope the rug dries before dark tonight. The colors in the rug are quite pretty once I beat the dirt out."

Lilia's gaze traveled around the room a second time. Her eyes misted with emotion. While she'd never seen such a dumpy little place, she'd also never had anyone work so hard to make things nice for her. For a moment, she wondered what sarcastic comment Wade would have had upon seeing the humble little room. She tried to picture her mother's reaction to the soddy's interior. She sniffed and touched her gloved hand to her nose. "You are all being so nice to me. Thank you. I don't deserve it."

A conk and a grunt of pain coming from the door behind her saved her from embarrassing herself by crying.

"This entrance wasn't made for men over five foot eight, was it?" Reverend Rich rubbed his forehead as he stepped inside the soddy.

Aaron grinned and placed his hand on his forehead too. "I know. I discovered the same thing when we arrived."

Reverend Rich grimaced as he gingerly touched his bruised forehead.

"Are you all right, Daddy?" Esther asked. "Here, let me look at it." She examined the bruise. "You'll be all right. You didn't break the skin."

The preacher snorted as if insulted. "It feels like I did!"

Esther laughed and reassured him that he'd feel better in no time. Reverend Rich grunted, then turned toward Caleb and Aaron.

"Got a wagonload of goods out here that needs unloading. Think you boys could give me a hand?" He gestured toward the door. "I need to get unloaded and return the buckboard to its owner before dark."

"Sure." Caleb dropped his tools and followed the preacher out of the house. Aaron followed the other two men, but not before exchanging a silent glance of a greeting with Lilia. Lilia looked quickly toward Esther, hoping she hadn't seen the exchange. If she had, the woman's face didn't show it.

Lilia gazed at the lovely touches Annie had put about the room, touches that made the place feel more like a home and less like a dungeon. Tears filled her eyes.

"Annie, this is so nice of you. You didn't have to do any of this, you know." Lilia knew she had been anything but kind to the former slave girl with the horribly scarred hands. And Lilia didn't fail to notice that the skin on those hands was withered from being submerged in water all afternoon, water used to scrub months of neglect from the walls and furnishings of Lilia's new home.

Annie's eyes sparkled. She wiped her soiled hands on her apron. "I know. Serenity wanted to help too, but . . ."

Lilia's heart softened. She started toward Annie as if to give her a hug, then stopped abruptly, realizing the social gaffe such behavior would be. Her face flushed with embarrassment. "I don't know what to say. Thank you."

Annie ignored Lilia's moment of awkwardness and gestured toward the narrow bed and the open trunk at the foot. "Serenity sent a pair of sheets and a blanket for you. And there are white Turkish towels in there as well. Aaron plans to put in a shelf over there." She pointed to the wall at the foot of the bed. "He's going to put wooden pegs beneath it so you'll have a place to hang your clothing. Oh, yes, I washed the curtains and when they dry, I'll iron them and rehang them before I go."

Lilia strode across the room to the cot and ran her hand over the brightly colored quilt. "I just don't know what to say."

Esther followed Lilia's example. "When they get those shelves made, Mama's rose patterned china will add a lovely touch to that side of the room." The woman turned in circles, a delighted smile filling her face. "This place is going to be warm and cozy when everything's done."

Lilia's composure returned. Only half serious, she replied, "I bet you wish you'd taken the job now."

Esther waved her hands in the air and shook her head violently. "Oh, no. You're welcome to the job. Teaching is not for me."

Laden with wooden crates, Aaron reappeared in the doorway. "Where do you want these?"

Annie didn't wait for Lilia to respond. She pointed to a spot near the foot of the bed. "Put them out of the way for now." Like an army sergeant on a parade ground, she stood beside the door and directed the men as they carried in the contents of the wagon. Esther started unpacking the food crates.

"Mama packed some fried chicken, potato salad, and soda biscuits in this basket for your supper after we leave." Esther placed the woven reed basket on the table.

"Speaking of which . . ." Esther glanced quickly about the soddy. "Where's the stove for cooking?"

Annie gestured toward the fireplace. "You're looking at it." Lilia stared in unbelief. She'd never cooked on an iron stove, let alone over an open fire.

Overhearing Annie, Aaron set a wooden crate down that he'd been carrying and turned toward Lilia. "Don't try to light the fireplace until I have a chance to sweep the chimney. Who knows what creature has chosen to set up housekeeping since it was last used? I'll be here to take care of that for you sometime tomorrow."

"Oh, I forgot to mention, the storm cellar is to the left of the house. We put a bucket of milk in there earlier for you. It will need to be dusted out as the ceiling is alive with daddy longlegs. It makes a great cold cellar as well as an emergency shelter during tornadoes."

"Tornadoes?" The term was new to the Southern-born lass. Lilia listened with only one ear as Esther explained about the violent storms that could sweep in off the prairie. But her mind was on other things. She wandered over to the stiff and scratchy, rope-tied sofa. She ran her hand across the furniture's faded and threadbare, green, silk upholstered arm.

Her appreciation of the room with whitewashed walls bounced back and forth between pleasure and contempt. She'd never imagine that she, a Northrop, could ever call such a place a home. Yet, regardless of the shabby furniture and the dirt floor beneath her feet, she enjoyed thinking of this place as home—at least for a few months. Beyond those few months, she preferred to forget for the time being.

-16-

A New Challenge

LILIA STOOD OUTSIDE THE ONE-ROOM SOD house she was to call home for the next three months and watched the two wagons rumble down the road, one toward town and the other toward Serenity Inn.

Esther had volunteered to stay with her for the night. "It's going to be lonely out here all alone," the young woman warned.

Lilia assured her she'd be fine. It wasn't as if she were truly alone. There were several inhabited soddies nearby. "I'm sure that if I scream for help, someone will come running," Lilia laughed. "My scream is so loud that you'd hear me in Independence."

Everyone had laughed with her. Before leaving, Pastor Rich had grown serious. "If you need anything, go see Elder Moore. He lives in the last sod house to the north."

Lilia had squinted in the direction he pointed. The glare from the sun blinded her vision, but at least she knew the general path in which to run, should it become necessary.

So much had been accomplished in a short time. Lilia appreciated the shelves Caleb and Aaron had installed. Aaron had taken the time to level the table and the chairs before loading his tools in the wagon. As Annie climbed into the wagon heading to the inn, she promised to return the next afternoon. "I'll show you how to use the bake oven in your fireplace. It's simple, really."

As the wagons disappeared from her view, Lilia felt totally alone, and more than a little frightened. She eyed the tall grass along the narrow path between her and the school building and thought, *Snakes!*

She remembered the time when as a small child she'd found a harmless garter snake curled up in the corner of her parents' front porch. Her father quieted her hysteria by saying, "Snakes are more afraid of you than you are of them." While she had never tested her father's theory, she realized she had to deal with the possibility of snakes lurking in the tall grass. It was either test her father's theory or become a prisoner in her new home. Even walking the pathway to the outhouse required brushing past the tall grass.

Determined to face her fear of snakes, Lilia hiked up her skirts with one hand, grabbed a stick of wood with the other, and headed for the schoolhouse, beating the pathway with the stick as she walked. When a startled field mouse scurried across her path, she screeched.

Her confidence grew the farther she walked. The hollow hum of the prairie's ever-constant wind whistled past her ears. Her single braid, once secured in a wad at the nape of her neck with hairpins, swung loose down her back making her feel like a small child. She skipped a few steps. She felt free.

For the first time in her life, no one was there to tell her what to do, where to go, what to say, or what to think. She lifted her skirts and took the six stairs leading into the schoolhouse two at a time. Upon reaching the landing, she whirled about in a circle. *How unladylike,* she thought.

She recalled earlier times, when her life had been simple and happy. Peace filled her soul as she gazed west. From horizon to horizon, prairie grass rippled in the breeze, an unending sea of gold.

She took a deep breath before entering the empty schoolhouse. While her soddy had been far from clean when she arrived, she was pleasantly surprised to find the interior of the school immaculate. Then she reminded herself of the weekly church services.

There were four rows of dark oak student desks, arranged from smallest to largest. She noted that the wood floor had recently been oiled. Three quarters of the way down the center aisle was a pot-bellied stove. A large basket half full of cow chips sat beside the stove.

On the chalkboard at the front of the room behind the teacher's desk was a message: "Welcome Mrs. Cooper." Lilia smiled. An American flag hung in the front right corner. She wondered if the star count included the country's newest state, California.

She ran her hand along the smooth, well-oiled surface of a wooden table along the back wall. On the table was a stack of writing slates and a wooden cigar box full of gray chalk. On the other side of the entry was a four-shelf bookcase. Several well-worn *New England Primers* occupied the top shelf.

Lilia leafed through one of the books. It wasn't so long ago that she'd learned to read from the same edition of the book. She scanned the titles of the books on the second shelf, all classics. The two bottom rows were empty. She suspected these shelves were where the children stored their lunches.

A faded map of the world, dated 1779, was mounted on the wall behind the bookcase. Red lines traced the routes of the early explorers.

A small table near the bank of windows held a metal washbasin and matching pitcher. An empty oak bucket rested on the floor beside it. She ambled to the front of the room, her hands clasped together behind her back. She pictured the seats filled with small, wiggling bodies.

She took inventory of the teacher's desk drawers. Equipment was in meager supply. She was relieved to find a pad of paper, a pen, and an inkwell filled with black ink. Realizing that the sun would soon set, she retraced her steps to the soddy. Tomorrow would be a new day.

The next morning Lilia was up before dawn. As she brushed her blond curls in front of the tiny pocket mirror she'd brought with her from Virginia, her stomach danced with excitement. She pulled her hair back into a tight bun and pinned it firmly in place at the nape of her neck. The last thing she wanted was for her pesky curls to escape their confines and feather about her face.

She stepped into her crinolines and put on her blue calico dress. It took her awhile to fasten the long row of buttons down the back and tie the matching bow behind her back. She needed to hold her breath when she reached the lower buttons. Her waistline was growing. Gratefully she slipped into Cora's ecru, crocheted vest then examined herself in the tiny mirror. She laughed. "Plump, that's what Daddy would call me."

Lilia removed a gold chain with an engraved gold watch from her trunk and slipped the chain over her head. The watch had been a graduation gift from her parents a few months previous. The delicate timepiece fell to rest on the bodice of her dress. She felt like a real teacher.

She ate the last of Annie's biscuits and drank a swig of water. She didn't have time to make tea from the packet of leaves Annie had included.

Grabbing her pale pink shawl, she bounded out of the soddy into the morning sunlight. Her heart pounded with excitement, the excitement reserved for the first day of school.

Her skirts flew in the breeze as she skipped down the pathway to the schoolhouse. Bounding up the steps, she flung open the front door. The night before she'd noticed the bell rope hanging inside the front door. Throwing her body into it, she jumped and pulled on the rope. The bell above her head gonged twice. The bass tone rang across the prairie. Within minutes children came from all directions.

Her knees shook and her voice quivered when she welcomed fifteen children to school. Carefully she recorded the names of the children on the pad of paper: three Tylers, three Pages, the Anders twins and their younger sister Beth, two Caveats, two Todds, the son of the preacher, and the only eighth grader—the painfully shy Sarah Farver.

As was the custom, the boys sat on the right side of the aisle and the girls on the left. Lilia began with the Pledge of Allegiance. Then she suggested they take their seats.

Sixth-grader Billy Caveat waved his hand frantically in the air. "You forgot prayer, Mrs. Cooper. We always start our day with prayer."

Oops! Lilia closed her eyes for a moment. She'd committed the first of what she knew would be many mistakes. "Of course, you're right, William. Thank you for reminding me. Shall we bow our heads and close our eyes?"

The children solemnly obeyed. "Dear Heavenly Father," she began in her most sacred tone of voice. "Be with us today as we study and learn. Amen."

The students' heads popped up in surprise.

"Our last teacher, Mr. Cady, always prayed for at least

five minutes every morning," twelve-year-old Jacob Moore informed her.

Rebecca's hand flew into the air. When Lilia acknowledged the child, she said, "One time Mr. Cady prayed for twenty-five minutes. I know because I counted the seconds like my daddy taught me how to do with lightning."

Lilia chuckled. "My, that is quite an accomplishment, Rebecca. I am impressed. You must like arithmetic."

A wide grin filled the child's face. "Oh, yes. I can add, subtract, repeat my multiplication tables up to twelve by heart, do long division, and do percentages. Mr. Cady couldn't even do that!" Two red braids high on each side of the freckle-faced girl's head bobbed in syncopation. The boys in the room groaned as if in pain.

Lilia silenced the boys with an arched eyebrow. "Good for you, Rebecca. That's handy information to know should I ever have a numbers problem I can't solve."

Rebecca glanced over her shoulders at the other students to be certain they heard the new teacher's generous compliment. Lilia pretended not to see Buddy Anders stick out his tongue at the precocious little girl.

"Teacher?" Thirteen-year-old Chip Tyler raised his hand. "Do you whomp the kids who misbehave?"

"Whomp?" Lilia asked in surprise.

"Whomp!" The boy restated his question. "You know, lick 'em for being bad?"

What should she say? Lilia hadn't given her plan of discipline much thought. "Personally, Chip, I prefer licking a licorice braid to a child any day."

The children laughed.

"I am sure you have many questions you wish to ask. I'll try to answer them as best I can."

The children tumbled over one another to learn more about their new teacher: "Where are you from? Where is Norfolk, Virginia? Where is your husband? How old are you? Do you have any brothers or sisters? Why did you come to Sugar Creek? Are you going to leave us and go to California like Mr. Cady did? Do you like gingersnaps? What kind of perfume are you wearing? When is lunch time?"

The morning disappeared faster than Lilia could have imagined. She hadn't planned on keeping the children past lunch, but they'd all brought their lunches with them and were eager to stay.

"Mama says," began ten-year-old Martha Caveat swinging her shoulders importantly, "that since she had to take the time to get us ready for school, we should have a full day of schooling."

Lilia laughed. "Well, I suppose it wouldn't hurt to find out how well you can spell and write, would it?"

Second-grader Kinder Tyler waved his hand shyly in the air. "I can write my letters real well. Do ya' wanna' see?"

Lilia smiled. "That's 'do you want to see,' Kinder."

"Sure." The boy grinned. His front teeth had only come in part way. "I'll look at your letters if you'll look at mine."

Lilia laughed and gave a delighted sigh. She was going to enjoy teaching these children much more than she'd imagined. "First, don't you want to have recess?"

The children cheered.

"All right then. What games do you like to play?"

Buddy Anders suggested Capture the Flag.

"That might be appropriate for the older children, but why don't we choose a game the younger ones can play as well?" Lilia asked.

"How about Red Rover?" Jacob suggested.

Lilia pursed her lips. "Isn't that as rough as Capture the Flag?"

"Yeah, I guess so." He knitted his brow into a frown. "Who wants to play baby games?"

First-grader Beth Anders leaped from her desk and planted her hands on her hips. "I am not a baby. And I can play Capture the Flag as good as any of you."

Lilia refrained from correcting the spunky little girl's poor grammar. "All right then, let's play Capture the Flag," she suggested. "You're dismissed for recess."

The children cheered and rushed from the classroom.

When she rose from the desk, Lilia saw Aaron Cunard standing in the doorway. "Hi, Teach," he said, grinning his crooked little smile. "How's it going?"

She blinked in surprise. "What are you doing here?"

"I'm here to clean your chimney, remember?"

"Oh, yes. Sorry." She shrugged her shoulders. "The children want to stay all afternoon."

"So I gathered. You're a pretty good schoolmarm."

She eyed him critically. "How long have you been standing here?"

"Long enough to be impressed."

"Can you start on the chimney without me?" she asked.

"It won't be as much fun." His eyes twinkled. "Tell you what, I have some errands to run. I'll be back around three o'clock."

"That sounds fine." Lilia smiled up at him. He towered over her by at least eight inches. "I'd better hurry out there before someone gets hurt."

Without a word, he stepped out of her way to let her pass.

Lilia joined the game of Capture the Flag in progress. Having Aaron watch the game several minutes from the porch of the school was unnerving. She wished he'd go away. But she refused to allow anything or anyone to distract her from her goal of being the best teacher possible for her fifteen children.

The afternoon flew by quickly. Soon it was time to dismiss the children. Her first day of teaching had come to an end without any serious problems. She felt exhilarated.

After the last child left for home, Lilia strolled back to her desk and surveyed the room. The floors were swept, the board cleaned, and the erasers clapped. The rows of desks were straight. Everything was in order for the Sunday church service.

A satisfied smile spread across her face. It had been a most enjoyable day. She adored the children. When the time came, it wouldn't be easy to hand them over to their "real" teacher. Lilia picked up her shawl from the back of her chair and started for the front door. She paused a moment to scan the room one more time before closing the door behind her. Yes, it had been a most enjoyable day.

She found Annie waiting for her at the bottom of the steps with a gunnysack full of apples. "I picked these on the way over here today." Annie held up one of the apples for her to see. "We can make an apple pie if you'd like."

The warm honey brown of Annie's face held a tinge of pink as she offered the apple to Lilia. "They have a tartness that is good for pies."

"Thank you, Annie. You have been so nice to me. I don't deserve your kindness."

Annie's eyes sparkled with happiness. "I enjoy doing things for people. You're Serenity's friend. I'd like you to be my friend too."

"I'd like that too."

As Lilia led the way down the pathway to the house, a battle raged within her, a battle between the prejudice of her upbringing and the face of kindness she saw in Annie. When they reached the house, Annie placed the sack of apples on the table while Lilia hung her shawl on a peg near the door.

So much of what Lilia had always believed was being challenged in this wild and strange place. Sometimes she felt as if she were under siege. In Sugar Creek as in Independence, being a Northrop meant nothing.

A thump sounded on the roof. Annie glanced in the direction of the noise.

Lilia pointed to the ceiling. "Aaron Cunard. He's sweeping the chimney. He volunteered," she added. Where would she be if no one had helped her? Why would the Richs, Serenity and Caleb, Annie, Aaron, even Serenity's in-laws go out of their way to take care of her? She couldn't understand it. She decided that it must be the custom of the prairie as Serenity had said.

"That was a smart idea using the crates as extra shelves for your food." Annie pointed to the wooden crates stacked on their sides, waist high beside the wet sink. Lilia had spread a pillow slip across the top as a dresser scarf. "They give you another work surface too."

"Huh? Oh, yes." Lilia removed a Mother Hubbard apron from a peg Caleb and Aaron had mounted near the fireplace the day before. She slipped the multicolored flowered apron over her head and tied the strings behind her back. "Actually, I got the idea from Mrs. Rich's pantry." Lilia rubbed her hands enthusiastically. "All right. Where do we start?"

Annie studied the shelves, then held up a large tin bowl and two worn paring knives. The kitchen tools were compliments of Cora Rich. "First we pare the apples," Annie said.

Lilia removed the brown-eyed Susans from the center of the table, along with the doily, while Annie dumped the sack of apples out onto the table.

"These are a bit small—perfect for pies," Annie said. "Larger apples bake up nicely. You simply core them and place a little honey and cinnamon in the middle. M-m-m!" She closed her eyes and smacked her lips.

The women's attention was again drawn to the noise above their heads. The loud thuds of Aaron's boots on the roof caused Lilia to wonder if the roof could hold his weight. She pulled out the chair opposite Annie and sat down.

"When I was a little girl, before my owner sent me to the fields . . ." Annie chose an apple and began peeling it. ". . . I remember sitting next to my mother—she was the head cook at the plantation. I'd watch her peel apples for pies." The peeling from Annie's knife spiraled down from the apple. "She could peel the skin from an entire apple in one piece." Annie frowned when her peeling broke and dropped to the table. "I've never been able to do that."

Lilia watched Annie's apple emerge from its skin, round and perfect. Annie quartered and cored the fruit, then sliced it into the large metal bowl. *I can do this*, Lilia thought. Tentatively, she picked up the second knife and an apple. As she peeled away the apple's skin, she cut off chunks of the fruit along with the peeling. The task was more challenging than she'd imagined. After removing the last of the apple's mottled green-and-red skin, she held up a deformed piece of fruit.

"Not much left to quarter and slice, huh?"

Annie laughed. "That's all right. You'll get better with practice." Annie's eyes twinkled with gentleness. "Paring apples is an acquired skill. Everyone has to start some-where."

Thunk! Thunk! Thunk! The noise came from the fire-place, along with Aaron's voice. "Lilia? Annie? Can you give me a hand?"

The two women hurried to the fireplace and peered up into the darkness. "What's wrong?" Lilia asked.

"Something's stuck in the chimney. I don't know if it's a bird nest or what, but I can't reach it. Would you open the flue for me please?"

"Sure!" Lilia called. She turned to Annie and asked, "What is a flue?"

"It's what allows the smoke to escape the chimney. Pull that lever beside you." Annie pointed toward a black wrought-iron lever on the stones next to Lilia's head.

"Before you pull it—" Aaron called.

Too late. Lilia yanked the lever downward. Without warning, an abandoned bird's nest dropped to the hearth along with a black cloud. Soot billowed from the fireplace. The women shrieked and leaped backward.

Lilia looked at Annie and burst into laughter. "Look at you! You're face is black with soot!"

"You are too." Annie pointed at Lilia and laughed.

"No!" Lilia rubbed her cheek. The palm of her hand was as black as midnight. "Oh no!" She dashed over to the trunk at the foot of her bed and snatched up her hand mir-ror. She blinked her bright blue eyes in astonishment. Annie was right. Her face was covered with soot.

Lilia gave a loud cackle. "Look at us! We could be sis-ters!" She doubled over with laughter. "If my mama could see me now! She'd be horrified. And what would the Norfolk society matrons think. A black Northrop!" She walked over to Annie and bowed from the waist. "Madam, may I have this dance?"

"Why yes." Annie curtsied. "I'd be delighted."

The two women moved through the steps of the quadrille with the grace of royalty until they both dissolved into laughter.

Suddenly, the front door flew open and Aaron burst into the cabin. "What happened? What is going on?" he asked. His face was covered with a coating of heavy black soot as well.

"Look at you!" Lilia gasped between bouts of laughter. Not only was his face coated, but also the front of his shirt and his hair.

"Look at me?" he sputtered, pointing a quivering finger at each of the laughing women. "Look at yourselves!"

Lilia dashed over to the wooden bucket of water in her wet sink. Feeling a little too frisky, she dipped her fingers into the water. "Want to wash up?" she asked, flicking water at the surprised man.

"Hey!" The droplets found their mark and produced streaks of soot that ran down his face.

"Want some more?" she asked, tantalizing him with a ladle half filled with water.

"You wouldn't!" He eyed her threateningly.

Annie recognized the devilish grin on Lilia's face and ran for the door. Aaron wasn't so inclined. He narrowed his eyes and sauntered toward Lilia. "You should never start something that you can't finish."

"I'm not afraid of a little water, are you?" Without hesitation, she heaved the ladle of water at Aaron's face and dashed for the open door.

The water hit its target. He gulped in surprise. "Why you little . . ."

By the time he emerged from the house, Lilia had hidden around the corner of the soddy.

Annie watched from the safety of the outhouse as Aaron emerged from the house carrying the water bucket. Rivulets of soot and muddy water ran the length of his face and clothes. He glanced first one direction then the other.

"I know you're here somewhere, you little minx!" Aaron shouted. "I'm going to get you sooner or later. You might as well take your medicine like a man—" He stopped short and reddened. "Er, like a woman."

Lilia peeked around the corner of the building and laughed. "You think so, huh?"

The bucket of water caught her full in the face. She screamed and stared at her dress in horror. Shaking her hands in the air like a cat does his paws after an unexpected swim in the pond, Lilia shrieked in disbelief.

Aaron burst into renewed laughter, as did Annie. For an instant, Lilia didn't know how to react. She'd begun their little game on a whim. Now she was soaked. Forgetting her age and position, Lilia reverted to the tomboy she'd been when she visited her grandfather's farm.

"I'll get you! I'll get you!" She danced up and down in frustration.

Aaron laughed and walked toward the well.

Suddenly Lilia threw herself at his waist.

He lost his balance and fell into the tall grass beside the pathway.

Lilia tumbled into the grass beside him. Immediately, she yanked a handful of grass from the sod and stuffed it down the neck of his shirt. Then, leaping to her feet, she ran to the soddy and locked the door behind her.

-17-

Pink Roses and a
White Trellis

LILIA STOOD IN THE DOORWAY OF HER LITTLE home, savoring a slice of Annie's apple pie. What a wild and wonderful day it had been. Her first day of school, the water fight, the apple pie, and the most amazing of all, discovering how much alike she and Annie were beneath their skin color. Who would think a coating of soot could remove generations of indoctrination?

Lilia laughed each time she remembered the startled look on Aaron's face when she tackled him. The poor man didn't stand a chance. He was totally unprepared for how she acted. She wondered what had possessed her to do such a thing.

Lilia had refused to open the front door until Aaron promised he wouldn't try to get even. She knew she couldn't stay inside forever. She needed the cow chips stacked outside her door to start a fire in the fireplace. And she had no fresh water left.

The cleanup had been almost as much fun as the water fight. It took gallons of hot water and lye soap for the three of them to remove all the soot from their faces, necks, and hands. If anyone had dropped by to meet the new teacher, they would have been horrified to find a man, a Southern belle, and a former slave scrubbing their faces and hands, and laughing together like old friends.

The bodice of Lilia's dress still showed signs of the afternoon's adventure, but the hearth and the fireplace were clean and ready to use before Annie and Aaron left for the inn.

Lilia watched as the last streaks of sun faded from the sky. She decided that sunset was her favorite time of day, especially on the prairie. Heaving a contented sigh, she drank the last of the chamomile tea from her cup. She couldn't remember when she'd been so tired, or so happy.

Sleep came quickly, as did dawn the following morning. Lilia had planned to sleep in since it was Saturday. But the sun had barely begun its journey west when someone knocked at her door. Worried something might be wrong, she hopped out of bed, threw on her robe, and opened the door.

It was Mrs. Page. She was carrying a kettle of hot stew. "I'm sorry I didn't get here sooner," she said. "I know you must have a busy day ahead of you and won't have time to cook, so I brought you some of my vegetable stew." The woman craned her neck trying to see inside the soddy. She appeared not to notice that Lilia was wearing her bedclothes.

Lilia thanked the woman and reluctantly invited her inside. Mrs. Page had barely sat down on the sofa when another knock sounded at the door. It was Mrs. Tyler, a meek little woman with stringy blond hair. She barely cleared five feet. The woman appeared shriveled, more by her circumstance than by her age, or so Lilia imagined. Mrs. Tyler handed Lilia a loaf of freshly made bread, then joined Mrs. Page on the sofa.

Lilia apologized for still being in her robe and night-gown, vowing to herself that as soon as her guests left she would drape a sheet around her bed for privacy in the future.

"That's fine," Mrs. Page confided. "Some days, it takes everything in me to get dressed, especially since Pearly, my youngest arrived. Hers was a difficult pregnancy." The woman paused and eyed Lilia knowingly. "I left the children at home with Abigail, except for Chip, that is. He's gone to town with his father."

Lilia liked Abigail, her only female seventh grader. She enjoyed getting acquainted with the two boys, Kinder and Chip. And she'd formed an opinion on Mr. Tyler the night she'd met him at the Rich's house. She wondered what the mother of his children might be like.

The women kept arriving at the house all morning, laden with goodies of every kind. During a lull in the stream of visitors, Lilia managed to slip into a dress, brush the tangles from her hair, and pin it in a bun.

Why these women waited until Saturday to welcome her she wasn't sure, unless they wanted to know whether or not their children would respond well to her. During the course of the day, she learned why Beth Anders didn't like squash and why the Tylers had abandoned their California dream. She discovered that Sarah Farver had noticed every detail about her, including the lemon-verbena perfume she'd been wearing. She also learned five different ways to take soot out of a cotton dress.

The biggest surprise came when Millie, the preacher's wife, mentioned the length of her morning prayers.

"I know plenty of ministers who think they have to preach the entire Book of Lamentations during their congregational prayers, but personally, I wonder if God doesn't tire of our pontificating," Mrs. Moore confided. "I'm always telling my husband that he needs to have mercy on Granny Hawkins' arthritic knees when he prays on Sunday morning."

The woman's eyes twinkled with happiness. Dimples appeared at the corners of her upturned lips. "If I didn't know better," the woman confided, "I'd say Jacob has a slight crush on you."

Lilia gulped. "Oh, really?"

"Really!" The woman rose to her feet. "I won't keep you long. I know you've had a string of visitors today. That's the way the people around here do, you know. It just took one woman to bring you some food this morning and the rest of the ladies rushed to do the same so as not to appear less generous. Oh, by the way, I would appreciate it if you would transfer the scalloped potatoes to another bowl and return the casserole dish as soon as possible. My mother brought the dish with her from Scotland. Well, gotta' go. My men will be home soon and hungry as bears."

The thought of being entrusted with a family heirloom frightened Lilia. She hastened to thank Mrs. Moore and suggested, "I can transfer the food right now if you'd like. It would only take a minute."

The woman gave Lilia's hand a motherly pat. "Nonsense. Enjoy." And she was out the door. Lilia watched her hurry toward her home and family.

The next morning, Lilia dressed for church with great care. Her clothes, her hairstyle, her every smile would be noted by her students and by their mothers. When Elder Moore prayed, Lilia remembered what his wife had said about the length of his prayers. By the end of the morning prayer, Lilia knew Granny's arthritic knees would be giving her trouble. They were singing the last verse of the second hymn when Aaron Cunard entered the building and slipped into the back row.

At the end of the service when Lilia filed out of church, Aaron met her and extended Serenity's invitation for dinner. He waited in the carriage while Lilia dashed home for Mrs. Farver's butternut cake to take with her to the inn. Then they were on their way.

Lilia entertained Aaron with anecdotes about the visitors she'd had the day before. "With all the food the ladies brought, I should stay home to eat some of it. Maybe you can take some home with you later today," she suggested. "Did I tell you that Mrs. Page said she'd supply me with a pitcher of milk each day and a pound of butter? That cold cellar will certainly come in handy."

Caleb and his father-in-law, Sam Pownell, were caring for the horses when Aaron and Lilia arrived at the inn. Knowing the women were preparing the dinner meal, Lilia hurried inside to help.

She found Serenity seated in the rocking chair by the fireplace, nursing Sammy. Josephine was slicing carrots to boil and Annie was stirring the gravy in a pan on the stove.

Lilia draped her bonnet and shawl on a peg near the door. "Annie, give me something to do."

Annie smiled, not so much at Lilia's offer, but at the looks of surprise on Serenity's and Josephine's faces. "Why don't you help Josephine set the table?" she suggested.

"Good idea. Now let's see, the silverware is in the pantry, right?" Lilia scurried out of the room before anyone could reply. "I feel like I've come home!" Lilia called from the pantry. "It's been a long time since I've been here."

While she and Josephine set the table, Lilia caught Serenity staring at her several times. Amazement was written all over her friend's face. Lilia smiled to herself. She knew how much she had changed in the time since she'd left the inn. She was glad to have her friend recognize those changes as well.

By the time Josephine rang the dinner bell outside the front door, the table groaned with hot, delicious-looking food. There was an air of celebration as they gathered around the table. Serenity placed Lilia between Aaron and Annie and across from the Pownells. As was the custom at Serenity Inn, they joined hands around the table for the blessing. Tears of shame filled Lilia's eyes as she and the former slave linked hands.

But Lilia's introspection on that point was cut short when she turned and extended her hand to the person on her left. Her reaction to taking Aaron's hand was jolting. They exchanged startled glances, then quickly bowed their heads for prayer, hoping no one else observed the exchange.

After the disastrous results of her marriage to Wade, she vowed that no man would ever touch her heart again. And that vow included the enticingly attractive Aaron Cunard. She couldn't deny the warmth of Aaron's hand and the flutter of excitement his touch triggered within her. Upon hearing "Amen," she snatched her hand from his. Throughout the meal, Lilia and Aaron avoided each other's eyes, even when they passed the dishes of food to one another.

Except for the awkwardness Lilia felt toward Aaron, an easy banter flowed around the table. The conversation began around the changes that had been taking place in Sammy, who was asleep in his basket on the floor next to

Serenity. At one point, Serenity apologized. "Here I go again, acting like a proud mother. I'm sure there are other topics of dinner conversation that we could enjoy beyond the sleeping and eating patterns of an infant."

"So how's the house coming?" Caleb asked Sam Pownell. Caleb put a spoonful of mashed potatoes on his plate and passed the bowl to Annie. "Be sure to let me know when you'll be ready to move in and I'll help."

"Me too." Aaron passed a plate of dill pickles to Serenity.

Across the table, Sam nodded his approval. "Thank you. That would be a big help. I hate moving!" He cast a good-natured grin at his wife. "By the way, I received a telegram from Dory and Abe on Friday. They've sold off everything and are on their way west."

"Really?" Serenity's eyes lit up with excitement. "When will they get here?"

"Before the first snow falls," Josephine replied.

Serenity explained to Lilia that Abe and Dory had been with the Pownells since she was Sammy's age. "Abe managed our estate in western New York and his wife Dory was our head housekeeper. She was my surrogate mother when I was a child." She turned to Josephine. "Their son must be quite big by now."

Josephine nodded emphatically. "I'm sure he is. Dory says he's a scamp."

Lilia grew uncomfortable when the conversation shifted to the morning's sermon on forgiveness.

"The hardest thing to get over after the death of my first wife," Sam admitted, "was my anger at God for taking her and my guilt for still being alive."

"I know what you mean," Serenity interjected. "I felt the same way. I thought God had taken Mama from me to punish me for the bad things I'd done." A wisp of a smile crossed her face. "It was Caleb's mom who helped me work through those feelings. She introduced me to a different kind of God—not a vindictive God but a God of love."

"All of us have experienced disappointments big enough to swamp a barge." Josephine glanced around the table. "And heaven knows there's enough in this world to be angry about." She placed her elbows on the table and her chin in her hands. "But, you know, when I was mad at my stepson for disgracing his father's memory, I could almost feel myself shriveling up inside, like a prune."

Lilia shifted her position and deliberately stared into the distance. Out of the corner of her eye she could see that Aaron was feeling uncomfortable as well.

"The other day," Serenity began, "I received the loveliest letter from Annalee Duran. She's the lady who sold us the inn. After the death of her husband, Annalee was bitter toward God. Anyway, she wrote that she's discovered God again, thanks to a Negro laundress on her father's plantation, a slave, in fact.

"While the woman scrubbed the family's laundry on a washboard, she would sing an old Southern hymn. The message of the song haunted Annalee until she gave her life back to God."

"What was the song the woman sang?" Sam asked.

"Wait. Let me get the letter and read the words to you." Serenity hopped up from the table and ran to the ladies' desk in the hallway. "Here it is! 'Amazing grace, how sweet the sound—'"

"That saved a wretch like me." Sam Pownell's rich baritone voice added the melody. "I once was lost but now, am found. 'Twas blind but now I see."

Lilia winced. It was the song she remembered hearing her grandfather sing while working at the anvil in his blacksmith shop. Memories of home ambushed her emotions. Tears filled her eyes. She had to get away. She was relieved when Aaron whispered an invitation to take a walk with him.

He held the door for her as she hurriedly put on her bonnet and gloves. "I'll be back to help with the dishes," she promised the women.

"Don't worry about the dishes. There are plenty of women here to help," Serenity called, grinning toward her husband over the newest wrinkle in the lives of her friend and her husband's brother.

As the door closed behind them, Aaron took Lilia's hand and placed it in the crook of his arm. They walked for several seconds before he spoke. "Were you as uncomfortable as I was with all the God talk?"

"Yes."

"Good. I'm glad it wasn't only me." He patted her hand affectionately as they walked. "I was brought up in a preacher's home. Believe me, I've had enough religion to last a lifetime!"

Lilia chuckled. "And I was brought up in a family where God was seldom mentioned, except at Christmas time, of course. Don't get me wrong, I love your sister-in-law and your brother, but—"

"I know. Most of the time it doesn't bother me, but every once in a while . . ." He kept his attention focused on the pathway before them. "Someday I'll give my parents' religion another chance, but for now, I have too much I want to do with my life."

When they reached the tiny cemetery at the crown of the grassy hill, Aaron helped Lilia onto the highest rock where they sat down.

She lifted her face to the wind and closed her eyes. The breeze was gentle. When the ribbons on her bonnet became untied, she started to retie it.

Aaron stopped her. "That bonnet must be uncomfortably warm on such a warm afternoon. I won't be offended if you remove it."

A piece of buckram that supported the rim of the bonnet did irritate the back of her neck. Lilia had been wishing she could be free of the white eyelet confection since the moment she put it on at the house. She removed the hat and dropped it on the rock beside her. She wrapped her arms about her knees and rested her chin on them. "I love coming up here," she said. "Though it's nothing like the views of the ocean from my grandpa's place outside of Norfolk, I feel an incredible peace when I'm here." She paused a moment, then asked, "Do you ever miss your home in New York State?"

"Not really. Itinerant preachers' families move a lot. How about you? What do you miss most about Virginia?"

She cast him a subtle smile. "This will sound crazy, but I think I miss my mama's rambling roses."

"Rambling roses?"

"Uh-huh." She closed her eyes and imagined the flower's pleasing fragrance. "Behind our house is a white picket fence to protect our kitchen garden from the local rabbit population. A matching trellis arches over the gate. Every summer the trellis is loaded with roses—the most fragrant roses in the world." Even with her eyes closed, she could feel Aaron gazing at her.

"Have you considered going back home now that . . ." His voice trailed off.

"Millions of times."

"What keeps you here?"

Sadness filled her heart. "I'm afraid we're back to the dinner conversation."

He gave Lilia a bewildered look.

She frowned and bit her lower lip. "My father is a hard man, Mr. Cunard. We exchanged strong words before I ran away with Wade. He said that if I left with Wade, I was no longer his daughter. I know him. He meant what he said."

"Are you sure? My daddy and I don't see eye to eye on lots of things, but I know he loves me with his whole heart—even now—"

"Now?" It was Lilia's turn to look bewildered.

"I tend a bar for a living. My daddy preaches against using alcohol of any kind." He dug the toe of his boot into the sandy soil at the base of the rock.

Lilia blinked in surprise. Everyone in her parents' social circle imbibed. "That's not so bad. My daddy loves his bourbon. And Mama, why Mama couldn't get through her day without her afternoon mint julep."

"Maybe so, but since I've been working at the bar, I've seen more reasons not to indulge than to use the stuff. I've seen the saddest cases of family men who've traveled all the way from places like Maine and Pennsylvania drink up all the cash that was supposed to finance their dreams and their trip west. They get a shot or two under their belts and head for the gaming tables."

Her smile faded as the thought of Wade invaded her mind.

"I'm sorry. I didn't mean—"

"No, you're right." She shook her head feverishly. "That's exactly what happened with my husband." She lifted her eyes to meet Aaron's. "Wade wasn't all bad, you know—not in the beginning." Lilia's eyes misted with tears. To camouflage her grief, she brushed aside a curl tickling her face.

"You miss him a lot?"

She gave a surprised snort. "Hardly. While I loved him once, he'd long since destroyed my love for him." She swung her face away from him. "Why am I telling you this? I'm sorry. I don't usually burden friends with—"

"Hey!" He reached over and gently turned her face toward his. "What are friends for?"

-18-

Shadows in the Night

At home alone that evening in her sod house, Lilia scolded herself for being so open with Aaron. "No! Didn't you learn anything from Wade?" she shouted at herself as she paced the room. "You cannot lose your head over another man! You have a child to consider." She ran her hands over her slightly protruding stomach. "Aaron Cunard might be a very nice man—he is a nice man! But Wade seemed terribly nice at first too, remember?"

She slammed the palm of her hand down on the wobbly table. Water splashed out of the flower arrangement and onto the doily. She strode across the room to her bed. She would take hold of her imagination. She would keep her feelings in check.

One by one, she removed the pins from the bun at the nape of her neck that held her braid. With each pin she reminded herself of the reasons she couldn't allow herself to love again. She unbraided her hair and shook it free, then ran her fingers through the cascade of blond waves.

"Teaching those children at the school tomorrow is the most important task you have to do right now," she argued aloud. "Standing here mooning over some dumb cowboy won't help you one bit with tomorrow's lessons." Wrapping her shawl about her shoulders, she grabbed the oil lantern and hurried outside.

A full moon hung heavy in the night sky. A faint white ring circled the moon warning of rain that was coming, if not that night, by morning. "I'd better plan for some inside games, just in case."

She tried to recall the rainy day games she played as a child. *Musical chairs. Charades.*

She skipped up the steps into the schoolhouse. The pot-bellied stove had cooled since the morning services. After setting the oil lantern on the edge of her desk, she lit two more lanterns to help chase away the dark shadows from the corners of the room.

Lilia picked up a piece of chalk and wrote tomorrow's arithmetic problems on the board. 2+1=____, 2+2=___, 2+3=___. She continued with increasingly more difficult problems, including figuring percentages.

On the teacher's desk were five books: a reading book, an arithmetic book, a geography book, a book of poetry, and a Bible—but none for the students. Recalling her personal library back home, she frowned. By the time she left home for the academy, she'd traveled to Canterbury, wept at the deaths of Romeo and Juliet, treasured the poetry of John Yeats, and listened in the night for the beating of "The Tell Tale Heart."

How could she excite these children about literature when they had no books? How could they learn to love reading like she did under such circumstances? If it weren't for the difficulties between her and her folks, she would have her parents send the books to her. *Don't get too carried away with these children. You're only temporary, remember?* She shrugged her shoulders and sat down at her desk.

The hoot of a barn owl caught her attention. She glanced at the watch on the chain around her neck. *Eleven o'clock? That can't be!* she thought. She held the watch to her ear and listened to its steady tick. The watch was working. She'd been at the schoolhouse for more than three hours.

She arose from the desk, extinguished the flames in two of the oil lanterns, put on her shawl, grabbed the remaining oil lamp, and headed out of the schoolhouse. As she descended the steps, she heard the owl hoot a second time, then to her right, another owl replied. *That's odd,* she thought.

As she rounded the corner of the schoolhouse, she spotted a point of light flickering from the area near the storm cellar.

"Hello?" Lilia yelled. "Is anybody there?"

The only sound she heard was the steady hum of the wind whistling through the prairie grass.

"Hello! I know somebody's out there." Every inch of her body was alert for danger. *Maybe it's just a few of the older boys playing a trick on me.* Gathering her courage, she called out again. "This isn't funny. Stop playing games with me."

Cautiously she inched her way along until she passed the storm cellar, then she broke into a run for the soddy. Slamming the door behind her, she swung the heavy wooden bar into the metal braces and pressed her back against the locked door. Her heart thumped inside her chest as if she'd been running. She struggled to slow her breathing.

Placing the oil lamp on the table, she ran to one window and closed the yellow gingham curtains. Then she rushed to the other window. As she reached up to close those curtains too, Lilia spotted a second flash of light coming from the storm cellar. She yanked the curtains closed, then threw herself on her bed and hugged her pillow. "Go away!" she gasped. "Go away."

Lilia trembled with fear. Memories of Wade and his brutality returned to her mind, bringing feelings of vulnerability and helplessness. For some time, she listened for she knew not what.

How long she'd been cowering in the shadows of her cabin before deciding to act, she didn't know. Finally, she sat up and listened. All was silent. She stood up, paused, and listened some more. When she heard nothing, she quickly undressed for bed.

To quiet her mind before turning in, Lilia crossed the room and lifted the corner of the curtain. Nothing moved on the moonlit terrain. Maybe she'd imagined the light. *Perhaps I saw some weird reflection from the moon.* The moon was unusually bright, despite the rings around it. Knowing she wouldn't sleep until she laid her fears to rest, Lilia tightened the ties of her robe and opened the door.

"I'm going to settle this once and for all," she muttered as she grabbed the oil lantern and stepped out of the soddy onto the pathway. Her bravado flagged the closer she came to the storm cellar. She whispered words of encouragement, assuring herself that the flash of light had been the result of a fanciful imagination.

Taking a deep breath, she lifted the heavy wooden door. The hinges squeaked in protest. Holding the oil lamp in front of her, she peered into the enclosed darkness and froze in terror.

"Don't!" A voice in the night behind her growled. "Don't scream!"

Scream? She couldn't catch her breath enough to scream. All she could do was stare at the frightening face of a giant colored man. His ebony skin glistened in her lantern light. Behind him she saw two or three women, another man, and two small children.

A touch on her shoulder from the hand belonging to the voice released the scream frozen within her lungs. Lilia's sustained, high-pitched shriek filled the night air for an instant before a hand clamped over her mouth. She tried to bite the hand of her assailant, but his grip was too tight. She kicked at his legs and dug at his arms and hands. As her attacker dragged her into the cellar, the large black man snagged the oil lantern from her hand.

She heard rather than saw the heavy wooden door drop into place. An oppressive combination of heat and body odor rushed at her, causing her to gag.

The man holding her against his body hissed in her ear, "Don't scream! If I let you go, promise me you won't scream."

Fighting nausea, she nodded her head feebly. His hand fell away from her mouth. She took in a huge gulp of air.

"I'm sorry I had to—" the man started.

She turned toward the voice and inhaled sharply. In the dim lantern light she identified her assailant—Elder Moore!

"What? You?" Her terror turned to outrage at the violation she felt. "Who are these people? What is going on?" She backed away from the two men who blocked her escape.

"I'm sorry, Mrs. Cooper. I had to silence you. Sheriff Prior and his men are out there somewhere." His eyes pleaded with her for understanding.

Being acquainted with her attacker made her bold. She planted the palms of her hands on her hips and glared. "I demand to know what is going on here?"

"Can she keep her mouth shut?" The black man queried through clenched teeth. The light from the lantern created ghoulish shadows on the man's angular face.

"I demand to know what's going on!" She stamped her foot and returned the black man's scowl.

"Mrs. Cooper, unfortunately you have fallen into the middle of an Underground Railroad transaction gone bad," Elder Moore explained.

A light of understanding flickered inside Lilia's head. Missouri was a slave state and Sugar Creek was a very short distance from the Kansas Territory, which was free. It made sense that fugitive slaves on their way to freedom would be transported across Missouri, regardless of the risk.

The preacher's actions suddenly clicked in her mind, "You! You're an abolitionist!" She whipped around to face the frightened huddle of people behind her. "These people! You're all breaking the law!" She turned and hurled her accusations in the preacher's face. "And you, a man of God!"

The preacher's expression remained unreadable. "There are man's laws, then there are God's laws. When they are in conflict, I choose to obey God's laws."

"Oh? How convenient that your God allows you to pick and choose which laws you'll obey." Lilia narrowed her gaze and lifted one eyebrow in a challenge. "Like a fox strolling through an apple orchard, isn't it? Nibble at one piece of fruit, then the next, regardless of the consequences to the orchard."

"I'm not certain foxes eat apples, Mrs. Cooper," he drawled.

"Who cares what foxes eat?" She clicked her tongue in frustration. "I'm sure you get the point. Now, if you will excuse me, I wish to return to my home."

The man holding the lantern shot a worried look at the preacher. "You can't let her go, sir. What will keep her from running straight to the Sheriff?"

The preacher shrugged. "I'm afraid releasing you, Mrs. Cooper, won't be possible any time soon."

"I beg your pardon?" She couldn't believe what she was hearing. "Am I to assume you are holding me prisoner down here?"

Elder Moore winced. "Not a prisoner exactly, more like an unwilling guest." He gestured toward a stack of flour sacks piled along the left wall. "You might as well make yourself comfortable. We'll be here for some time."

Lilia snarled, then plopped down on the flour sacks. She folded her arms across her chest in an act of defiance.

It seemed important to Elder Moore that Lilia understand. He gestured toward the frightened runaways. "These people are fleeing a plantation in Georgia. Let me introduce you to Mr. and Mrs. Hancock and their son, Buck; Mr. and Mrs. Fredrick and their two children, Camilla and Roland. And this is Porgy and Piney Winslow; they're newlyweds. Their master had lost each of these men to a neighboring plantation owner in a card game. Fortunately, they learned of it before their owner delivered the men to their new master."

The woman introduced as Piney silently pleaded with Lilia. Lilia averted her gaze to the floor.

"And the man holding your lantern is Mr. Ned Ward, one of the only free blacks to settle in this part of the state before Missouri passed the law that prohibits free blacks to do so," Elder Moore explained.

"Preacher . . ." Mr. Ward sided up to Elder Moore and mumbled something into his ear.

Lilia pretended not to listen.

"If we keep Mrs. Cooper down here and the Sheriff comes knocking on her door, won't it be suspicious when no one answers?"

"Hmm." The preacher's eyes narrowed in thought.

"You could be right. However, we need to keep her here until, uh, the next conductor arrives and our cargo is on the move once more."

Ned Ward shifted his weight nervously from one foot to the other. "We need to move the cargo immediately. Once they're across the state line—"

"I know Ned, I know. I'm as impatient as you are, but you and I only know our segment of the route. We wouldn't know where to deliver the cargo once we crossed the border. I think it's wise to wait for the next conductor."

The only abolitionists Lilia had ever seen were the newspaper cartoon characters that depicted them as devils with horns, pitchforks, and tails. She tried to ignore the two men as they discussed their situation. *If I get out of here alive,* she vowed, *I will march into Sheriff Prior's office and tell everything! Elder Moore and this Ward man can't treat me like this and expect to get way with it! I'll see them thrown in jail. They'll be sorry!* She settled into a serious pout.

Several minutes of silence, except for the youngest child's sporadic whimper, passed. Lilia smiled at the little boy. The child's eyes were round with fear. A part of her longed to gather him into her arms and assure him that he was safe. The other part of her couldn't get past the fact that these people, including the boy with the frightened eyes, were runaways and law breakers. Her father would be horrified if he knew she were in the vicinity of such people.

Three raps on the cellar door startled her out of her thoughts. She started to her feet only to have Ned Ward force her to sit down while Elder Moore hurried to open the door.

The cold night air rushed through the opening. Lilia inhaled gratefully. Her scalp tingled with fear as the new conductor made his way down the four steps into the cellar.

"Douse that lantern!" the stranger snarled.

Instantly Ned Ward extinguished the flame, but not before Lilia caught a glimpse of the stranger's face. *Aaron Cunard? No, it couldn't be,* she argued. But she knew it was. Relief replaced her fear.

"Aaron?" she called out in the darkness. "I'm so glad you're here. You won't believe what these men are doing—"

"What's she doing here?" Aaron snapped.

"The lady didn't give us much choice." Elder Moore attempted to appease Aaron Cunard's irritation. "She stumbled upon us. We couldn't let her go, knowing what she knew."

"Aaron?" The truth of Aaron's involvement began to seep into her brain. "Are you one of them? Are you an abolitionist too?"

He sighed. "I'd rather you had not found out about our dealings, Lilia. This has nothing to do with you."

"Nothing to do with me?" She leaped to her feet. "Wonderful! Then am I free to go?"

"Not right yet, I'm afraid. The sheriff and his posse were sniffing around the Tyler's place when I sneaked past. They know something's up. I tethered my horse behind the Anders' place."

"Aaron! I demand that you release me immediately!" She could barely contain her indignation. This man whom she trusted with intimate details of her life was betraying her.

"I'm sorry, Mrs. Cooper, but I cannot allow you to leave at this time!" His voice was hard and impersonal. "Please sit down and be quiet. Ned, you'd better lower the door again. Voices travel in the night air."

Mrs. Cooper? Where was all the tenderness that he demonstrated earlier? Was it an act, like Wade's pretense of loving her to get his hands on her father's money? Was she so stupid to fall for another man's lies? The questions spun in her mind like leaves trapped in a summer dust storm.

The minutes dragged on. She leaned her head against the dirt wall of the storm cellar and closed her eyes. Never again would she allow a man to fool her. She would teach the child within her the lessons of deceit she'd learned at the hands of men.

The silence and the warm stale air lulled her into a twilight sleep. At the sound of the cellar door opening, she shot awake. A gust of fresh air flooded into the underground chamber. She gulped the cool, clean air greedily.

Aaron stuck his head out of the cellar and listened. "It's all clear," he whispered to Elder Moore. "Send them out."

Elder Moore beckoned to the fugitive slaves. "Come. It's time to complete the last leg of your journey to freedom."

Silently, the three families filed out of the cellar. Elder Moore followed them up the steps where he remained, giving the fugitives time to make good their escape. When he descended the steps, he extended his hand toward Lilia. "Mrs. Cooper, may I help you?"

Furious, she batted his hand away and scrambled to her feet on her own power. "You, sir, are a cad and a bounder! If it weren't for those fifteen children, I would be out of here come dawn!"

"I am sorry." The man stared at the ground. "I know you don't believe me right now, but I am sorry."

"Save it for the sheriff!" She hissed before gathering her skirts in her hands and stomping up the steps.

"Mrs. Cooper." Elder Moore caught up to her and leaned forward. "You understand we'll have to close the school immediately if anything happens to any of the board members."

Lilia stopped. She glared at the man beside her. *Was that a threat?*

Elder Moore bowed and walked away.

Lilia watched him disappear into the night. *Close school? What would she say to the children?* Her agitated interior mood directly contrasted with the calm night air. Stars twinkled in the sky. The moonbeams made the ripening prairie grass appear white, like a blanket of snow. Without stopping to appreciate the beauty, Lilia fled along the pathway to her home.

Once inside the cabin, Lilia slammed the door and locked it. Then she cried. She cried from the fear she'd experienced, from the disappointment about Aaron, and from the powerlessness of her situation. She cried until sleep overtook her.

When she awoke, Lilia discovered that she had fifteen minutes to wash, dress, and eat breakfast before school started. Like a whirlwind, she whipped through her morning routine. Running and stumbling over dirt clods, she arrived at the school in time to welcome the first arrivals.

-19-
Unexpected Turn
of Events

 LILIA HAD NEVER IMAGINED HERSELF AS A teacher, but after one week, she knew that when the real teacher arrived, she would miss the classroom and the children terribly. When Cora Rich sent an invitation with Mrs. Page to spend the weekend in Independence with the family, Lilia accepted the invitation with glee.

She dreaded meeting either Aaron or Elder Moore after the last week's fiasco. Having come to no conclusion about the best course of action toward either man, Lilia had done nothing about her late night adventure. *Maybe I'll see the sheriff in town and then I'll know what to do.*

On her Sunday afternoon walk with Esther, the two women ran into Annie who asked Lilia how she was doing.

"We missed you at dinner today," Annie volunteered.

Lilia could feel color rising in her face, but she couldn't tell Annie the real reason she had no intentions of visiting the inn anytime in the near future.

The weeks flew by. Lilia continued to enjoy her position as teacher. As to the weekends, she always had an excuse for not dining with the Cunards. The evening she first felt her baby move, she yearned to go to Serenity and tell her the exciting news. But the four-mile walk to the inn deterred her.

One morning during the second week of October she awakened to a glistening, white frosted world outside her front door. While the frost was gone before the ten o'clock recess, the world began to turn brown in preparation for winter.

The days passed quickly as every Friday afternoon, when she returned to her little sod cabin after school, she found bundles of garden produce and baked goods beside her door. Elder Moore had told her when she took the job that the people of Sugar Creek were a generous lot. "As long as you find food at your door, you'll know they like what you're doing for their children," he'd said.

Not having a large mirror proved to be an advantage for Lilia. She couldn't view the day-to-day changes in her profile. The waists on the dresses Cora Rich had altered were now straining against the buttons. With the weather growing colder each morning, Lilia wore the vest for more than a cover-up. She was glad that Cora had included a blue quilted jacket that buttoned down the front.

Annie dropped by Lilia's place once a week, usually on Mondays, with a freshly baked pie or a loaf of bread or what she called a dish of apple grunt. The two would laugh and talk together about the happenings at the inn and Lilia's experiences with the children. Lilia loved hearing about Sammy. But she ached to see him for herself.

One Monday the Cunard's carriage stopped in front of her soddy just as she dismissed the children from school. Caleb was driving and Serenity sat beside him in the driver's seat. "Hi, are you busy?" she called, scrambling down from the carriage before Caleb could help her. "I have missed you so much. What's going on?"

Lilia threw herself in Serenity's arms. "I've missed you too," she wailed. "I'm sorry but I've been so busy and I've had several dinner invitations. . . ." Her voice trailed away when she realized that her friend wasn't buying her excuses.

Lilia glanced past her friend into the carriage. "Where's Sammy?"

"Annie stayed with him so I could come. I was hoping to kidnap you and bring you back to the inn for dinner. Joseph Blackwing brought us a giant wild turkey and we've been baking it in the oven since early this morning. It smells so good." Serenity cast a teasing glance at Lilia. "What do you say? Close up the school building, grab your bonnet, and come on. I'll promise you one of the drumsticks."

Serenity knew how much Lilia loved turkey drumsticks.

"Are you having any other guests?" she asked hesitantly.

Serenity shrugged. "Not that I know of. There've been no guests staying at the inn since the beginning of September."

That was all she needed to hear. Lilia grabbed her bonnet and hopped into the carriage beside Serenity.

"You certainly are agile for being five months pregnant." Serenity laughed. "I can hardly tell you're pregnant at all."

Lilia laughed. "My students keep me from getting too fat and too lazy."

Caleb flicked the reins over the horses' backs and the carriage rolled forward.

"You seem to be enjoying being a schoolmarm. It becomes you." Serenity chuckled knowingly. "What do you plan to do once the new teacher arrives?"

Lilia felt the usual heaviness whenever she thought of leaving Sugar Creek. "I'm not sure. I've heard rumors that the new teacher is on her way even as we speak."

"You know you are always welcome at the inn. Having you there during the winter months would give me someone to talk to during the day," Serenity confided. "Caleb has enough work in the shop to keep him busy until spring and Annie will be returning soon to my folks in town. It seems she has a gentleman friend."

"Really?" Lilia squealed and clapped her hands. "That's fabulous. Who is he and where did she meet him?"

"Let's see." Serenity thought for a moment. "His name is Ned Ward. He's a free Negro. He works at the docks." She frowned. "I'm not sure how they met, probably at church. There is a small Negro church in town."

Ned Ward? The memory sent shivers up and down Lilia's spine. She wrapped her arms about herself and shuddered.

"Are you cold?" Serenity asked, turning around in the seat. "I have one of Sammy's afghans back here somewhere. Here!" She handed a blue-and-white crocheted blanket to Lilia. "Wrap up in this."

The dinner with the Cunards was delicious. She and Serenity had so much to share and Lilia couldn't keep her hands off Serenity and Caleb's precious little son. As she smiled into his trusting blue eyes, she thought about her own child and realized how eager she was becoming to meet him or her.

Before Lilia left the inn, Serenity invited her to attend revival meetings being held in Reverend Rich's church in Independence. Esther had mentioned the meetings earlier.

"We'll be glad to swing by and pick you up each evening," Caleb assured her.

During the ride home, Lilia considered the invitation. Her evenings were lonely. She'd borrowed and read every book in Sugar Creek, save the school's Bible. She recalled the religious revivals that had come through Norfolk. They resembled a circus—lots of music and color. They were the best entertainment for miles around.

When they arrived at her home, Lilia told Caleb that she would love to attend the meetings.

As Caleb's carriage disappeared into the darkness, Lilia realized how much she hungered for human companionship. Watching the way Serenity and Caleb enjoyed their son together reminded Lilia that her child would not experience a daddy's love.

She grew sad as she remembered the games she and her own father enjoyed. Taking walks to the docks to see the tall ships on Sunday afternoon had been her favorite time with him. On the way home, he would stop at his favorite pub where the owner would give her a handful of horehound candy. The pub was their special secret since Lilia's mother didn't approve of her husband taking their daughter into the "devil's den" as she called it.

The rest of the week flew by in a fury of activity at the school. The children were making maps of the United States and its territories for geography class. Lilia had asked the school board for a roll of butcher's paper and some colored chalk.

She'd pushed back the school benches and spread the paper out on the floor. The children had eagerly thrown themselves into the project.

With the revival meetings in Independence, the church services in Sugar Creek had been suspended so Lilia could safely leave the artwork in the middle of the floor over the weekend.

On Friday night, she'd finished a slice of bread with honey butter on it when the Cunard's carriage pulled up to her front door. Lilia slipped into her jacket, threw on her bonnet, grabbed her gloves, and ran for the carriage.

Caleb drove while she and Serenity sat in the backseat with Sammy. Lilia told her friend about the maps and about the children's excitement over the project. In a short time, the carriage came to a stop outside the brown, shingled Baptist church. By the number of the carriages and wagons gathered outside, many people had already arrived.

While Caleb parked the carriage, the women hurried inside the church to find a good seat. Lilia was waving to the Todd children when Serenity tugged at her sleeve. "Come. Aaron saved us a seat."

Aaron? She'd never expected to run into him at a revival meeting! Lilia drew back. Serenity acted as if she hadn't picked up on Lilia's reticence. Taking Lilia by the arm, she whisked her to the third row on the right. And before Lilia could protest, she found herself seated between Aaron and Serenity.

Uncertain after their last encounter, Lilia glanced out of the corner of her eye at Aaron. He cast her a brief, impersonal smile, then returned his attention to the activity in the front of the church. *All right,* she thought. *If that's the way you want to play out this evening, fine!* She snapped her face forward and lifted her nose in the air.

She'd imagined their next encounter, but she'd never thought it would be in a church. She pictured him begging for her forgiveness for the way he'd treated her. She wouldn't forgive him right away, of course. She would make him suffer a while, then maybe, if he were convincingly repentant. . . . That's the way she'd imagined their next meeting. Instead he acted indifferent to her presence.

The audience sang the old hymns with gusto. When the soprano soloist screeched on a high note during the special music, Lilia cringed and fought the urge to shudder. She cast a quick glance toward Aaron, hoping she'd adequately suppressed her reaction to the sour note. By the wry grin on his face, she knew he'd read her mind. They smiled, successfully swallowing their desire to laugh. Aaron reached into his pocket and dropped a coin into the offering basket when it was passed.

Reverend Rich introduced the visiting evangelist, a returned missionary from Asia. The man told of the poverty he found in places like India and Burma. Lilia was horrified when he told about young wives, thirteen and fourteen years old, being burned alive on their husband's funeral pyre, of baby girls being tossed in the garbage dump at birth, of five-year-old boys being forced to work with the elephants and being trampled to death under their feet.

"God loves these people, every one of them. And He loves you too, so much that He died on a cruel cross to save you from your sins." The speaker pointed at the congregation. "That's right. Your sins, and your sins, and your sins!" When he pointed straight at Lilia, her face flushed with embarrassment. She shrank down behind the lady in the pew in front of her.

"He knows everything you've ever done. And He loves you anyway," the man continued. "Like a father pities his erring son, so the God of the universe sees and pities His children and is eager to forgive them of their sins."

Lilia squirmed in her seat. The man's piercing dark eyes bored into her soul. She glanced about for an escape, any escape. Sammy was asleep on his father's lap. Serenity sat snuggled close to Caleb. To make it to the aisle she would have to climb over both.

Behind her, she caught the eye of Rebecca Page. The little girl grinned and waved. Lilia responded in kind, realizing that escape was no longer an option. If she couldn't escape physically, Lilia decided she could escape mentally. Unfortunately, no matter how hard she tried, her thoughts kept returning to her parents' home in Virginia, especially to her father.

A nudge on her left brought her back to the little brown church in Missouri and to Aaron who was standing.

"Excuse me," he whispered as he brushed past her knees. Where was he going? When he squeezed past Serenity and Caleb, they looked ecstatically happy. Upon reaching the aisle, Aaron turned left toward the front of the church instead of turning right toward the door as she imagined he would.

Several other worshipers, including her seventh grader, Jacob Moore, were also going forward. Sarah Farver, the eighth grader who barely spoke above a whisper, joined the growing number of people kneeling before the altar.

The organist began playing and singing a hymn. "Just as I am, without one plea but that Thy blood was shed for me. . . ."

Lilia's eyes misted for an instant, and then she reminded herself that the song wasn't about her and her sins.

"O lamb of God, I come, I come."

People around her were weeping. A man two rows behind her noisily blew his nose. More than ever, Lilia wanted to leave, to run from the confusion she felt inside of her.

Those who had gone forward returned to their seats. The evangelist invited everyone to return the next night, then he prayed.

The worshipers filed quietly out of the church. Upon reaching the door, Lilia greedily inhaled the night air. When the evangelist shook her hand, she mumbled something and hurried past. Aaron and the evangelist shook hands. The preacher welcomed him back into the fold.

Fold? What fold? she wondered. *What is a fold anyway?* "What was that all about?" she hissed as Aaron led her away from the crowd.

"It's a long story."

"Much like the drama you involved me in awhile back?" She slathered her words with sarcasm.

He gazed down at her as if trying to decide what to say. "Can we find a place to talk?"

Mrs. Anders from Sugar Creek interrupted before Lilia could answer. Beth, her youngest, wrapped her arms about Lilia's legs, pulling Lilia's dress close to her body. "I love you, Mrs. Cooper," she said.

Lilia hugged the child. "I love you too." Lilia tried in vain to gather extra fabric around her midsection. She could see questions forming in Mrs. Ander's face. That spelled trouble.

Aaron tipped his hat at Mrs. Anders and smiled. "It looks like Papa has the carriage ready. George, go find Buddy." The woman tapped her son's shoulder. "Tell him Papa is ready to leave. It was nice seeing you again, Mr. Cunard." Mrs. Anders took Beth's hand and led her to the waiting carriage.

Other parents from Sugar Creek stopped to greet the teacher and look over the young man by her side. When

Caleb pulled up in his carriage, Aaron and Lilia broke free from the crowd. Serenity and Sammy were already on board.

Caleb hopped down from the carriage and hugged his brother. In a broken voice, he said, "I am so proud of you. Do you know how thrilled Mama and Daddy will be?"

Aaron nodded and swallowed hard. "Thanks. I've got a lot of decisions to make in my life, don't I?"

"That's between you and God, Aaron." Caleb pounded his brother on the back. "That's between you and God."

The emotional moment between the two brothers ended when Sammy let out a wail. Caleb looked up at his wife, then shook his brother's hand. "Gotta go. Sammy's getting hungry."

Caleb helped Lilia into the carriage, then leaped into the driver's seat and took the reins into his hands. Aaron glanced toward Lilia, then up at Caleb. "Brother, I need a favor from you. If you're not comfortable with this, it's all right, but would you be willing to take Lilia to the outskirts of town, then let her ride back to the inn with me?"

Caleb shot a surprised glance at his wife, then at Lilia. "Is that all right with you, Lilia?"

"Yes." The words stuck in her suddenly parched throat.

At the outskirts of town, after the last carriage disappeared toward home, Caleb reined the horses to a stop and waited in the darkness for Aaron to catch up. Lilia could hear Sammy hungrily nursing at Serenity's breast. Her insides shook like jelly; her breath came in short gasps at the thought of the planned rendezvous.

Within a few minutes Lilia could hear a carriage approach and slow to a stop beside them. She dared not look until she heard Aaron's voice. "Lilia, if you'd rather not . . ."

She gazed into his questioning eyes and gave him her hand. He helped her from the carriage and into his two-seater buggy. "I'll bring her straight home, I promise," he called after his brother.

The horses ambled slowly along the dusty roadway. For several minutes, neither of them spoke. Curious, Lilia asked what had happened to Aaron at the church.

Aaron tried to explain, but the young woman who had no spiritual background couldn't understand.

She could see a change in him, but she couldn't understand it. "I can't believe you've become one of them!" she scoffed, trying to raise his ire. "I suppose you'll be preaching the gospel as you mix drinks."

"No. After tonight, I can't go back to that job."

She clenched her fists at her sides. His betrayal by becoming a Christian suddenly bothered her more than his illegal activities. "What will you do for money? Start charging by the head to run fugitive slaves across the border?"

"Of course not!" He looked at her sharply. "I've been thinking of opening a carpenter's shop."

"A carpenter's shop?" She threw back her head and laughed aloud. Her bonnet slipped off her head. Embarrassed, she fiddled with the ties, which had somehow gotten knotted. In frustration she yanked the bonnet from her neck. "A carpenter? The next thing I know you'll be preaching out on the hillsides."

"Don't be sacrilegious, Lilia. When I helped build the Pownell's place this summer, I discovered I enjoyed working with wood. I'm quite good at it too."

"Jolly good for you! Why are you telling me all this? It has nothing to do with me."

"Maybe not." His eyes became strangely sad and his voice turned into a whisper. "For some reason it's important to me that you understand who I am and what I'm about."

She shrugged and folded her arms across her chest.

"Tonight changed my life in many ways, but not in one. I will continue to help fugitive slaves escape to freedom. On that point I am committed."

"So?"

"Just wanted you to know." He slowed the horses to a stop beside the barn. The light shining from the inn's windows looked warm and inviting. He climbed out of the buggy and reached with strong arms for Lilia. "And thanks for not running to the sheriff."

"I . . . well . . ." Lilia couldn't begin to explain to herself why she hadn't said anything to anyone. How could she tell this gorgeous man?

He took her by the arms. When her feet touched the ground, she stood face-to-face with Aaron. He looked like a man toying with the idea of kissing a woman. If she swayed slightly forward, she could close the gap between them.

The neigh of his horse brought her back to reason. "Thank you, Mr. Cunard, for the ride." Her voice was heavy with emotion.

He stepped back, placed her hand in the crook of his arm, and escorted her up the pathway to the house. At the door, he tipped his hat toward her, turned, and left.

She stepped inside to find a curious Serenity and a bemused Caleb. She could tell that Serenity ached to ask her dozens of questions. When she automatically went to remove her bonnet, she realized that she'd left her bonnet in Aaron's carriage.

"I'm quite tired," she explained to Caleb. "If you could take me home right away, I would appreciate it."

"Of course!" Caleb spurred into motion.

Serenity touched her friend's arm. "Lilia, would you care to borrow one of my bonnets? It's cold out there this evening."

"No, uh, thank you. I'll be fine," Lilia insisted.

~20~

The Letter Home

AARON ARRIVED IN HIS BUGGY THE NEXT evening to take Lilia to the meeting. She blinked in surprise but allowed him to help her into the vehicle.

Along the road she smiled and waved uncomfortably when they passed the Tylers and the Moores. "I will be scandalized in front of my children and their parents," she sputtered.

Aaron laughed. "It's broad daylight. I have an open carriage. What do they expect us to do?"

"That's not the point," she insisted. "Surely you know how tongues wag in small towns."

He urged the horse into a trot. "Relax and enjoy the crisp autumn evening. This Indian summer we've been enjoying will be gone by morning, I'm afraid."

In a short time they were filing into the packed church. Serenity and Caleb had saved them a place near the front. Right away Lilia noticed the change in the way Aaron got involved in the worship and the singing compared to the evening before. Feeling more out of place than ever, she questioned whether or not she'd attend another meeting.

However, she did attend the next meeting, and the next,

and the next, and the next. Each meeting ended with the same song, "Just as I Am, Without One Plea." Each night she watched people walk to the front of the room as Aaron had done and give their hearts to God—whatever that meant. And on the way home, she listened as Aaron expounded excitedly on the evangelist's message.

The second Saturday night arrived, the last meeting of the series. The evangelist would be moving south to Fort Scott, Kansas. As Lilia mumbled the words to "O God, Our Help in Ages Past," she struggled to make sense of the confusion she felt.

The same soprano who'd sung every night failed to hit the high C at the end of her solo once again, but the congregation rewarded her with a generous "Amen" anyway. Reverend Rich opened the service with prayer. He asked God to open the eyes of the blind and the ears of the deaf that they might respond to the Holy Spirit's call. Then the evangelist rose to speak.

He told a story about a selfish son and a loving father. Every word seemed to be pointed straight at Lilia. "Your Father loves you. It doesn't matter how far you run, you can't outrun His love. It doesn't matter how bad you've been, how grievous your sins, He loves you and waits for you to come back to Him." The evangelist leaned over the pulpit, staring straight at Lilia. It was as if the man could read her mind. "Imagine the pain your Father feels when He sees you hurting and lonely in your sin. Imagine how He aches for you because you doubt His love is strong enough to forgive you. His love is big enough to look beyond your past toward a glorious future with Him."

Lilia tried to tune out the message by thinking of other things—the arithmetic papers she needed to grade before morning, the bread she had rising on the stove, the chipmunk making a nest in the eaves of her house—but always her attention returned to the preacher and his message of love.

When the organist began singing and playing the familiar closing song, Lilia found herself leaping to her feet. She'd intended to slip out the back door when she reached the aisle. Instead she felt herself being propelled down the aisle toward the pulpit.

Part way down the aisle, someone took her hand. She looked and saw it was Aaron. Tears glistened in his eyes; a cockeyed smile wreathed his face.

What are you doing? she argued with herself. *You are being totally unreasonable. Next thing you know you'll be one of those Bible-thumping, Scripture-quoting Christians you've always joked about.*

She looked into the evangelist's eyes. His smile was one of knowledge and compassion. After a short prayer, he sent them back to their seats.

Lilia floated as if in a dream. She was hardly aware of Serenity's hug when she returned to her seat. What had she done? Whatever it was, Lilia had to admit she'd never been so filled with peace or experienced such joy as she did that evening.

The cold wind blew in off the prairie as Aaron's buggy whisked her through the night toward Sugar Creek. With his one arm about her shoulders and a carriage blanket tucked about their legs, they stayed as warm as possible. Yet by the time the carriage stopped in front of her sod house, they were both shivering from the cold.

He helped her down from the carriage. Again they came face-to-face.

"Come inside for a cup of herb tea?" she asked.

"I probably shouldn't. Your neighbors are bound to notice."

She fumbled with a button on his suede jacket. "So? Their real teacher will be arriving by the end of next week. They don't need me anymore."

She led him into the soddy and handed him the tea-kettle. "Could you fill this with water while I get the cookie jar? Annie sent over a package of oatmeal cookies two days ago and I can't eat them all."

When he returned with the water, she could wait no longer. "Aaron, I have so many questions to ask you. What happened back there in the church tonight?"

"What do you mean?"

"I couldn't have stayed seated in that pew for anything. It was as if Someone put a hand in the middle of my back and pushed me to the altar. I don't understand."

He glanced down at his hands folded in his lap. "You experienced the touch of the Holy Spirit."

"Excuse me?"

"You know, the Holy Spirit—God?" The surprise on his face surprised her as well.

"I'm sorry but this religion thing is new to me. I've never heard of this Holy Spirit of yours."

"How do I explain?" He frowned. The only sound they could hear was the wind whipping around the corners of the building. "How do I explain? The Holy Spirit is like the wind in your face. You can't see it, but you can definitely feel it. That's what happened tonight. You couldn't see the Spirit, but you definitely felt His power. Does that make sense?"

"I'm not sure. All I know is that it was like, how can I say this? Love! An overwhelming love, drawing me and I had to respond. Does that make any sense?" she asked.

Aaron's eyes filled with tears. "Very much so."

"Why are you crying?" she asked.

"I've never heard it put so beautifully. I've seen thousands of people respond to the Holy Spirit's call, but I've never heard anyone describe the experience so perfectly." He reached across the space between them and took her hand.

"As long as I live, I will never forget tonight," he said. He rose to his feet. "I must be going. We don't want to give your neighbors cause for worry about your virtue, do we?"

Lilia chuckled as she stood up. It had been a long time since anyone had worried about her virtue. She released his hand and scurried to the door. "Thank you, Aaron, for tonight . . . and for not giving up on me. I have a lot to think about. There's a Bible at the school. I think it's time I get acquainted with it." She bit her lower lip. "There is so much I don't understand."

He ambled to her, his gaze never leaving hers. "You are a remarkable woman, Lilia Cooper. When you decide to do something, you go at it full force, don't you?"

"Is there any other way to live?"

At the door, he stopped. "Will I see you again soon, now that the meetings are over?"

Lilia's mind was in turmoil. She'd experienced too many strange and wonderful feelings that evening. She needed time to weigh them against what she knew, or at least thought she knew. "There's a good chance my last day of school will be next Friday and I'll be moving back to Serenity Inn. I'm sure I'll see you there." She tried to smile.

He studied her face for a second. "How are you feeling about that?"

"Sad—happy, I don't know. It's not that I haven't been expecting it to happen. Besides, this baby is becoming more and more obvious." She glanced down at her waistline.

"If I can help you move, let me know." He kissed her cheek and left.

She stood in the doorway watching until she could no longer see his buggy or hear the horse's gentle trot. Instead of returning to her house, she snagged her shawl off the wall peg and dashed to the schoolhouse. Once inside she fumbled around until she located and lit an oil lantern. She then found the Bible.

Seating herself at the desk, she opened it at random. She scanned the page and decided to begin reading Psalm 51. It looked to be as good a place as any other to begin. "Have mercy upon me, O God. According to Thy loving kindness . . . cleanse me from my sin."

That's what she hungered for, to be pure and innocent again. To be forgiven, totally forgiven from her endless list of sins! A wail burst from Lilia's throat that startled her.

"Oh, Father God, I do give myself to You, sins and all." She didn't know how to pray like the preachers did, with all the thee's and thou's. Instead she let the words tumble straight from her heart. She didn't even stop to wonder if God could hear her simple prayer. After this week of meetings and her experience tonight, she was sure that God existed and that He was interested in her.

By the time she finished praying and reading, Lilia knew what she had to do before she could sleep. She took out a tablet of paper from the top drawer of her desk, removed the ink pen from its cradle, and dipped the point into the ink well.

Dear Daddy and Mama,

I don't know if you ever want to hear from me or see me again after all I've done. Regardless, I am so sorry for the way I hurt you both. Daddy, I am sorry Wade stole your coins and squandered them before he died. Will you please forgive me? I have asked God to forgive me and He has. Now, I need to know that you will also forgive me. Even if you never want to claim me as your daughter, I need your forgiveness.

I am living outside of Independence, Missouri. I teach school in Sugar Creek, at least for the next week, then the regular teacher will arrive from the East, and I will go to live with my friend Serenity at an inn she and her husband operate—Serenity Inn.

Wade was killed while trying to steal a horse from the Shoshone Indians. I am six months pregnant with our child.

I haven't written because I couldn't see how you could ever forgive me for betraying you as I did. Tonight I attended a revival meeting and the preacher told about a boy who left home like I did. He ruined his life and squandered his father's money. And when he came to his senses, he returned and his father welcomed him with open arms. Is that too much to hope for?

She dipped the pen in the inkwell and continued writing.

Please know that I love you both. I don't know how I can ever repay you for the loss of your coins, but God willing, I will try. I will start by including two dollars and fifty cents in this letter. I know it's not much, but it's all I have at this time.

All my love,
Your daughter, Lilia

She stopped, stared at her signature, crossed out it out, and wrote, Eulilia Northrop Cooper.

Early the next morning she walked to the Moore's home. She knew Elder Moore went into town early on Saturday mornings. Mrs. Moore met her at the door and invited her into the kitchen. She was surprised to find Aaron and Elder Moore sitting together at the kitchen table, along with Ned Ward. The men leaped to their feet.

Pasting a bright smile on her face that belied her true feelings, she handed Elder Moore the letter, along with a silver dollar. "I hope I'm not interrupting something important, but I was wondering if you could mail this for me. I hope the dollar will cover the cost."

Elder Moore assured her that the dollar would see the letter to its destination.

Lilia glanced at the two other men. They appeared as uncomfortable as she did. Aaron refused to meet her gaze.

"Mrs. Cooper, it seems the last time the four of us were together, things didn't go too well," Elder Moore hemmed. "I hope there are not hard feelings."

Lilia cocked her head to one side and sniffed. "I was muffled and dragged into a cellar where I was held captive for who knows how long. Then I was forced to be an accessory to a crime I didn't condone. Tell me, gentlemen, how can I not have hard feelings?"

Aaron looked at her in surprise. "But Lilia, I thought after last night—" Suddenly he reddened. "Not that there was a last night. I mean after your experience with God."

"My experience with God changes a lot of things in my heart, Mr. Cunard, but I haven't abandoned all my previously held beliefs."

"No, of course not. I just thought . . ." Aaron searched for the right words to say.

"Aaron, my boy." Elder Moore threw an arm around the young man's shoulder. "The lady is right. We do owe her an apology for our actions, however necessary they were at the time. Mrs. Cooper, please accept my humble apology for my ungentlemanly behavior."

Lilia nodded. "Your apology is accepted."

Ned Ward apologized as well.

When he finished, Lilia assured them that she forgave their misbehavior, but that she still wasn't sure whether or not she should inform the sheriff about their operation.

Aaron shot a quick glance at Ned, then at Elder Moore. "Lilia, you have to promise us—"

"I don't have to do anything, Mr. Cunard." She smiled up at Elder Moore. "Sir, I understand your teacher will be here before the end of the week."

"Yes, that's the latest word we have from her."

"Then I will finish out the week for her and move before the weekend so that she can get settled in time to start teaching school on Monday. I suppose your deeds are safe until then. Once my job is over though . . ." It took all of Lilia's strength to deliver her resignation. She couldn't imagine waking each morning without looking forward to another school day.

"The parents and students have appreciated all you've done in the classroom." Mrs. Moore rounded the corner of the table and stood next to her husband. "They absolutely adore you."

Lilia choked back her tears. "Thank you, Mrs. Moore. I adore them as well."

The woman cast Lilia a conspiratorial look. "Now that you will no longer be my children's teacher, I can ask. Tell me, when is your baby due?"

"In March."

The woman gave Lilia a squeeze. "I thought so. Let us know when you deliver. The ladies of Sugar Cove are making you a few little things for the baby."

"How very nice. Thank you."

Lilia made her good-byes and walked back to her house. She felt good about the letter, good about her confrontation with Elder Moore, and good about the ladies' acceptance of her and her pregnancy.

She wondered how many other parents had noticed her pregnancy. If Elder Moore had wanted to, he could have confronted her and possibly forced her to quit teaching earlier. But he harbored her and protected her just as he did the escaping slaves. As she entered her soddy, she said aloud, "Must be God's love. I have a lot to learn."

The week passed quickly. On Thursday night, the school board called a special meeting to thank Lilia for her services and to welcome Miss Turner, the new teacher. As Lilia made her way out of the schoolhouse, Kinder Tyler, the most rambunctious of the lot, ran after her. "Mrs. Cooper. Mrs. Cooper, I'm going to miss you. You're the best teacher I've ever had."

Lilia kissed the boy's cheek. "You're going to like Miss Turner. She seems very nice."

"That's what my mama says, but you'll always be the best to me."

The board decided Friday would be only a half day of school to give the children time to say good-bye to Lilia and to allow the two teachers time to confer. While she and Miss Turner talked, Caleb and Aaron loaded Lilia's belongings on a wagon. Annie and Serenity supervised the men.

Lilia walked down the pathway to the little sod house for the last time. She refused to look back at the building where she'd experienced such happiness. The night before she'd spent time reading several of the psalms of praise she'd found during her short spiritual journey. Remembering them gave her courage.

As she swiped at her tears, she scolded herself for being so sentimental. *It's not as if I'm going far away.* She could see the children any time she wanted. But she knew it would be different once she was no longer their teacher.

For the woman accustomed to playing tag with fifteen children, the days at the inn dragged by slowly. Lilia helped Serenity with the daily tasks, but once the snows came, there wasn't much beyond food preparation and cleanup that needed to be done. Lilia had too much time on her hands.

Having access to Serenity and Caleb's library helped. Aaron visited the inn every Sunday afternoon. And each week after the meal, she and he would walk up the hill, sit side by side on the rock, gaze at the horizon, and talk. They talked about their childhoods and their dreams. She shared with Aaron the exciting Bible texts she was discovering. Aaron shared with her what he was learning as apprentice to the best carpenter in Independence, a black man named Bo McNair.

Lilia missed Aaron's visits when the snow got too deep for his horse to make it through. Secretly she'd been hoping to receive a letter from her father, but none came.

The world outside the inn was cold and stark. Except for the barn, the chicken house, and outhouse, Serenity Inn looked to be the only place on the face of the earth. Even the rabbits, whose fur had changed to white, were no longer scurrying up to the kitchen door for handouts.

Caleb tried to clear the road heading toward town, but as fast as he'd clear a stretch, the wind would fill it in again. The holidays drew near. Serenity did her best to decorate the place for Christmas. She cut the shape of a bell out of a sheet of red tissue paper she'd been saving and hung it over the door. With red yarn, she hung a swag of braided grasses and apples above the fireplace.

While Lilia missed Aaron's visits, she appreciated having time to get acquainted with her new God. And she discovered she was getting to know herself as well. Who was Eulilia "Lilia" Northrop Cooper anyway? Going from schoolgirl, to wife, to mother-to-be, to widow, to schoolteacher, to lady-in-waiting had happened so quickly she hadn't had time to adjust. She also slept a lot.

On Christmas morning Serenity, Caleb, and Lilia sat down to a breakfast of pancakes and blackberry syrup. Suddenly they heard a knock at the door.

It was the Blackwings. Joseph opened his heavy blanket and dropped a large trout in Caleb's hands. "For dinner," Joseph announced. "Merry Christmas!"

As he and Gray Sparrow removed their heavy animal-skin robes, the jangle of sleigh bells reverberated in the room.

Caleb glanced toward his wife. "Who can that be?" Caleb and Serenity hurried to the window.

"Who is it?" Lilia asked, feeling too sluggish to follow their example.

"Oh my! I don't believe it!" Caleb exclaimed, rushing to open the front door. "What are you folks doing here?"

The sleigh pulled to a stop in front of the inn. Out jumped the Pownells and Aaron. As Serenity and Caleb greeted her parents, Aaron strode toward Lilia. He took her hands in his. "I missed you."

She felt all aflutter, like a schoolgirl. "I missed you too."

Josephine rushed to pick up Sammy who was playing on the rug in front of the sofa. Sam, Serenity's father called, "Hey, Aaron, maybe we should bring in all those packages from the sleigh."

Still in shock, Serenity stood near the door. "How in the world did you get here?" she squealed. "I thought the road was impassable."

Aaron laughed and winked at Lilia. "It was until a bunch of us got together and cleared it enough to allow a team of horses and a sleigh to get through."

~21~
The Desires of Her Heart

CHRISTMAS PROVED TO BE ONE LILIA WOULD always remember. She felt so at home with the Cunards and the Pownells, and yes, the Blackwings.

When Josephine announced that Abe and Dory had arrived from New York just ahead of the blizzard, Serenity squealed with delight.

"Dory wanted to come with us today," explained Josephine, "but she's pretty exhausted from the long trip and coming down with a bad cold. Abe insisted she rest a few days before coming out to the inn. Annie insisted on staying in town with them. She knew you'd understand."

"But, of course, I understand. You tell Dory to stay in bed until her cold is better." Serenity shook her head. "We don't want her coming down with consumption or something."

Serenity's father chuckled aloud. "Don't you worry about that. Old Abe will rein her in."

Josephine nodded. "He's the only one who can, I assure you. She is one determined lady." Then as an afterthought Josephine added, "And I love her dearly."

Lilia mused over the exchange regarding the servant Dory. They talked of the woman as if she were one of the family. She had to admit to herself that she'd never felt so close or protective over any of her parents' slaves. In the past she would have been disgusted by such familiarity between the help and the gentry. Slowly she was beginning to understand about loving God and loving other people, regardless of their race or color. Lilia knew she had a long way to go, but, as Serenity had told her many times during the last few weeks and months, God is a patient God. Like a gardener tending His fledgling plants, He gives His children time to grow.

When it came time to open the presents they'd brought, Lilia couldn't believe the gifts she received. From Josephine and Sam, she received a baby blue, flannel-lined silk robe. When Gray Sparrow handed her the soft white, woolen baby's blanket, sweater, and hat the Indian woman had knitted, Lilia burst into tears and threw her arms around the surprised woman.

The gift from Aaron meant the most to her—her very own Bible, inscribed with her name in gold on the front cover. At Sugar Creek, she'd used the school's Bible. At the inn she'd been using Serenity and Caleb's family Bible. She trailed her fingers over the black leather cover. Her own! She had trouble believing it was actually hers. Lilia's breath caught in her throat when she read the message Aaron had written inside the cover.

"12-25-1851. To my precious friend, Eulilia. May the words of this Book bring you closer to your God, and may God bring us closer to one another. Respectfully, with love, Aaron. Hebrews 13:5."

Slowly Lilia released her breath and smiled lovingly at Aaron. "It's perfect. Thank you so much."

As she readied herself for bed that night, Lilia reverently turned the onionskin pages with the gold edging one at a time. She found the text Aaron had written in the dedication.

"I will never leave you, nor forsake you." Was he speaking for God alone? Or did he apply the promise to himself? Lilia didn't dare consider the possibility. She'd been fooled before. She couldn't afford to be fooled again.

Aaron and the Pownells stayed overnight at the inn. Joseph Blackwing and his wife stayed as well, at Serenity and Caleb's insistence. After a late breakfast, Aaron whisked Lilia away from the kitchen chores for a walk to their rock.

The path was obliterated by drifting snow. After several tries, Aaron admitted defeat. They found refuge from the constant wind inside the barn with the horses. He cupped her face in his hands. "I wanted to be alone with you long enough to let you know how beautiful you are and to tell you that I love you."

Lilia shook her head. "No, Aaron. I'm not beautiful. My body is swollen—my face, my hands, my ankles, not to mention my stomach. I look more like a duck than I do a woman."

"No, no, no, you're wrong." He again captured her face in his hands. "I've never seen you look more lovely. And I do love you." He pressed his forehead against hers. "You may think it's too soon after Wade or something, but I'm not asking for a commitment. You have enough to worry about with that baby coming soon. I just want you to know that I love you, deeply, fully. And when the day comes that you're prepared to love me in the same way, I'll be here for you."

Lilia was shaken to the core of her being. Aaron was the greatest male friend she'd ever known. But love between a man and a woman—that was a different matter all together.

When she opened her mouth to explain, he touched her lips with his index finger.

"No, not now. Don't say anything now. You need more time." He traced his finger around her lips. "Promise me you'll think about what I said." Leaning forward, he brushed his lips across hers. Her breath caught at the gentleness of his kiss. She blinked from surprise.

Aaron straightened and extended his arm toward her. "May I escort you, madam, to the inn?"

Lilia replayed the interlude in the barn again and again during the next few weeks. Occasionally she'd slip away to the barn to relive the breathtaking moments.

Aaron continued making trips to the inn either on Saturday or Sunday of each week, regardless of the weather. Though she never asked, Lilia hoped each time that he would be carrying a letter from Virginia when he arrived.

During his visits, he never again mentioned their conversation in the barn. To Serenity and Caleb, Lilia and Aaron appeared to be nothing but good friends. And during the week, Lilia never brought up his name to the Cunards.

It was the second week of February when Sammy came down with a bad cold. By the following Monday, the cold had lodged in the child's chest. Frightened by the fever that spiked during the night before, Caleb headed for town to fetch Doc Baker. All day, Serenity held the child, cooled his brow with cold water, and sang his favorite nursery songs to him.

Outside, a blizzard blew in from the west. Realizing that no one had milked the Cunard's two cows, Lilia bundled up in Caleb's old mackinaw, put on his second pair of boots and a pair of mittens, wrapped a scarf around her head, and waddled to the barn. She hung on to the guide rope stretched between the two buildings.

That she'd never milked a cow didn't stop the determined young woman. Many times she'd seen Serenity and Annie do it. And while it took some time, she finally got the hang of it. She lugged the full bucket of warm milk back to the inn.

Realizing that she needed to make a side trip to the outhouse beyond the pantry door, she carried the bucket to the pantry and slipped out the back door to the outhouse. Carefully she held onto the guide rope until she reached the building, took care of her business, and started back to the inn. Suddenly she felt herself falling. As her hands flew into the air, she lost the guide rope and fell in the snow.

When she got up, she couldn't find the rope, nor could she see either the inn or the outhouse. Snow swirled in white masses, stinging her eyes. Which way should she go— left, right, backwards, forward? Hearing Onyx barking to her right, Lilia started in the direction of his bark only to hear him barking in another direction. She turned that way, then another and another, until she was totally disorientated. She stopped to listen again. This time she heard nothing, not the dog nor the wind. All was silent.

Frightened, she closed her eyes and prayed, "Dear Father, You promised never to leave me or forsake me. You know where the house is. Show me the way, please, for my baby's sake." Pausing to take stock of her situation, she set off to her right. When she ran into the trunk of a tree, she knew she'd gone the wrong way. The only tree she could remember being near the inn was a scraggly oak beside the road on the way into town.

She dropped to her knees and felt for the tracks of a horse's hooves. When she failed to find tracks, she stood up and headed toward what she hoped was north. Suddenly she smacked into the tree trunk a second time. This time she hit with such force she fell backward in the snow. Her head hit a rock and the white blizzard disappeared into total darkness.

When Lilia awoke, she was in her bed at the inn and Gray Sparrow was leaning over her. "What happened? How did I get here?"

Serenity rushed to Lilia's bedside and handed her son to Gray Sparrow. "Oh, darling, you're finally awake. If it hadn't been for Joseph finding you in the snow bank, you would have frozen to death. How did you get all the way down by the creek?"

Lilia started to explain when her stomach cramped. She doubled over in pain. "I think I'm having the baby," she gasped.

"No, it's too soon," Serenity argued. "You're just over-wrought from your frightening adventure."

"How's Sammy doing? Is his fever coming down? Is Caleb back with Doc Baker yet?" Lilia felt as if she was babbling, but her questions kept coming.

Serenity tried to answer them all. "Sammy's doing much better, thanks to the salve Gray Sparrow rubbed on his chest. The fever seems to have broken. And no, Caleb has not returned with Doc Baker." Serenity straightened the covers about Lilia's shoulders. "You need to rest for a while. Gray Sparrow will stay with you while you sleep." She kissed Lilia on the forehead. "I'm so glad you're safe! How do your fingers and toes feel?"

"All right, I guess."

"Well, just rest." Serenity gathered her son from Gray Sparrow and tiptoed from the room.

Gray Sparrow sat in the rocking chair by the window.

Lilia turned on her side to face the woman. She wanted to thank her for saving her life, but another strong cramp gripped her abdomen. "Gray Sparrow," Lilia gasped, "I think my baby's in trouble."

The Shoshone woman shuffled to the side of the bed, pulled back the bed covers, and placed the palm of one hand on Lilia's stomach. Gray Sparrow grunted, then padded from the room.

Within seconds Serenity whipped into the room, her face drained of color. "Gray Sparrow says you are in labor."

At that moment, the women heard the front door of the inn swing open, followed by the stomping of snow-covered boots. "Caleb, is that you?" Serenity rushed from the room and quickly reappeared with Doc Baker. They found Lilia in the throes of another contraction.

Lilia had never experienced such pain. Serenity and Gray Sparrow stood at the head of her bed taking turns holding her hand and mopping her brow while the men—except for Doc Baker—waited in the great room.

The night dragged by interminably for the mother-to-be. Between contractions, Lilia closed her eyes and recited all the verses she'd learned during the last two months. When Serenity realized what Lilia was doing, she began to repeat Scripture with her.

Lilia relaxed when Serenity repeated Psalm 23. Lilia's contractions grew closer together until they merged into one long contraction. Doc Baker told her to give one more push.

Lilia screamed and it was over.

The doctor held the limp bluish form of a baby in his hands. "It's a girl." Lifting the infant by the heels, he smacked its bottom. "Breathe child! Breathe!"

Lilia screamed! "What's wrong? What's wrong with my baby?" She tried to sit up so she could see.

Finally the infant let out a mewling cry. Her skin began to turn pink.

"She's all right?" Lilia demanded. "My baby's all right?"

The doctor handed the child to Gray Sparrow. "I'm not sure. She's very small. Only time will tell." He returned to his task of caring for Lilia.

"No! No! I can't lose my baby. Please God, save my baby," Lilia wailed, tossing her head from side to side on the pillow.

Gray Sparrow returned to Lilia's side and placed the infant in her weeping mother's arms. Lilia could still see a faint tinge of blue to the child's skin.

Stroking the baby's arm, Lilia began to sing to her daughter.

The baby opened her bright blue eyes and gazed intently into Lilia's.

"Hello, beautiful. I'm your mommy. Did you know that you are the most beautiful baby in the entire world?" Lilia laughed and added, "No offense, Serenity. I think I'll call her Anne after my mother. Anne Louise Cooper, that's a good name. Don't you think?"

"Louise is my middle name." Serenity beamed with delight.

"I know." Lilia grasped her friend's hand as they both gazed at the tiny child.

The news of the birth of Anne Louise Cooper traveled throughout the area, along with details about the fragile nature of her birth. Friends began arriving the morning after the snowstorm subsided with presents, but more importantly with prayers for the child's survival.

From Independence and Sugar Creek, a steady stream of well-wishers, who called themselves "family," packed down the snowy roads. Aaron was one of the first to appear. And he would leave Lilia's side only when Serenity pushed him out of the room.

When little Anne refused to nurse, Gray Sparrow formed a nipple out of a piece of cotton gauze and filled it with sugar and water, then tied it off with a string. The infant greedily slurped the sweetened fabric.

The prayers and the visitors continued until Doc Baker declared the infant to be out of danger. When the word got out, Lilia's friends, her students, and their parents gathered around her bed and held what Cora Rich called a praise service. They sang, read Scripture, and prayed. At the end of the celebration, Reverend Rich took the child into his arms while Elder Moore placed his hands on Lilia's head. Together they asked for God's blessing on the woman and the baby. When they filed out of Lilia's room, Serenity insisted Aaron leave as well.

"Don't you have somewhere you need to be, little brother?" Serenity asked. "Besides, Anne is getting hungry."

Color crept up Aaron's neck into his face. He said good-night to Lilia and promised to return the next day.

Lilia gave him a tiny wave as Serenity changed baby Anne's diaper. As she handed the infant to its mother, Serenity said, "That boy is smitten with you. You know that, don't you?"

It was Lilia's turn to blush. Avoiding Serenity's eyes, she guided her child's tiny mouth to her breast.

Serenity paused at the foot of the bed. "And how do you feel about him?"

Lilia frowned. "I'm not sure."

Serenity bustled about the room for some time, picking up blankets, folding diapers, and adjusting the shade on the window. "Does he know you're not sure about how you feel?"

"Yes."

"I love Aaron very much," Serenity warned. "I don't want to see him hurt by anyone, even by you, my best friend."

Lilia didn't answer. What could she say? Every time she thought deeply about the subject, an overwhelming fear engulfed her. After Serenity left the room, Lilia talked to her nursing child. "I love you, little one. And I always will—that I know for sure." To herself she said, *But God is going to have to let me know it's all right to open the part of my heart that died. I don't want to rush and make that decision myself. I'm too scared.*

On the first day that she was allowed out of bed since Anne's birth, Lilia had one thought in mind—wash her hair. When she told Serenity, she added, "Better yet, why don't we do each other's hair like we did at school?" No one was around but the two of them. Caleb was in town delivering parts to a wagon that he'd repaired.

After a little coaxing, Serenity agreed. While Serenity heated the water, Lilia scrounged through her trunk for her favorite bar of lemon-verbena soap.

The women had a delightful time washing each other's hair, then drying it before the fire. At noon, they ate toast and bowls of Serenity's lentil soup. Serenity decided to take an afternoon nap with her son. Lilia placed her daughter in a large wicker basket beside the sofa, then sat down and brushed the snarls from her hair. The warmth of the afghan covering her and the crackling of the fire in the fireplace quickly overtook the new mother. Stretching out on the sofa, she drifted off to gossamer dreams of running through spring green prairie grass. Her long golden curls blew free about her shoulders in the gentle breeze.

Her dress and matching crinolines made of the sheerest of silk rippled about her in a diaphanous cloud of petal pink. Like a child of ten, she flung her arms in the air and twirled in circles. When she stopped spinning she saw Aaron standing at a distance holding out his hand and calling to her.

"Lilia, come to me. Lilia. Lilia."

"I'm coming, my love. I'm coming to you." But no matter how hard she ran, she couldn't get any closer to him.

"Lilia. Lilia?" His voice was much closer this time. "Lilia."

She could almost feel his hand caress the curls clustering about the sides of her face. "Lilia, wake up." She'd never experienced such a deliciously real dream.

"Lilia, honey. She is fast asleep."

To Lilia, his voice sounded as if he was talking to someone else. He wasn't looking at her anymore. She frowned.

"Lilia, please wake up. There's someone here to see you."

Suddenly she snapped awake. Her body jumped and she sat up. For an instant she couldn't remember where she was. She blinked. Her eyes focused on Aaron's surprised face.

"Sorry, I didn't mean to startle you."

She leaned hard against the back of the sofa. "Who? What?" She blinked again.

"Lilia, wake up. It's me, Aaron."

"What are you doing here?"

"I brought someone who's anxious to see you."

Her hands flew to her hair, which was flying loose about her shoulders. "Who? No, wait. Give me time to get presentable. My hair is a mess. I just washed it."

Aaron chuckled. "I don't think this guest will mind if your hair isn't styled." He turned his head to speak to someone behind him, but Lilia continued protesting.

"Sir—" She reached for her hairbrush, which had fallen to the floor beside the sofa.

Another hand grasped the ivory handle before hers. When Lilia's fingers brushed against the fine blond hairs on the back of the hand, a shock ran through her.

She looked up into the face and gasped. "Daddy!" Lilia couldn't breathe. Sobs burst unbidden from her. "Daddy?" she whimpered. "Is it really you?"

"Yes, sweet one." The rotund, middle-aged shipping magnet gathered his daughter into his arms, crushing her against his rough woolen overcoat. The aroma of his shaving soap inundated her nostrils. She was a little girl again being rescued from danger by her daddy. As he clung to her, he repeated over and over, "Lilly-bell, dear sweet Lilly-bell."

A gurgle from baby Anne startled both of them.

"Daddy, I want you to meet your granddaughter, Anne Louise."

The man released his daughter and turned to gaze in awe at the tiny form of his granddaughter. "She's an exact replica of you, Lilly-bell," he said. "So pink and perfect."

Lilia reached for her father's hand. "Oh, Daddy." Again her tears began to flow. "I thought I'd never see you again. When I didn't hear from you, I thought you—"

"Wouldn't forgive you?" The man shook his head and looked at his daughter through love-soaked eyes. "What a silly goose you are. I never stopped loving you, not for a minute." He sat down beside her on the sofa. "There is nothing you could ever do to keep me from loving you."

"But your coins." She buried her face in his shoulder. "I'm so sorry."

"Coins? What coins?" He gently lifted her face to his.

Embarrassed, she tried to avert her eyes.

"Lilly-bell, look at me! I don't remember any coins. All I remember all these months is missing you."

"Oh, dear." Lilia threw her head back against the sofa and flung her arm up, covering her eyes. "Oh, I was so foolish. Everyone tried to tell me and I wouldn't listen. I don't deserve your forgiveness. I don't deserve to be your daughter!"

"Nonsense! You're a Northrop through and through. Did I ever tell you about the time I ran away from home? How did you think I got started in the shipping business?"

Lilia sniffed and glanced about for a handkerchief. Aaron handed her one.

"This young man—he's a lifesaver. He asked the telegraph operator to contact him if any telegrams came in for you," Mr. Northrop explained.

Mr. Northrop clasped Lilia's hand in his, caressing her fingers with his other hand as he spoke. "I was stranded in St. Louis during the last snowstorm. I managed to get passage on a coach heading for Independence. Unfortunately, the stagecoach broke a spoke in Sweet Springs. That's when I discovered that you folks had telegraph service and I sent you a telegram."

Aaron circled the sofa and sat on the floor beside Anne's wicker basket. Lilia's father and Aaron exchanged looks of mutual admiration.

"Your young man, here, got my message and wired back immediately that he was on his way to get me. He came all the way to Sweet Springs with a horse-drawn sleigh and brought me directly here to the inn."

Lilia threw herself in her father's arms. "I am so glad you're here. I missed you so much. I couldn't understand why you didn't answer my letter."

"Honey." He stroked her head and back. "I left home the same day your letter arrived. I almost had to tie your mother to the front door to keep her from coming with me. Your brother convinced her that it would be a difficult trip because of the weather and that she would slow me down. As it turned out, Carter was right."

"I'm just so thankful you're here." Lilia snuggled closer to her father's side.

"Well, you can thank your young man. I'd still be stranded in Sweet Springs if he hadn't rescued me."

Lilia looked at Aaron with new appreciation. Something deep inside her began to thaw. She wanted to ask Aaron a million questions, to say a million things, to hug him a million times, but all she could manage was "Thanks so much!"

Turning again to her father, Lilia said, "Aaron and his family have been wonderful to me. His sister-in-law operates this inn. She was my roommate at Van Horne's. Serenity Pownell Cunard. You and Mama met her when you came up to the school for parents' weekend, remember? Her father was a New York congressman."

"Oh, yes, Congressman Pownell, a Northern politician with definite opinions regarding slavery, if I remember right."

Lilia shot Aaron a quick glance. "That's right, Daddy. He and his wife live in Independence now."

"So, Lilly-bell, tell me everything. You wrote that Wade Cooper is dead?" Her father's eyes narrowed at the mention of her former husband's name.

Aaron rose to his feet and excused himself. "I think I'll surprise my brother when he comes back from town by doing the evening chores for him."

Lilia smiled in appreciation. Talking about Wade was difficult at best, but talking about the way he treated her in front of Aaron would have been humiliating.

Lilia clung to her father throughout dinner that evening. Secretly she resented having to leave his side to nurse Anne. But when she returned and placed the little child in his arms, Lilia forgot her temporary unhappiness. It was obvious to everyone that grandfather and granddaughter loved each other at first sight.

After dinner, Lilia felt slightly uncomfortable when Caleb took out the family Bible, read a text, and then prayed. Would her father understand the changes she'd made?

At the end of the prayer, Lilia's father looked first at Caleb, then at Serenity. "Lilia told me all about the way you folks took care of her after her husband's demise. You and the preacher's family went way beyond your responsibility. I want to thank you."

Serenity's eyes sparkled. "What else could we do? She's family."

He rubbed his lower lip over his mustache. "That's just it. She's not family. To be honest, I doubt I or my wife would expend ourselves for someone who is not a blood relative."

Caleb was lifting a hand to speak when Lilia interrupted.

"Daddy, Serenity and her husband believe we're all God's children and it is our God-given responsibility not only to help one another, but to love one another." She cleared her throat before continuing. "The Cunards regularly dine with a Shoshone Indian couple. The jerky you enjoyed in the gravy tonight was a gift from them."

Lilia had never put the thoughts she'd had during the past few months into words. She took a deep breath. "Since I've come to Serenity Inn, I've gained not only a great friend in a former slave named Annie, but a sister." She cast Aaron a quick smile. "Thanks to the Cunards, I've learned so much about love. Such love changes a person."

The older man ran his hand over his mustache and beard. "Well, whatever the reason, I do thank you. To show my gratitude, I would like to give you this." He reached into the breast pocket of his suit jacket and pulled out a leather pouch. "Here." He placed it on the table in front of Caleb. "I understand you have plans for expanding the inn. This should help."

Serenity gasped when Caleb turned over the pouch and twenty gold coins clattered onto the table. "Sir," Serenity said, "We can't take this. Lilia is like a sister to me. Besides, she more than earned her keep, helping with the daily chores."

The wealthy businessman looked at her with dismay. "Consider it payment for my stay here until the roads clear and I can take my daughter and granddaughter home to Virginia."

Serenity and Caleb stared down at the table while Lilia cast a worried glance out of the corner of her eye toward Aaron's suddenly rigid profile.

~22~

Love Blooms

By March, most of the winter storms had passed and the steamboats on the river began transporting adventurers and gold seekers to Independence. Families began arriving at the inn once more.

Mr. Northrop was anxious to return to Virginia, but he was also aware of baby Anne's fragile nature. The luxury of the riverboats would make the trip relatively safe for the young child. Lilia had been debating whether or not to return to her parents' home. She longed to see her mother and to show off her good-natured, infant daughter to the family. Then there was Aaron. It was clear that he loved her and the baby and that he loathed the idea of her leaving Independence.

He came to see her almost every day during the week before she was scheduled to leave. Lilia tried to explain to him her need to heal from her own wounds and to help heal the wounds she'd inflicted on her family. And Aaron tried to understand, but Lilia wondered if he really did. Friends like Annie and Esther didn't, though they tried.

In the evenings, Grandpa would watch the baby while the couple strolled to the cemetery, talked, and prayed together. The more time they spent together the easier their conversation flowed. Lilia had even told Aaron that she loved him.

While sitting on what they'd come to call their rock, Aaron had kissed her a second time. Although she'd never talked about it, Lilia feared having too much physical contact with him. She didn't trust herself after Wade. Aaron seemed to sense her reserve, for which she was grateful.

Late one afternoon while they sat at their rock, Aaron again declared his love for her. This time he asked her to marry him.

A tear slid down her cheek as she touched his cheek and kissed his lips. "Aaron, there is nothing I'd rather do than marry you. . . ."

He gazed steadily into her eyes, flexing and unflexing the muscles in his jaw.

"But, I'm terrified! I rushed into marriage the first time and I vowed not to do it again." She couldn't believe she was saying this. Of course she loved him. She felt the familiar loving feelings. "I went by my feelings last time. This time I have to be sure, not only for me, but for the sake of my daughter. I can't make another mistake. I have to know with my mind that you are the right one. Do you understand?"

The pain in Aaron's eyes broke her heart. "No," he said. "You love me and I love you, isn't that enough?"

"Aaron, how can I explain? I must be sure that our marriage is God's plan too. Isn't that what you've been teaching me these last few months—to wait for God's direction in our lives?"

He drew her into his arms and buried his face in her shoulder. "But surely you know I'm not Wade. I can't bear the thought of having you leave me. And Anne, I've come to think of her as my own daughter."

With her hands, she lifted his face until their eyes met. "If God is in our union, nothing will keep me from being with you. Can you believe that?"

He drew away from her. She knew he was hurting. Placing his elbow on one knee and his chin in his hand, he stared at the sandy soil at the base of the rock.

What could she say? How could she let him know that she craved his touch? That it took all of her resolve to keep from melting into his arms at that very moment? "Love me enough to give me three months—June. That's not too long, is it?" she pleaded.

Aaron straightened and sighed. "I'm sorry, Lilia. I know you're right. I'm being impatient. It's just that I've waited so long already." He stood, then drew her into his arms. "Take all the time you need, darling—my gift to you. I'll keep on waiting." His eyes revealed the compassion and love she knew was in his heart.

"Thank you," she whispered. "Right now, I love you more than I thought possible."

She closed her eyes and lifted her face to meet his. What began as a kiss of desperation and fear changed to one of passion and love. The intensity of the kiss shocked Lilia. As much as she'd loved Wade, she'd never responded to his kisses in such a powerful way. Her exciting little trysts with Wade had been just that—trysts.

When Aaron's lips left hers, she felt bereft. Imperceptibly, she swayed against him. He gave a low moan in his throat and drew her closer. "June will be here before we know it," he whispered, nibbling lightly on her ear. "I long to keep the promise to you that I wrote in the cover of your Bible."

I will never leave you, nor forsake you. She'd repeated the words every night since he gave her the Bible at Christmas.

"As long as God gives me breath."

Aaron was so different from Wade. Why couldn't she let go of her fear and trust him? She despised herself for putting him through such torment. Then she remembered Anne and her resolve hardened. No, she had to be sure God had ordained their love. She vowed she would be sure.

Before Lilia, baby, and Mr. Northrop boarded the riverboat heading east, Aaron shared with her and the others a house plan he'd been secretly sketching in pen and ink. It was of a simple clapboard cottage surrounded by a white picket fence.

"I'm not sure where to build it yet," he admitted as he pointed out the details of the house plan, including the master bedroom and the nursery next to it. "I think a trellis would be nice arching the front gate." He stole a quick glance at Lilia. "I want to plant rose bushes on each side of the trellis—pink ramblers, I think."

Lilia blushed and averted her gaze.

He continued. "I've heard tell, Mr. Northrop, that Virginia grows extraordinary roses, especially the rambling kind."

Lilia's father eyed his blushing daughter, then Aaron. "Virginia ramblers can be difficult to transplant."

"Oh, I don't know." Aaron rolled his tongue along the inside of his cheek. "Tender loving care can make an incredible difference in the health of rose bushes as well as people."

The next morning Aaron picked up Lilia and her father at the inn. Due to the limited seating in Aaron's buggy, Annie, with dishcloth in hand, Serenity, toting her son on her hip, and Caleb, with his arm casually draped around Serenity's shoulders, said their good-byes at the inn.

As the buggy pulled out of the inn's driveway, Lilia wondered which of the women she'd miss most—Serenity, her very best friend, or the gentle, unassuming Annie. The thought was almost comical when she recalled how she'd felt about Annie the first time they'd met. *What a difference God makes,* she mused.

Before driving to the docks, they stopped at the Richs' house to say good-bye to Esther, then at the Pownells' to say good-bye to Annie. Lilia fought back a wave of tears as she watched a somber-faced Aaron kiss baby Anne good-bye. The child gurgled and pulled on his earlobe.

When Aaron handed the baby to Lilia's father, Lilia rushed into his arms. She buried her face in his strong, protective chest. He took her face in his hands and kissed her gently, first on her forehead, then on the tip of her nose, then on her lips.

"Never forget how much I love you," he said, his voice reduced to a scratchy whisper.

Lilia could only nod and sniffle. Gently, he ran his pinkie finger along the side of her face. "You can still change your mind," he whispered. "I'll make an honest woman of you whenever you say." He smiled as tears filled his eyes. "I'm sorry. I promised myself I wouldn't do that."

"Do what?"

"Beg you to stay. You have good reasons for wanting to wait. And it can't hurt to give our love time. I will write, you know."

Lilia, who'd never been concerned about money before, frowned. "That could get pretty expensive, Aaron."

His grin widened. "All the more reason to keep our separation short."

"Along with a billion other reasons," she added, a teasing glint in her eyes.

Lilia's father carried Anne a short distance away while Lilia talked. Lilia reached into her reticule for a linen handkerchief and dabbed at her tears. "Going home for a spell seemed like such a good idea—once . . ."

Aaron tilted her chin until their eyes met. "And it still is. Giving God time to work with both of us will be rewarded. If I didn't believe that, I'd never let you go."

"Let me go?" A slight edge came into her voice.

"No, I didn't say that right. I will never force you, my love, to do anything. Force and love don't go together. But I would be on the next train out of here and be there to meet you when you dock in St. Louis."

"You'd do that?" Lilia's eyes sparkled.

"In an instant, if I didn't support your decision to go home and help God heal the wounds in your family."

She dropped her head and nodded.

"The way I see it," he continued, "our love will grow stronger and healthier after you've laid all your anger and pain to rest."

A frown creased Lila's brow. She took a deep breath and let it out slowly as she sighed, "You're right. I know . . . I know . . ."

The moment was broken as the riverboat helmsman sounded the horn, warning the passengers to get on board for departure. Panic filled Lilia's face as she looked into Aaron's face.

"This is it," she whispered. "This is it." Lilia had never felt such agony as she did knowing she was saying good-bye to the only man who loved her for who she was and who she was becoming. "I don't know what to say . . ."

She trembled as Aaron, focusing on her lips, leaned forward. She closed her eyes and lifted her lips to meet his. The warmth of his kiss brought a new wave of tears to her eyes. Wade had never kissed her so tenderly. His kisses were punishing and demanding, not gentle and yielding.

It took the second and final blow of the riverboat's horn before they stepped apart. Neither spoke. Aaron picked up Lilia's hatbox and handed it to her.

Then, taking her arm, he escorted her to where her father and baby Anne were waiting. Aaron scooped Anne into his arms and kissed her, then relinquished her to her mother's arms.

Aaron cleared his throat while Lilia buried her face in the baby's soft flannel blanket. Then he shook Lilia's father's hand. "It's has been a pleasure meeting you, sir. I hope to see you again in a few months."

"And I you, Mr. Cunard. You're a fine gentleman, one whom I would be proud to have as a son-in-law, if my daughter so desires."

"Thank you, sir." Aaron attempted to clear his throat a second time. "Take care of those precious girls of yours."

The man grinned. "You can count on it!" His eyes twinkled with delight. "The nice thing about rambling roses, son, is they transplant well any time of year." Mr. Northrop winked and chuckled aloud. "A word of advice. I wouldn't wait too long. You know what they say about faint hearts and fair maidens, don't you?"

Aaron looked shocked. Lilia clicked her tongue in mock irritation at her father. "Daddy!"

Mr. Northrop took the child from Lilia's arms and escorted his daughter up the gangplank. Lilia could feel Aaron's gaze resting on her as she climbed the plank. She'd never walked such a long gangplank before in her life, or so it seemed. Each step took her further and further from the gentlest and kindest man she'd ever known. Was she doing the right thing? Should she bolt back down the plank before it was too late? "Oh, God, I am so confused. Am I walking away from the only peace and happiness I've ever known? It was here I met Aaron and it was here I met You. Will You be as real and as close to me in Virginia as You've been in Independence?"

These weren't new thoughts. She and Aaron had discussed them again and again since she'd made her decision to return to Virginia.

When Lilia stepped onto the deck, she turned and looked down into Aaron's tear-stained face.

"I love you," he shouted over the noisy steam engine and the crowd of well-wishers.

She waved and blew him several kisses. "I love you too!"

—Epilogue—
Virginia
Ramblers

 On May 30, 1852, Aaron was rubbing the final coat of wax on the carved oak mantle in the parlor of his newly built cottage on the outskirts of Independence when the town's telegraph boy knocked on the open front door.

"Telegraph, Mr. Cunard." He handed the telegraph to Aaron and left. An instant of fear coursed through the young carpenter's mind as he opened the envelope and withdrew the yellow folded paper. *Is something wrong? Did something terrible happen?* he wondered as he unfolded the telegraph. Taking a deep breath, he read, "Roses blooming—stop. Ready to transplant to Independence—stop. All doubts gone—stop. Anne misses you—stop. So do I—stop. If you still love me and want me, I'm ready to transplant to Missouri—stop. Completely yours, Lilia Northrop Cooper, Norfolk, Virginia."

With a whoop and a holler, Aaron grabbed his jacket and hat, bounded from the house, taking a minute to shut the door behind him. He saddled his horse and made for Serenity Inn to share the good news.

Caleb and Serenity assured him they would prepare the new house for Aaron's bride while he was gone.

"There's not much to do . . . well, maybe there is. There's still a lot of sawdust around, though I do have a few odds and ends of furniture because I've been living there since I finished the roof and windows."

Serenity laughed and gave her brother-in-law a big hug. "Don't worry, dear brother, Annie and I will have your new home spotless and ready for the three of you when you arrive. We're so happy for you."

Aaron nodded his head like an excited boy of twelve. "I know. I know. And the best thing is I know that God is in this marriage. We did everything His way." His eyes glistened with tears of joy.

Caleb, choked up with emotion, nodded and pounded him on the shoulder. "I'm happy for you, little brother."

"Thanks. Now I need to get back to town to finish up some business and buy passage on the morning train." He paused long enough to exchange glances with his brother. "I wish you all could be there, at the wedding . . ."

"Me too." Caleb cleared his throat. "Mom and Dad will be so happy."

"Yeah, I know. Ever since I told them of my conversion and of Lilia's heart change, Mom's letters are filled with such happiness. She said it was as if a heavy burden had been lifted from her heart."

"Sounds like Mama," Serenity whispered. They'd all missed the elder Cunards and their little sister Becca since they moved to California.

"If only Lilia could have met Mama," Aaron said.

"Some day, little brother, some day," Caleb assured him with a hearty thud on Aaron's back.

On June 1, 1852, before boarding the train for St. Louis, Aaron Cunard wired his reply. "Prepare roses for transplanting—stop. See you soon—stop. Kiss Anne for me—stop. I love you too—stop. Forever yours, Aaron.

On July 1, 1852, the *Norfolk Weekly News* printed the following announcement: "After a small family wedding in the bride's parents' rose garden, Mr. and Mrs. Aaron Cunard and their daughter, Anne, by Mrs. Cunard's first marriage, left the home of Mr. and Mrs. Chauncy Northrop, the bride's parents, for the groom's home in Independence, Missouri. The groom's parents, Reverend and Mrs. Eli Cunard, reside in Sacramento, California.

"The lovely bride wore her mother's French, ivory lace wedding gown. Mrs. Cunard carried a nosegay of pink rambling roses from her parents' garden and a gold-tooled white leather Bible. The bride's infant daughter, Anne, wore a pink dimity gown sprinkled with embroidered white roses. Mrs. Cunard's brother, Chauncy Northrop Jr., and Mrs. Cunard's cousin, Elizabeth Bender, attended the couple. Reverend Horris Filben presided. A small garden reception followed.

"The happy couple and child will honeymoon in Richmond and Washington, D.C. before leaving the east for their home in Independence, Missouri.

"The bride's mother, Mrs. Northrop, informed our reporter that she and her husband are planning to visit their children and granddaughter, Anne, in the spring of 1853."

Lilia folded the newspaper clipping and slipped it in the couple's family Bible. She placed the Bible on the light-stained oak stand in front of her open parlor window. Lacy white panels fluttered in the warm early autumn breeze. Her eyes misted as she watched the love of her life water the four scraggly twigs that would, come spring, produce a crop of pink Virginia roses on the plains of Missouri.

Slowly, she gazed about the simply furnished parlor. Wherever she looked, Lilia could see Aaron's handiwork— the mantle, the staircase, the rocker beside the hearth. All spoke of his concern for detail and his love of beauty. She smiled at the mound of multi-colored pastel yarn laying on the navy-print upholstered sofa. Would she ever master the knack of crocheting in time to finish the blanket her sister-in-law Serenity was helping her make for her and Aaron's first child? Idly, she rested her hand on her flat stomach and pulling back the curtain, she returned her gaze to the man kneeling beside the trellis archway in front of her home. He looked up from his gardening and waved. A tender warmth flooded through her.

"I found a green shoot," he called excitedly.

She laughed and waved. He'd worried that the precious rose bushes would not survive the transplant. She assured him the roses were tougher than they looked. Given tender, loving care, they'd do fine.

When the couple arrived home from Virginia, Serenity and Caleb had thrown a large wedding reception for them, inviting all their friends. Their pastor, Reverend Rich, had offered a special blessing on the newlyweds, on baby Anne, on their new home and on the spindly twigs that would one day produce blossoms that would bring joy to the Cunard home and to all who would pass by their humble haven.

Lilia traced her index finger over the gold leaf words— Mr. and Mrs. Aaron Cunard—on the front leaf of the white leather-bound family Bible. Her husband cared for the scraggly rose bushes with the same tenderness he cared for her and little Anne. She'd prayed the same prayer a dozen times since their Virginia wedding. Lilia whispered again, "Thank You, dear Father, for loving me and rescuing me from my own foolishness and from the life of misery I would have had with Wade. You couldn't have placed this Virginia rambler in better, gentler hands than Aaron Cunard's."

also available from
THE SERENITY INN SERIES

It's the touching story of an aristo-
cratic, rebellious young woman
named Serenity. Set amidst the tumul-
tuous years prior to the Civil War,
Serenity's Desire is a romantic, adventurous, and spiritually riveting story
of one strong-willed woman who
must come to terms with the injustices of the world and depend on
God's comfort to finally achieve
serenity within herself.

0-8054-6373-9

Passion, love, and turmoil abound in the
second volume of the Serenity Inn series.
After receiving her inheritance, Serenity
finds herself wondering if her friends sin-
cerely accept her or are simply after her
money. Coming of age, Serenity struggles
with the issues of independence, true
acceptance, and love.

A novel filled with wonderfully interest-
ing characters of the pre-Civil War era
who welcome readers into their lives to
experience the romance and adventure that can only happen
at Serenity Inn.

0-8054-1674-9

available at fine bookstores everywhere

also available from
THE SERENITY INN SERIES

Josephine Van der Mere is a rich and beautiful widow and a staunch supporter of the abolitionist cause. But when an encounter with a familiar face leads to blackmail, Josephine must enlist the help of her friends to keep the struggle for freedom alive in this riveting installment of the Serenity Inn series.

Join Annie, Abe, Serenity, Caleb, and the rest in this bright, romantic adventure as Josephine braves the trials of the frontier and discovers that her true fortune lives in the love of another.

0-8054-1675-7

available at fine bookstores everywhere